Laurie Brooks

Selkie Girl

Alfred A. Knopf
New York

THIS IS A BORZOI BOOK PUBLISHED BY ALFRED A. KNOPF

Visit us on the Web! www.randomhouse.com/teens

Educators and librarians, for a variety of teaching tools, visit us at www.randomhouse.com/teachers

The Library of Congress has cataloged the hardcover edition of this work as follows:
Brooks, Laurie.
Selkie girl / Laurie Brooks.
    p. cm.
Summary: When sixteen-year-old Elin Jean finds a seal pelt hidden at home and realizes that her mother is actually a selkie, she returns the pelt to her mother, only to find her life taking many unexpected turns.
ISBN 978-0-375-85170-4 (trade) — ISBN 978-0-375-95170-1 (lib. bdg.) —
ISBN 978-0-375-89144-1 (e-book)
[1. Selkies—Fiction. 2. Seals (Animals)—Fiction. 3. Orkney (Scotland)—Fiction.
4. Scotland—Fiction.] I. Title.
PZ7.B79659Se 2008
[Fic]—dc22
2008003547

ISBN 978-0-375-84385-3 (tr. pbk.)

Printed in the United States of America
November 2010
10 9 8 7 6 5 4 3 2 1

First Trade Paperback Edition

Random House Children's Books supports the First Amendment and celebrates the right to read.

This story belongs to you, Joanna.

THE SELKIES

In the distance, four searching eyes lift above the water and gaze toward the land. The darker of the two creatures makes a snuffing sound as she clears water from her nostrils and sniffs the summer air. The sun cuts through the low-lying clouds, blazing across the sea in dark, watery jewels.

The two animals float motionless on the surface, then in tandem, they dive deep beneath the water, their bodies gliding effortlessly through the waves to a cooler layer of the sea. Their movements mirror each other perfectly, two becoming one.

At a silent signal, they swim again to the surface and look toward the shore. Just ahead lies the skerry, jagged points of black rock jutting above stones made smooth by the pounding of the sea, its only inhabitants squawking puffins and cormorants. But the two animals looking toward the skerry know that soon it will be dotted with hundreds like themselves. They are selkies, the spotted seals that call the northern waters of the Orkney Islands home. Lying in the sun, their sleek coats glistening, mouths pulled up at the corners as if to say, *I belong here, too,* for the seals make their home on both land and sea.

Beyond the skerry, the rocky coastline gives way to the beach that borders the green and gold of Shapinsay Island. The island rises, sheer cliffs circled with beaches, rolling up to grassy hills and fields of wildflowers.

"It is time," the red-spotted seal whispers to her sister.

"The waiting is over," the darker selkie replies in a language only the seals can understand. "Now it can begin."

The two dive a second time, and as they plunge through the water, their noses point purposefully toward the skerry that stretches between the North Sea and the coastline of Shapinsay Island. There is a new urgency in their movements, for just ahead, on a huge rock jutting out above the channel, stands the small figure of a girl looking out to sea. As the selkies watch, in a single movement, she dives into the icy water and swims toward them.

Part One

THE LAND

CHAPTER ONE

*H*eart beating hard, breath ragged and sharp as thorns, I run toward the beach, where all the world is water, calm and safe and whole. Blood pumps through my legs as I jog down the path, and the wind, not to be outdone, races with me. The damp of sea spray stings my face, but I welcome it. The sound of water playing on the shore feels like home.

My feet splash in the shallow ripples that wash up blue-green seaweed, cold but woolen soft, dark and deep with secrets. I stand knee-deep in the sea, content. Breathing slowly, until my heart quiets and my eyes clear, I search the horizon.

The selkies are nowhere in sight.

I shove back the annoying curls that cover my eyes and scan the shoreline to the rocky cliffs. The day is unexpectedly clear. I can see for miles. Even through the mist, the tip of the skerry winks at me. Visible only at high tide, it points a stony finger out to sea, the final extension of the island.

I begin to run again, and the pounding of my feet drums a rhythm in the sand that keeps time with the waves.

I know they will come. I know they will come.

Could I have missed them? What if they were looking for me and I wasn't here? Devil take those annoying chores.

I know they will come. I know they will come.

What if they think I forgot them? As if such a thing is possible. I've thought of little else all year.

The sand gives way to slippery boulders, jagged in disarray, as though they have been thrown in anger by some huge hand. Perhaps they were the expression of some giant's temper, once upon a time. Oh, to have the power to hurl such boulders, to hear the crack and crunch of stone meeting stone at the water's edge. That would make them listen, and I would change everything.

I squint across the ocean's surface, hoping for some sight of them. My hand has found its way to my mouth, and I feel a single sliver of fingernail that I've somehow overlooked. One quick bite and it is gone. Mither tells me it is a horrible habit, but I can't help it. Besides, I never bite my fingernails when anyone else is around. It draws too much attention to my hands.

I carefully arrange the extra-long lace sleeves Mither has sewn onto my dress to cover my hands. Gathering the extra fabric in my fists, I settle myself on a huge boulder worn smooth by the pounding waves. It thrusts out over the sea, a flat extension rounded into a hollow with a curved backrest, just right for perching above the waves. I have named it Odin's Throne, in homage to the great Viking god of war.

Here I can dream undisturbed, high above the concerns of the others. I wonder who else has sat here as I do, dreaming of other worlds; a young woman who traveled with the Pictish armies that invaded from the south or perhaps a Viking warrior once rested here. I close my eyes and imagine his approach in a huge carved ship, sails filled with the frigid north wind. I stand with the warriors, leaning into the hard gale.

But I am not a killer. I am not like the others. I am glad not to be a destroyer of innocent creatures.

I think of the latest argument with Grandpa, and my forehead wrinkles into a frown. Why is he so stubborn? Why won't he listen to me?

"We must stop the cull," I told him. "Why don't they call it what it is—the kill? The selkies have a right to survive, as we all do."

I pictured the yearly birthing of the selkie pups, the beach littered with their bodies, white and new, the darker forms of their mithers nestled nearby. The pups must be born on land and suckled for six weeks until they are old enough to swim. But many never have the chance to reach the safe harbor of the sea. Before the pups are old enough to be led into the water, the island men gather for the cull in the cover of fog where the helpless babies lie on the beach with their mithers. The men raise their clubs over and over, bringing them sharply down on the heads of the pups, killing them one by one. A well-placed blow to the head is all it takes, and the pure white of their coats is stained red with blood. A hundred pups die before the killing is over, the beach transformed into a crimson graveyard. By the time Midsummer arrives, the rain and the ocean damp have washed away all traces of the slaughter and the beach is pristine again, as though the cull never happened. The others can have their Johnsmas Foy without giving a thought to the killing that took place only weeks before.

"Some pups survive," Grandpa argued. "No one wants the selkies to die out completely."

"No?" I answered him. "They have a strange way of showing it."

Each year as the cull approaches, I make my argument, and each year Grandpa calmly explains to me why the seal babies have to die. "Selkies are greedy creatures, you see, and hardy, too, with few natural enemies. If we didn't kill some of the wee ones, there'd be so many they'd eat all the fish. We'd have no herring to fill our nets. And with no herring, we'd starve. It's a question of survival, Elin Jean."

"We could eat bread and vegetables," I always counter. "That'd be food enough. We are the greedy ones, killing the selkies to have all the herring for ourselves."

"The selkie pups must die, and that's the way of it. Always has been the way of it."

I care nothing for the way of it. I only want the selkies to be safe. "It's wrong to kill defenseless babies. I don't care what you say."

That's when Grandpa falls silent. His rocking chair wears a groove in the beaten dirt floor. He continues in a softer tone, "I don't like it any better than you, Jean." Grandpa sighs, and his sadness pours into the room. "When I was young, I was all for the money the pelts would bring, like the others. Now I've no stomach for the killing."

Like Grandpa, Fither never takes part in the cull, a fact that makes me proud. But when I try to tell him, he offers me a strange, crooked grin and turns away without reply.

I bite at the remaining bits of nail on my thumb. It has begun to bleed. I suck on the wound to make the bleeding stop and drop my hands in my lap. *Stay there, ugly things. Why must you always be in the way?* I rearrange my sleeves over my hands.

Still no sign of movement on the horizon. I glance at the quiet of the beach below me. The others have gone home to prepare for the Midsummer's Eve festivities. Good. When the selkies come, we'll be alone and peaceful-like.

Where are they?

Maybe now that I'm sixteen, they'll think me too old to swim with them or that I don't care for them anymore. They might think that I'm like the other girls, busy dreaming of a handsome lad to come courting, of making a good marriage and settling down in a crofthouse big enough for a family.

I imagine the scenario and it makes me laugh.

Excuse me, sir, you'll have to take the other road; there's a line of suitors blocking the way here. Haven't you heard? They're lining up to ask Elin Jean's fither for a dowry of land and the privilege of her hand in marriage. We're all waiting by the road here to see who she'll choose.

Hah! Not bloody likely. As if I'd want any of those dullards. I'd rather be an old maid.

An image of a dark-eyed boy walking up the road slides into my mind and will not take its leave of me. I close my eyes and see his shoulders squared against the wind and his hair blown off his face, revealing the dark skin and high cheekbones of the travellers. Tam McCodrun, who appears in my dreams, both waking and sleeping. Uninvited, he makes himself comfortable in my thoughts even though I know there is no hope that I could ever nestle into his heart and find a home there. I'd as surely be courted by a king. Did he not rebuff me at Sinclair's yesterday?

I hated to be sent to Sinclair's store. I always ran into someone I knew, or some witless children had a fine time giggling and snickering at me. Once I was chased home by several girls who tried to rip the sleeves of my dress so they could gape at my hands.

But Mither needed a needle, and I could not begrudge her that, so I agreed to go. I had a bad feeling as I trekked the distance over the soft hills to Sinclair's, so when I arrived, I waited for a bit before going in, lurking around the side of the stone building to watch the comings and goings. My hope was to enter the store when no one was there, buy the needle, and make a hasty exit before I was seen. After watching several shoppers leave, I took a chance and entered the store.

I scanned the interior, but it was empty except for old Widow Sinclair, the proprietor, standing behind the counter.

"Good day, Mrs. Sinclair," I mumbled, and ducked out of sight behind a row of goods, heading for the books displayed at the back of the store.

"Elin Jean?" she called to me. "Will you not be asking after my health? And you such a polite girl, too. Well, I won't make you beg. The swelling in my joints never stops reminding me that I'm half in the grave, and I've a nasty toothache, but I'm as well as can be expected at my age, praise St. Magnus."

Ignoring her, I lifted a book off the shelf and felt the tooled leather alive in my hands. I ran my fingers over the leather cover, wishing for the thousandth time that I could disappear into one of these stories. The pages would lift apart, revealing a pathway to a world beyond Shapinsay Island where no one knows me, anywhere no one stares or whispers about me.

I felt his presence before I saw him. Standing not ten feet away, Tam McCodrun was staring at me. Held loosely in his hands were several kitchen knives. I turned away, unable to look at him, bracing myself for the anticipated round of taunting. I prayed he would go away. I prayed he would stay.

When he spoke, his voice was low, meant only for my ears.

"It's always the books you're wanting to see." I could not tell if it was a question or a comment, but it was offered without a trace of cruelty.

I ventured a glance over my shoulder. He held my eyes for a moment, then stuffed his hands deep in his pockets and looked away, studying the jars of nails gathering dust on the shelves.

"Tam!" called Widow Sinclair. "Those knives won't sharpen themselves. You've work to do."

For a long moment, he stood defiantly, a smirk stretched across his lips. I saw his knuckles go white as he gripped the knives and strode off toward the front of the store.

Hands shaking, I slid the book back in its place on the shelf and traversed the back of the store until I was in the aisle that led to the exit, thinking only to be quit of the place. I peered around the tall shelves to the front of the store. Tam was poised at the door.

"What say you, Jean?" the widow called to me. "Will you walk with this ruffian and put him out of his misery?"

I felt my face go red, and my chest thumped with a heart that had grown too big to fit there. My mind raced for some way to stop her blathering. I charged to the front of the store, where she stood enjoying herself as if watching a troupe of street players in Kirkwall town.

I opened my mouth to speak, but Tam was quicker. "If I wanted to go walking with the Selkie Girl, I'd ask her myself. And I mean you no disrespect, Widow, but mind your own business. I'll be bringing your knives back tomorrow." And he was gone, the door slamming behind him, end of story.

I dig my toes into the pebbly surface of the hill. Giddy God. I'm a fool and half again a fool. Surely the selkies know I'll not be thinking of such things. No young man will come courting me, certainly not Tam McCodrun. Not even one of the lowest status. None would dare. My life will not be lived in the world of men and women, the world of families and babies and belonging. The outcast must find another way.

On the horizon, the light glints off the misty rocks of the skerry. And then I see them and my heart lifts.

I know them straightaway, even at this distance. Their spotted coats mark the sea in bright ovals, weaving in and out of the dark water of the voe. Once, twice, they dive and resurface, traveling toward the rocks that form the skerry.

Scrambling to the outermost reach of the cliffs, I wave my arms high over my head. "I'm here!" I shout, but the selkies continue to swim doggedly toward the skerry as if they haven't heard me.

Impatient with the waiting, I shrug out of my woolen dress, careless of my misshapen hands, now naked in daylight's unfriendly stare, and I dive up and out, plummeting into the icy water. The leap takes me safely away from the assemblage of jagged rocks below, and I enter the water like the cut of a knife.

It feels warm.

Eyes open, I eagerly navigate the distance that separates me from the selkies. I know they will be waiting.

I am the one they have come to find.

CHAPTER TWO

*N*ear the end of the skerry, I search for movement below the water, disturbances in the tides that signal the selkies' presence.

Nothing. Where are they?

Then I feel them slide alongside me in the water. My heart is thudding so hard it pounds the bones of my ears. I turn on my side and gaze at the Red. She gently touches her nose to mine. Through the rush of liquid that surrounds us, I can see the Red's kind face, gently sloping curves, and huge emerald eyes filled with affection. The Black, who flanks her sister, offers me a nearly imperceptible nod of welcome.

Together we swim, traveling out past the calm waters of the voe into the churning tides of the North Sea, circling around each other in random patterns, enjoying the freedom of the water. Then we break the surface to breathe the sweet ocean air, and dive again. Navigating down to the deeper water, I imagine I can remain underwater as long as the selkies beside me. If only I could. I would stay in the sea and never return to the land.

Through the shifting tides, we spin and glide, facing each other, then drifting apart, my hands reaching out to touch their feather-soft fur. I swim to the surface to breathe when I must, then dive again and again to be near them, until I am exhausted. Reluctantly, I climb onto the rocky sanctuary of the skerry. I'm shaking the dripping tangle of chestnut hair out of my eyes and concentrating on taking great gulps of sea air so that I can rejoin the selkies when a marvelous event holds me transfixed on the slick surface of the skerry.

The Red and the Black haul out onto the rocks, fur ruffled straight up to catch the sun. They maneuver their round bodies carefully until they lie on either side of me, their eyes wide with feral kindness. I can hear their breathing.

"You've come," I whisper, quiet as church, still afraid to move. "I knew you would come." I look from one to the other, drinking in the nearness of them, on land beside me for the first time.

"You are my true friends," I whisper, although I had not meant to say it out loud. "Let the others have their sport of me. Let St. Magnus show them the way to hell."

The selkies blink their languid eyes and tears run freely down their cheeks. Cautiously, I reach out, fearing that even the smallest movement might frighten them away, but the Black pushes a cold nose into my palm. The Red lays her damp head on my arm, and her tears fall on my water-cooled skin.

I run my fingers along their smooth bodies, their rounded animal heads. My heart is near to bursting with renegade love for these quiet creatures who never come near humans, no matter how curious they might be about the ways of the land. Selkies are curious by nature, but they know too well the dangers that follow the path of humans—the harpoon, the sharpened spear, the impenetrable net that foretells a swift and certain death.

And yet they lie here beside me.

Trust me. I will keep you safe. "Don't be afraid," I soothe. "I pledge on my life. I will not let harm find you. Not now, not ever."

The Red's sloping head swivels toward her sister with a knowing look. The Black meets her gaze, and the two creatures turn to me. In that moment, I realize that my life is tied inexplicably to theirs.

"Tell me why you are here," I ask, looking from one to the other. "I want to know."

The lapping of the waves on the rocks is the only answer.

"Why have you never come near me before?" I persist. "Why now?"

The selkies exchange another look, and fresh tears flow.

"Why do you weep? Whatever you want of me, I will do. Anything."

The intelligence in their faces leads me to expect an answer. If they could speak, their voices would be sweet, gentle with understanding, but they lie silent beside me.

I lean my head on the Red's sloping back and drink in the wonder of her. I am aware of the sharp smell of the sea, the cool north wind, the uneven surface of the rocks on my back. Most of all, I am content to be so close to the two selkies who have returned to swim with me each year.

A circle of sunlight moves across me. I close my eyes and listen to the selkies' breathing.

The Red's supple head lifts up from the curve of my arm and she sniffs the air. Her body stiffens, and she moans the long, low bellow of her breed, a sound that signals danger. The two creatures turn to me for a last look, dipping their huge heads in a ritual of goodbye, and in a single twisting movement, they dive and swim swiftly away from the skerry.

"Wait," I cry out. "Wait for me."

I search the horizon for danger but can see nothing of concern. Diving into the sea, I swim as quickly as I can to catch up. I sense them just ahead, navigating their bodies ever deeper toward the North Sea. As I plow through the water, the need for air expands my chest until I think it will burst, and I know I have to surface.

My head breaks the water. Air rushes into my lungs. Taking deep breaths to prepare to dive again, I spy the cause of the selkies' sudden flight. Rapidly approaching the skerry is a wooden fishing boat, its sails tipped deeply aft in the wind.

Giddy God, I think, ducking under the water. I mustn't be seen.

The selkies are nowhere in sight, far beyond the voe by now, safely in the North Sea, thanks be to St. Magnus. I swallow the bitter disappointment of losing my friends until next year. It swells in my throat until I think I will choke on it.

At least the selkies are safe. For now. I think of them in danger and my body tightens. "I will keep you safe," I whisper to the North Sea, the tides curling under me. "No matter what, I will keep my promise."

CHAPTER THREE

The currents are calmer in the voe, so the distance back to the beach is an easy journey. I am careful not to cause too much movement in the water or surface more than necessary in case I am being watched. Near the rocky inlet, I venture a look above the water.

No one is in sight.

To my left is a clear view of the beach that rings the island. To the right the huge boulders that house Odin's Throne protect me from spying eyes beyond. I risk a stealthy glance over my shoulder to where the boat had been.

There. I see it, bobbing in the currents, coming about to catch the wind that will sail it into the harbor.

I swim the last distance to the shore, careful not to scrape my knees on the shallow rocks. Satisfied that I am hidden from view, I creep out of the water and hide behind the rocks, watching the boat as it sails out of sight. Then, cautiously, I make my way up the rocks and retrieve my dress. I pull it over my head, arrange the long sleeves over my damp hands, and scramble for the path to home. As my feet cover the distance along the cliffs, they drum my silent wish. *No one saw me. No one saw me.*

But what is that sound?

Someone on the beach beyond Odin's Throne. No, several people, laughing. But not spontaneous merrymaking like Grandpa enjoys over a glass of ale with his friends. A darker kind. Ridicule, cruel laughter that grows out of hurting someone. Or something. It is familiar.

Then I hear the unmistakable sound of a selkie cry.

I bolt, running over the slick rocks toward it. As I round the bend, nearly losing my footing, I peer cautiously below to the other side of Odin's Throne. Iain and John Firth are throwing stones at the unfortunate selkies sunning themselves in the cove. Cumbersome on land, their thick bodies lumber away from their tormentors toward the sea, their wide eyes pleading for mercy as they flop desperately to the safety of the voe. Several of the cows, nursing mithers with their young, move more slowly than the others. Lying on the sand, helpless, is a lost pup who survived the cull. In the skirmish, he has panicked and become separated from his mither. White body pumping along the beach, he yelps pitifully for his lost protector. One of the boys lifts a wooden club and runs toward the straggler.

"No!" I shout, half running, half falling down the path to the beach, skirts flying, rocks scraping my thighs. The startled boys search for the source of the interruption.

"Don't kill him. Please. Wait!" Arms flailing for balance, I plow through the damp sand and scoop the surprised pup into my arms, where he struggles for freedom from my determined grip. Ignoring the boys, I carry the pup to the water's edge.

"There you are, little friend," I croon, laying the creature in the shallow water. "Go on. Find your mither."

Just beyond, selkies bob in the water, out of harm's reach. The terrified pup swims doggedly to the waiting group. His mither guides him to her with short barks and moans.

I tug the long sleeves of my dress over my hands and turn to the boys. "You ought to be ashamed of yourselves. How can you be so cruel to helpless creatures?"

"How can we be so cruel?" mocks Iain, a wiry, red-haired boy with the pale skin of his Viking forefathers and arms that hang too long on his skinny frame.

John, who dangles a club at his side, frowns with exasperation. "You've no right to be muckin' about in our business, Selkie Girl! You've made me lose a skin!" His voice is still changing, and his reddened cheeks reveal patches of stubble, the early beginnings of a beard.

"I'm glad of it," I throw back at him. "I hope you never get another pelt as long as you live."

Iain snickers, and the two boys move toward me. Then I hear it, the shameful rhyme that follows me wherever I go. "I warn you once, I warn you twice, I warn you out the glowrie's eyes," the boys chant, and the sound fills the beach with relentless purpose. *Drive her away. Drive away the Selkie Girl.*

Humiliation colors my cheeks. My mind races with a hundred retorts, but the words lie dry as dirt in my mouth. I drop my head, and my hair mercifully covers my face. Even these boys can make me feel as small as the grains of sand on the beach.

But I stand my ground.

"Maybe you'd do some witching for us," John suggests, laughing.

"Aye. Let's see some witching."

"Aye, swim, Selkie Girl!"

"Leave off now, lads." Tam McCodrun's shadow blocks the sun. I can see his bare feet chuff through the sand. He looks at me with eyes smooth as stones, and his dusky hair travels in curls to his shoulders. His clothes hang on his thin frame, his shirt badly in need of a wash and his trousers ripped and tattered up to his knees. A vest, sewn together from scraps of cloth that once might have been as colorful as island wildflowers, is faded, barely reminiscent of its former glory. The son of gypsy peddlers, he wears his honor around him like a coat, and I love that most about him. It doesn't matter to Tam that gypsies occupy the lowest status among the others. He carries himself like the son of kings. Ragged clothes enhance his authority as naturally as his hair is tossed by the wind. Tam McCodrun has risen above his low station with deeds of daring and rebellion, his reputation as a daredevil eclipsed only by tales of his mutinies against authority.

I want to be him.

He spreads his bare feet wide, toes dug into the sand. His black eyes look up and down my body. "Lads, lads. Leave off now. She's already been for a swim by the look of her."

The expression on his angular face is unreadable. I search it for clues, and he holds my gaze.

Do you understand? I ask silently. Oh, to have such a champion, to have such power. I curse the dripping curls that proclaim my swim.

"She was just protecting her own. That's only natural," says John.

"That's the only natural thing about her," adds Iain savagely.

"Aye. The rest of her is misbegotten." John slaps his club rhythmically onto his open palm. "Let's run her off the beach." The boys' raucous laughter blows up and into the wind, carrying its malevolent intent, a carrion bird closing in on its prey. My heart drops on the sand and lies there, hot and exposed.

"I said leave off." Tam's voice echoes with a rich authority, and the two younger boys fall silent. "Go on with you now," he adds dismissively.

"Go away, Lass Who Swims in the Sea, stay away from thee and me!" shouts John as he heads down the beach. Iain pushes him down, and the two laugh.

"Swim for us, Selkie Girl, and we'll toss Tam in after you!" More laughter.

"He'd sink like a stone, Iain," says John. "He cannot swim!"

Tam's reply comes quick. "The sea is for fools and fishes." His face splits open in a smile, handsome and guileless. "Go home before I run you off the beach myself!"

I hear the boys' laughter fade as they follow Tam's order.

Uninvited tears sting my eyes. If only I could disappear. If only Tam could see me as more than the Selkie Girl, the brunt of a hundred pitiful jokes, a victim of these embarrassing, youthful brutes.

I venture a look at him and see that he is studying his tanned feet chuffing the sand. What is he waiting for? If he's expecting a thank-you, he'll wait all day and night, too, before I'll be offering that. I didn't ask for his help.

For a moment, I am paralyzed with fear of another rebuke. I have asked nothing of him and will ask nothing in the future.

I bolt up the path, tears blinding my sight. Tripping, I fall hard on the rocks. Before I can scramble to my feet, Tam is beside me. "Are you hurt?"

I won't answer. I won't give him the chance to hurt me again.

"Careful on those rocks," he murmurs, quiet-like, and I feel his warm breath on my cheek. "I've fallen myself many a time and have the scars to prove it."

The softness in his voice leaves me breathless.

"Safe home, bonny girl," he whispers, and his lips graze my cheek.

For a moment, he looks at me as though nothing separates us, not even the sea air. I search his expression for signs of a miraculous transformation, but he wears the same confident grin.

Then he lopes down to the beach, his body set in an easy repose.

No, I must be mistaken. It cannot be. But I know it for sure and no mistake. Tam McCodrun kissed me.

CHAPTER FOUR

Clutching the lace sleeves of my dress, I fly along the path to home. What a strange, unpredictable day! *Be careful now, go slow. Don't jump too fast.* I tend to believe the best, my treacherous, optimistic nature leading me, so I often blunder into situations that might better be approached with caution. I know that about myself, and it makes me wary. Grandpa says that I have an idealistic soul, but from past experience, I have learned that spinning potentially bad circumstances into golden opportunities is not as easy as it might seem, and often unsuccessful.

In spite of these rational thoughts, a sliver of joy runs through me like the rain, and a grin crawls across my face. I laugh out loud and fall into the wild daisies that rim the path, all vibrant yellow and white.

I kindly invite you to stay forever, unexpected, life-changing day. St. Magnus, tell me, what has changed? What has brought this day?

I watch the light crawl across the sky. Tam's face appears in the puff of clouds above me, and it is smiling. I grin back, made foolish with hope. Smoke from the crofthouse mingles with the clouds and makes me think of home. Like the daydream it is, Tam's face dissolves into a passing cloud.

Maybe I won't go home. Maybe I'll stay forever in this moment and avoid all of it. Tam and I will take a boat to the mainland. We'll board a ship and travel around the world. Our stateroom will have gilded furnishings and a huge feather bed that parts like the waves when we fall upon it.

Tam and I, alone every night of the voyage, will lie awake long after the others have fallen asleep, talking of this and that, telling stories and laughing at little things that have happened during the day. We will have secrets that no one else knows. We will know each other as well as one person can know another, and we will love what we see.

Such a beautiful dream. Such a beautiful lie.

I brush the grass from my shoulders. Mither will be looking for me. I imagine her sitting by the window that opens out to the sea. Here she enjoys the dual benefits of the morning light and a dazzling view of the sea. The entire landscape is available to her from this chair, and it is well known in the family that this is her favorite spot.

Much of Mither's day is spent on her feet, doing the multitude of chores the croft demands, but there are times when quiet work is required, sewing and mending, carding and winding wool to make sweaters for the cruel winters. Then she sits in this spot, hands moving deftly through the wool, eyes fixed on a place far out to sea, listening to the faint sounds of the selkies singing their songs of summer.

Ahead, the crofthouse waits, perched on a rise that tumbles into a verdant meadow that rings the sea. Rectangular in shape, fashioned with stone and thatch, the crofthouse is home to our entire family, people and animals alike, so that even in the cruelest weather, our horses, sheep, and goats are nearby, warm and safe. Our living quarters consist of two rooms—a main room, which houses our kitchen and living area, and the ben end of the house, where our box beds are built into the stone walls for privacy and warmth. The emerald grass in front of the low-slung house is interrupted by a black-furrowed vegetable garden, where Mither nurtures, through the short growing season, beans, beets, spinach, and turnips. Potatoes and onions thread their roots deep in the loamy soil, and a prize rhubarb patch yields succulent fruit Mither sweetens with treacle and folds into tarts for Sunday supper.

Behind the house, golden fields of wheat dip their heads in the wind, and in a stone-fenced field beyond, the chubby bodies of sheep and goats graze on the determined grass. Only scrubby bushes block the view, for the trees have long ago been harvested to fashion household furnishings and boats, leaving the landscape visible from the cliffs to the sea.

Dotted along the front of the house are Mither's flower beds. Lovingly tended daisies and delicate Queen Anne's lace mingle together like partners at a dance. One bare spot of earth stands as the reminder of a wayward goat that managed to escape the paddock. It munched contentedly on the young buds until Mither threatened the amazed creature with a broom, chasing it back into the field, accompanied by Grandpa's delighted laughter.

The sea wind is cool at my back, and I am drawn to its comfort. I think of the selkies who have given me their trust. I will never be far from the sea. Here is a roaring power to be reckoned with, this channel where the wild North Sea meets the mighty Atlantic. At odds with each other, the two bodies of water collide, churning into waves that can rise to forty feet. As changeable as the weather that reigns over it, the channel rests, mild as a newborn lamb, until the wind shifts it into raging tides that can catch the most experienced sailor unawares. And in a storm, the waves stretch as tall as mountains, white peaks battling for domain over the waterway. Even the thought of these storms humbles the others. What the sea gives up, it must take away, they say. And the truth of those words is born of bitter experience. Each year families lose fishermen to the sea, gobbled up in the wild storms, bodies lost forever beneath the tides.

The sun breaks in bright lines through the clouds and lies amiably on my damp shoulders. I steal another glance at the sea, thinking of the white-capped quilt that beckons me to lie in its embrace, my companion and safe harbor, the home of my friends.

I lean my body into the whine of the wind and start again down the path toward home. Below me, Grandpa waves from the entrance to the byre, then disappears into the interior. I hear him run his bow over the strings of his fiddle for a quick tuning, and satisfied, he plays a jig that reverberates through the air, buoyant as the arrival of Midsummer.

The music tumbles out the open window and runs through me until a fierce energy builds in my bones and my feet map a course of their own, dancing down the path. I enter the open door of the croft in a promenade over the hard-packed dirt floor, brown hair swinging over one shoulder, then the other, and I am one with the wild rhythm of the music.

I catch a glimpse of Mither, illuminated by the dual light of day spilling through the window and firelight, soft from glowing peat, her gnarled hands poised midair in a dance of their own.

Grandpa increases the tempo, faster and faster, until I feel like I might whirl myself through the thatched roof, my arms bending like stalks of grain whipped by island gales. This is freedom. No boundaries, no rules, no expectations. Tam's face appears in my mind. We are dancing, eyes locked together. I hold the image as the music transports me to a place where I am content.

Grandpa is a stylish, fine fiddle player, facile with the fingering and sensitive to the shifting moods of the music.

Like Grandpa, I am a fool for music. The melodies run through me like a strange elixir. Since I was a small child, dancing has been my passion. My family has told me that my dancing is unlike any of the traditional island dances, wilder and more spontaneous, without plan. I cannot dance like the others, the steps stiff and regimented. When I dance, my body tells me where it will go and I follow.

Grandpa reaches a crescendo, and on his cue, I leap and land, silent as a cat, as he bows the final notes with a flourish. He gently tucks his fiddle underneath his arm, leaving his hands free to clap vigorously in a tribute to our shared performance. "Well done, me," he boasts proudly. "Well done, you. There's none can dance the music to life as yourself."

"Aye," echoes Mither, settling into her window seat. "She's the gift in her, our Elin Jean."

"The best dancer from Shapinsay to Kirkwall town."

"What does it matter if no one ever sees it?" This comes out sharper than I intended. It is an old wound, one that refuses to heal. I adjust the long sleeves of my dress over my hands and concentrate on making myself invisible.

Mither and Grandpa exchange a look. Grandpa reaches into his vest pocket and produces his ever-present wooden pipe. Like an old friend, it nestles comfortably in his palm as he touches a match to the bowl, and the sweet smell of tobacco skims about the room.

"Just you wait," Grandpa declares, an annoying twinkle playing in the corner of his eye. His cheeriness irritates me. He is sweet, I admit, but he is forever trying to jolly me up. His intentions are as transparent as glass, and I only end up feeling worse. Does he think I don't know what he's trying to do? He accuses me of being sunny, his word for my temperament, but he is the one who is forever spinning false happiness out of gloom.

"Waiting. Always waiting. When will the waiting be over?" I say this mostly to myself, not expecting or even wanting an answer.

Grandpa snorts. "When you're stone-dead, buried in the ground and cold as the fishes."

"Then you're wishing you had the waiting to do," Mither adds hoarsely, as though talking takes more energy than she can spare. Mither is often ill, sometimes for days at a time. Even when she is up and about, like now, every task strips her of strength. Lately, she has been detached and morose, as though some great weight pushes her away from us, and I worry about the cause. It has been so long since I heard her laugh that I am beginning to think I have never heard it at all. But I remember the sound of it, rich and open like plowed earth, and I long to hear it again.

Grandpa nods, pondering Mither's comment, I suppose, because they exchange one of their looks, as if they are in perfect, unspoken agreement. Once I cornered Mither with my opinion about this understanding between them. "Why do you and Grandpa even bother to talk? You read each other's thoughts before you say them."

"Your grandpa understands the world better than most," Mither told me. "He takes the time to watch and listen, then thinks about the meanings. It's no hardship to agree with a man as thoughtful as your grandpa."

Grandpa blows rings of smoke, one inside the next. He sends the ovals toward the ceiling, and they follow willingly until they collide with the lingering haze from the cooking fire above and their perfect circles distort and disappear. I know what Mither means about Grandpa being thoughtful, but I think it must be something more. I take the time to watch and listen, but no such meaning comes to me. I only end up feeling more confused.

Mither sighs and stands, tossing a ball of wool into the basket at her feet. Before she closes the lid, I see a corner of shimmering blue-green fabric curled up in the basket. What is that? I thought I had seen all Mither's sewing projects. She interrupts my thoughts before I can ask her about it. "And where were you this morning, Elin Jean? Your fither was looking for you."

A wave of fear knifes through me. I compose my face into a mask. "Out for a walk, is all," I say evenly. After all, it's not really a lie. I did go for a walk.

Mither gathers up my tangle of damp curls. "A fine nest for the birds you have here."

"A bit dampish, if you ask me," adds Grandpa, handing Mither a clean cloth to hurry the drying. They know I've been in the sea. I'm sure of it. It is Fither who mustn't know.

Mither burrows the cloth into my hair and then moves to the cupboard to fetch her seashell comb. Delicate and pearly, it is her prize possession. Most of the combs on the island are made from seal bones, but Mither won't allow anything in the house made from the killing of seals. Gentle creatures should be allowed to live in peace, she says, even if the price is our having to do without.

"Come to me," she beckons. "Your hair goes all far-flung-like when you're dancing wild."

There is no need to say more. Mither is a willing conspirator in keeping my secret from Fither. She has always been the peace-keeper in the family, the buffer that stands between two stubborn factions, Fither and me.

I sit on the low stool in front of the warm hearth, and Mither works the comb slowly through the mass of curls that fall down my back. She hums deep in her throat until the song she has sung to me since I was small emerges, low-pitched and husky.

Mither's song. I am too old for lullabies, but Mither's voice is oddly soothing to me. I close my eyes and drift to a calm place as she sings.

> *Voices whisper with the wind*
> *Of places you have never been,*
> *Singing songs of ebb and flow,*
> *Of secrets you will someday know.*
> *Selkies gliding in between*
> *Tides that play upon the sea,*
> *Calling you to come along,*
> *Beckon you to sing the song.*

"Listen to the sea," I sing with Mither. "There is a land far beneath. Awaken from your sleep to the mysteries down below."

Midsummer's Eve. All year I have waited for this night. I have reached the age of sixteen, when island girls can take part in the Johnsmas Foy, the grand celebration that signals the coming of summer, the time of the midnight sun, when daylight lasts through midnight and darkness lays claim to only a few short hours. After the shadowy winter, with its short daylight hours, the warm sun always feels like a miracle. Is it any wonder that the others greet its appearance with reveling until dawn in a celebration of the bright days of summer to come?

How can I convince Fither to let me go to the foy? How can I explain why I must go? This past year the days and nights have blended into one another with little difference, sleeping, eating, chores, the same routine day after endless day. I'd rather die than live this life another year. This year I will go to the foy, even if Fither says I cannot. This year I will not be left behind.

"What is it, Peedie Buddo?" I didn't realize I had pulled away.

"Nothing."

"Nothing?"

"Sometimes I have the strangest feeling, walking through the days sleeping-like. I'm awake, and yet I'm dreaming, all at the same time."

"You are waiting for the knowin'. All of us are searchers until we find it." Mither looks toward the sea. "Someday you will know your place in the world and what you are meant to do in it. From that day forward, everything will be different."

"Worse is more likely," Grandpa grumbles, drawing on his pipe.

Mither's eyes search for mine, and I reluctantly meet them. "Eyes green as the sea and thoughts twice as deep," she says. "You will find the knowin'."

"A brown-haired lass, there's none so fair. Neither golden nor black locks can compare," rhymes Grandpa.

"Don't be saying that," I snap at him. "You're only feeling sorry for me."

Grandpa adjusts his body in the woven seat of his rocking chair. "I mean you no disrespect. I like rhyming, is all."

I think of the boys on the beach saying those cruel rhymes.

"I hate rhymes," I say. "All of them."

CHAPTER FIVE

*R*hyming has taunted me since the day I decided to go to school. I had learned, during the long Orkney winters, all Grandpa could teach me. I could manage columns of numbers in my head, although I hated the precision and finality of figures, and I could describe the complex geography of the islands that dotted the Scottish coast. I had put to memory entire sections of the Orkneyinga Saga, the stories of how the islands were settled by the clash of Norse raiders and Pictish warriors, but I knew there was more to know than could be learned within the walls of the croft. Why was the sun in evidence for more hours in the summer than in the winter? Why did sheep dung coax the flowers from their stems and urge potatoes to bulge with life? Why did some unlucky lambs die in the spring, stillborn as they burst from the womb? And the questions that burned white-hot inside me, until I thought I would burst into flames from the inside out. Why do we keep to ourselves? Why does Mither never go to town? Why is it that neighbors never knock on our door to chat about the weather or borrow some staple for supper? Why are we different from the others?

No one would answer these questions. My parents were adept at dodging them, and if I pressed, they simply stopped speaking. I learned from Grandpa that my parents meant no harm, that the questions upset them terribly, and he cautioned me to stop asking. Although I did as I was told, I remained tortured by their cruel choice to refuse me this knowledge.

Grandpa did his best to respond to my endless questions, but he frequently threw up his hands. "Now, what purpose does the knowing of that serve?" he'd complain. "Why would a wee one like yourself need to know such things?"

I never spoke of it, but I suspected the questions were beyond his knowledge, too, so to spare his feelings, I quietly accepted his inability to answer them. I kept my questions stored, waiting for the answers I was sure I would someday find, but I wondered why the other children trooped off to school in the cool mornings while I had to stay at home. I longed to join them.

I imagined them sitting in neat rows, facing a brilliant teacher from the mainland, speaking of the wonders that lie beyond tiny Shapinsay Island, of Shetland and the Faroe Islands congregating farther north, of the Norse countries to the east and the cities of Scotland to the south. And west—what lies beyond the cruel North Sea? Surely the teacher would know.

I begged Fither to let me go to school.

"No, lass," he barked each time I asked, and the creases around his mouth grew deeper with annoyance. "Your mither needs you here about the croft. There's work to be done."

So I waited until evening, and as Fither drank his ale, his face softening in the firelight, I doubled my pleas. It was more than knowledge that beckoned me. It was the desire to be like the others, carefree with worldliness. I watched them on the road every morning, until the thought of joining them haunted me, and I fretted myself into a constant state of agitation.

Fither stood firm. "Stay away from the others," he ordered. "Do you hear me, Jean? They are not like us." And although I opened my mouth to protest, I was silenced by the furor of his tone. How are they not like us? I wanted to know. Why are we different? No matter how often I asked, the answer was always the same. "Stay away from the others."

Until I turned eight years old. I think of it now as the time when everything changed, the year my innocence yielded to hard truth. If I'd been an obedient child and accepted Fither's order, that might have been the end of it, but now I know that it was bound to happen. My restless nature would not be still, and so one day, on a crisp spring morning when the buds concentrated on pushing up through the warm earth, I followed through on a carefully laid plan.

I woke before first light, pulled on my best woolen dress, and tiptoed silently into the early-morning air, closing the heavy door quietly behind me so as not to wake my sleeping family. I positioned myself behind a stand of scruffy bushes that bordered the road and waited, munching on a slice of bannock I'd brought for breakfast. I thought of the day that lay before me like a feast, the teacher's welcoming smile, books to devour, and above all, being with the other children I had watched so often passing by.

After I had watched the sky grow light, waiting so long I thought it must grow dark again, I was rewarded with the sound of laughing children marching up the road. I crouched out of sight until the group had passed, listening to their chatter. Then I joined them at the rear, just as I had planned, as though I had been acquired, like a damp leaf clings to a shoe. For a few precious moments, I was one of them, and the warmth of it filled me with contentment.

Ahead, a group of boys stopped to wait for the slower children to catch up.

"Who's that?" one of the boys called out, pointing at me.

The others turned to look. I smiled and dipped a curtsy according to plan.

"Good day to you," I offered. "May I join you on your way to school?"

I remember the squawk of kittiwakes circling above in the brief silence that followed. Then a towheaded girl with bright pink cheeks blurted, "It's the Selkie Girl."

"Aye. The one who's misbegotten," said one of the older children.

"Her mither's a witch," another child whispered.

I watched them form a rough circle around me, chattering and spinning a tale of me that I had never heard before.

"No one knows who her people are . . ."

". . . or where she comes from."

"Her parents never posted the banns for marriage."

"She swims in the sea!"

Wait, I am like you! I am like you! I wanted to scream at them, but the words turned to sand in my mouth, and I stood silent, staring at the shine of my boots.

"A selkie girl. That's what she is."

"Selkie Girl, Selkie Girl," the children began to chant. A small boy pushed me, then a bigger girl. I fell to the ground as the children crowded around, jostling each other for a better position, as if I were a freak on display at the fair. An older boy pushed through the crowd. He roughly grabbed my arm and pulled back the sleeves of my dress. He held up his prize so the others could see my hand. I struggled to get away, but he held me fast.

"Look! Look at the webs!" he shouted.

"Ahhh," the children breathed at the sight of my webbed hands, horror and delight mingling together in their faces.

"Witch!"

"Witches aren't allowed at school."

"Or selkies." This clever remark sent a wave of laughter over the group, encouraging the fun.

Oddly, it was one of the littlest girls who threw the first stone. She was too young to understand the meaning of the event unfolding on the road. It was a playful thing, done without a moment's thought to the consequences. The rock bounced harmlessly off my arm. It stung like nettles, but I remember thinking, *That doesn't hurt, not really.*

Another rock hit my back. Another was thrown at my ankle. Another and another flew, hitting me all at once, and I understood. I covered my face and head as best I could, but not before I caught a glimpse of their mouths stretched wide with hate. As the stones flew, I heard them chanting, "Hie thee, Lass Who Swims in the Sea, stay away from thee and me." And as I scrambled to my feet and ran, I heard them chattering behind me, like gulls that look haughtily down from the highest rocks, as if to say, *Ha-ha. We're the highest now.*

You can imagine what happened next. When I returned home, bruised and bloody, a gash opened across my temple, Fither knew without my telling him what had happened, and he forbade me ever to leave the borders of the croft.

The others had made me a prisoner. Devil take them all.

CHAPTER SIX

The stoning was the beginning of it, but not the end. Often the children would call out their cruel rhymes as they passed our croft. We ignored them, as if they were a pulled muscle or a hangnail, and eventually, they wearied of it. But even now, years later, the sound of rhyming, even Grandpa's love of verse, causes the hair to rise on the back of my neck and the muscles in my shoulders to hunch up for a fight.

Grandpa's eyes study mine, glazed with hurt. He didn't mean to insult me with his rhyming. I know that. He wasn't thinking of my humiliation at the hands of the others because it was long ago, but the memory of those cruel rhymes returns to me more often than I like, and I feel sick with shame at the thought of it.

Mither gives my hair a final tuck, taming one loose strand. I shrug her hand away.

"It's what's inside of you that matters," she says. "You know that, Elin Jean."

"No one cares about my inside. They're too busy gawking at the outside."

Grandpa rises, stretching the kinks out of his joints. "The lads and lasses'll take notice of your dancing this night at the foy." His smile stretches wide.

"I can go? I can go to the foy?"

"There'll be a full moon this night. It'll be a celebration like none before, the torches of heather lighting up the beach, the dancing and singing until dawn. And one young lass, proclaimed by all, the finest dancer in the Orkneys."

I grab his sleeve and force him to face me. "Are you saying I can go? Tell me, Grandpa."

"I'm the elder in this house, am I not? Would you be expecting me to go to the foy alone and you sixteen?"

I heard it plain as day. *I'm the elder in this house,* he said.

"I can see the looks on them," he whispers, closelike, before I can say more. "Eyes wide as saucers with the surprise." Striking a pose, Grandpa imitates the crackling voice of nosy Mrs. Muir. " 'Have you ever seen the likes of that dancing? More wondrous than the skelly sun hitting the cliffs of Hoy! Who is she, that bonny lass?' And me saying proudlike, 'Who else? That's my granddaughter, Jean.' "

"But the others," I say. "What if they hate the dancing and think me a fool?"

"What a bulder of nonsense," says Grandpa, his arm slipping around my shoulders. I can smell the tangy scent of him through his wool vest. "I'll be there beside you, and you, dancing the music to life, what choice will the others have but to love you as I do."

Grandpa reaches for his fiddle and begins a tune, one of my favorites, but I cannot dance. I am bombarded with fear and hope. Holding sway over them both is my resolve. As the music saturates the room, I imagine the foy, the chance to go at last. Tam will be there. He will see me dance.

I take Mither's waist and swing her around the room. She is as light as a child. "I can go to the foy, Mither, I can go!" I shout, over and over, dancing with her until the crofthouse door flies open unannounced and daylight spills in behind a tall figure. Before my eyes adjust, I know the slant of his shoulders outlined in the doorway.

"What's this?" The dark furrows of Fither's face gleam with the day's labor.

"Nothing, Fither," I say quickly.

"A bit of fun, Duncan, is all," Grandpa offers.

I slide toward the door to the byre. I might have the chance to escape, but he catches me.

"Hover you now, lass. What's your hurry?"

A flutter of fear rifles through me. "No hurry, Fither." I look down at the floor to avoid his eyes. I can feel his disapproval surround me like the pungent odor of smoked fish. He shoulders out of his coat and hangs it on its peg near the door.

"Sit you down, then. I'd be having a word with you." Fither wraps his lanky arms around Mither. She allows a brief kiss, then dips away, deftly avoiding his embrace.

Fither sighs loudly, making all of us aware of his disappointment at her rejection. "Pale as the evening sky and twice as lovely," he murmurs to Mither's back.

Mither turns and gives him a crooked look. "A lie is harder to tell in the long haul than the cruelest truth." She tucks a strand of graying hair behind her ear.

"The truth! There's a slippery fish," says Grandpa, and his chuckling eases the tension in the room. "Just when you've caught it up, it slides away from you."

But Fither is as determined as always in his courtship of Mither. "I only know what my eyes tell me, and my heart. You're as bonny as the first time I laid eyes on you. And when I'm working in the fields, I'm only thinking of being home with you. A warm fire, a good stew, and yourself, altogether what this crofter needs."

Fither engages in this lovemaking every day, so concentrated in it that the world could come to an end and he'd hardly notice. I inch toward the door. A few more steps and I'll be gone.

"Jean!"

Garn. No escaping now.

"Come here, lass. Sit you down."

I sit obediently on the low stool by the fire, my heart thrashing like a trapped animal.

"James Leslie saw you this morning swimming out beyond the voe. That is forbidden. You know that, Elin Jean."

Giddy God! It was James Leslie's boat I saw this morning!

"Please, Fither. I can explain."

"I'll not be hearing explanations for what you know is wrong."

His voice drones on, but I am not listening. I already know the lecture by heart, and even if I agree, he will continue as if I do not. Better to be silent. That horse's ass, James Leslie. Why couldn't he hold his infernal tongue? I pick at a piece of loose skin around my fingernail and bite it off.

"I've told you and told you," Fither goes on. "Even the finest swimmer in Orkney must respect the tides. They change in a peedie minute and pull the strongest swimmer down into the blackness. Only a fool tempts the sudden tides beyond. Is drowning what you're after?"

"I know the tides," I murmur.

"What's that?"

"Nothing, Fither."

"Not even a half-wit swims in the sea. There's reasons for that, lass."

I am more than familiar with the reasons. I have been raised on tales that chronicle the dangers of the sea. All the Orkney folk know well the price the sea demands from those who take their living from it. The sea will give up her treasures for the table, seaweed for the gardens, and seal oil to light the cruisie lamps, but she will take her reward. Each year fishermen are lost to the sea, bodies washed up on the shore, blue and white with death, or worse, never found for proper burial. The sea is both nurturer and enemy, the proprietor of the others' deepest fears.

Fither's angry voice cuts through my thoughts. "Answer me, Jean. Why did you swim out beyond the voe? Is it a watery grave you'd be after?"

He speaks of it as though it is a choice, but it is not.

"I cannot help myself," I answer. "Something pulls me down to the beach and into the sea."

Fither's body goes taut, and I feel the anger rising from him like steam off water at the boil.

"I'll not stand for it. I'll not have you risking your life when the fog rolls in and you cannot see beyond your nose."

This much is true. The fog can fall suddenly, so thick it covers the harbor for half a mile out so that even the seal oil lamps cannot penetrate the soupy air. Fishermen have no greater fear than being caught at sea when the fog sets in. With no landmarks to guide them, they might take a wrong direction, heading out to the raging channel, rather than sailing into the protected waters of the voe. The island people spend countless time and energy predicting the weather and its capricious nature. It is a matter of more than a little concern. Lives are risked on foretelling the whimsical weather patterns.

"None of the others would dare swim in these waters," Fither admonishes. "You must leave your childish play behind and take responsibility for your own safety."

"I had to swim out to the skerry." The minute the words leave my lips, I regret saying them. There's no chance I can make him understand.

"Had to? What were you thinkin', lass? What possible reason could you have to do a foolish thing like that?"

I am silenced by this question, but Mither answers quietly from her corner of the room. "The selkies were calling her, the Red and the Black."

I shoot Mither a look of gratitude for this defense, but she is looking at Fither. I seize the chance to press my argument. "They came back, Mither, just as you said they would."

"Aye, at Midsummer's tide."

Then the words tumble out as fast as I can form them before the moment passes. "One red as the sun going down, the other dark as peat. Noses lifted straight out of the water like they were looking for something."

"There are hundreds of selkies in the voe this time of year, alike as one another," Fither scoffs.

"It was the Red and the Black and no mistake. Their eyes were human-like. They were crying."

"Nonsense! It was only seawater dripping." Fither's face hovers inches from mine, and I shrink from his fury. He is wrong, but he refuses to see it.

"Selkies cry just as humans do and for the same reasons, longing for what's been lost and cannot be found," answers Mither, and I want to hug her for understanding.

Fither studies the floor, and we wait. "What's to be done with you, Jean?"

"I try to stay on land, Fither, but then I'm aching for the feel of the water and the pull of the waves."

"You listen to me." Fither's hands dig into my shoulders. "I'll put a stop to this, even if I have to lock you away. Do you hear me?" Fither releases me with a push, and I fall backward off the stool.

Oh, please God, no, don't lock me away, not now, not the night of the foy. Please, St. Magnus, no.

I grab the hem of his jacket and bury my face in it. "Don't lock me away, Fither. I won't swim again. I promise." This babbling is a lie. I cannot stay away from the sea, but I will say anything at this moment to lure him away from his threat.

"Jean!" The sharpness in his voice startles me, and when I look up, I see that my sleeves have fallen back and my hands, still clutching his coat, are exposed. I hide them behind my back and continue as if nothing has happened, hoping to distract him, but dread crawls up my spine like a spider. "I'm sorry, Fither," I say quickly. "It was the Midsummer sun and the calm of the water. I'll not be forgetting again."

"Give me your hands."

Dear God, make me disappear.

Mither takes hold of Fither's arm. "Duncan, have your ale," she coaxes. "It's waiting. I've freshly baked bannock. You must be hungry." Mither lifts the cloth covering from a cakelike loaf, and the rich smell of bread drifts through the room. My stomach growls. How strange to be hungry at a time like this.

Grandpa hurries to agree with Mither. "Aye. I'm thirsty as a landlocked fisherman. All the world looks brighter with a full stomach and a pint."

Fither glares at Grandpa. His sharp features glow red in the firelight, whether from the heat of the coals or the fury of his argument, I cannot be sure.

"I'll not be dissuaded." Fither holds out his hands as if demanding payment for a debt. "Give them to me."

I see the sun glittering on Tam McCodrun's bare shoulders, his black eyes smiling at me.

"Show me your hands!" Fither shouts, and I see that his hands are balled into fists at his sides. He has lost patience, and I am postponing the inevitable.

Reluctantly, I offer him my hands. The house is still, as if holding its breath with me.

"Webbed," he says, his voice hoarse with defeat. "They've grown webbed again."

CHAPTER SEVEN

$\mathcal{M}$y hands lie small and naked in Fither's callused palms. At first glance, they look ordinary, the salty hands of a girl who lives by the sea, but closer inspection reveals the transparent webbing that extends to the first knuckle of each finger. Between my thumb and forefinger, sheer tissue connects the space.

"Fetch my gully knife," Fither commands, but no one moves.

"It's no good to cut them," Mither pleads, the edge in her voice revealing her fear. "They'll only grow back like always."

Like always. How many times has Fither cut the webs? The cutting began before I can remember, when the webs were nothing more than tiny flaps of infant skin. Mither has told me they hardly bled at the first cutting and Fither crowed that this would be the end of them. But within a few days, a nearly imperceptible layer of skin re-formed between my baby thumb and first finger, red and angry at the insult. Each day, as the webs regenerated, Fither examined their progress, waiting until they were healed to safely cut them again. But no matter how often he cut them, they always grew back, determined as weeds, and Fither despaired of ridding me of them.

As I grew, the cutting occurred less often, the danger of infection discouraging Fither, until it shrank to a yearly ritual. As another year marked my life, birthdays became a cruel reminder of my deformity. Once, I hardly remember how old I was, Mither could not stanch the flow of blood from the cutting. She stayed with me long into the night, pressing cloths on the wounds, while Fither paced, muttering unintelligibly to himself.

At dawn I woke to hear my parents engaged in a terrible quarrel. Fither's voice pierced the morning with shouting. Mither sobbed without restraint. In my box bed, I pulled the covers over my head, but I could still hear the sounds of their fighting.

Finally, exhausted with accusations and blaming, they fell silent. But tension crowded the house until I thought I would explode from the pressure of it. Eventually, they reached an uneasy truce, but a cold distance remained between them. I never knew what transpired, but the ache between my fingers healed into an itch, a constant reminder that it was all because of me.

"You'd have me do nothing!" Fither roars, bringing me back from my reverie. "She's sixteen now, time to make a good marriage to a crofter with land, home, and hearth. She'll need more than a dowry to fetch a husband."

Mither lays a calming hand on Fither's arm as though gentling a wild thing. "Even if you cut her hands clean off, she'll never be like the others."

"Who will she be like, then?" Fither's question hangs unanswered, echoing off the four walls that define my life.

I close my eyes and will them to stop arguing.

"I cannot bear to hear the others laugh and make sport of her," Fither confesses grimly. "I will not stand idle, seeing her married off to some tinker without a sturdy tub for washing or a strip of land to keep his family fed. Is that what you'd be wanting for our Elin Jean?"

"I'd be wanting her to marry for love." Mither's voice is firm, edged with her own barely controlled anger. "I've heard tell of one who lost his reason for love, of a crofter who took a stunder to love a lass with nothing but herself to offer. And that was enough."

Fither's body sags as though some tightly held strings have been loosened. He walks to the hearth and pokes the burning peat bricks, throwing up a shower of sparks. One thrust is enough to wake the fire, but Fither jabs them over and over until they dissolve into shreds of glowing coal.

Grandpa breaks the silence. "Those ponies'll be wanting to be fed." He lifts the woolen cap that is his year-round companion from its hook by the door. His back is stooped more than usual as he pulls the cap over his head. Grandpa despises arguments, finding any excuse to avoid them. And he cannot bear the cutting. I think he is afraid of it.

"Don't run from it, Grandpa," Mither pleads. "There's those here who need your help."

Grandpa sighs. "Dunna cut her, man. There's naught to be done for it. You cannot change what nature has meant to be."

A single tear slides down Mither's face.

This is my fault. I look at my hands, and the webs sneer at me, self-satisfied with their importance. In that moment, I hate my hands more than I have ever hated anything, even the others. If I could kill them, I would. "Cut them, Fither," I demand. "I want to be like the others."

Fither covers the distance to the cupboard in two long strides and lifts the gully knife from its dark interior. He takes the leather strop from its hook and runs the blade at an angle up and down. It makes a brisk, shushing sound as it slides over the surface of the strap. *Shhurt. Shhurt.*

A shaft of light glints off the metal and shoots across the room. I lay my hands on the rough-hewn table, fingers spread wide. "It does not hurt too much, Mither."

"That's a good lass." Fither is calm now. His hand hovers over mine, the knife held firmly. "Hold your hands steady. Steady now."

I am in the North Sea, diving deep into its welcoming embrace. I feel the velvety touch of fish, whisper-soft, and the quiet thrum of the tides. I hear the door slam, Grandpa escaping into the byre.

Fither positions the knife above my hand. He hesitates.

Giddy God, what is he waiting for?

"Cut them!" I scream.

"No!" Mither wrenches Fither's arm away, and the knife clatters to the floor. "Cutting her hands will not keep her from the sea." Mither's face is wild and streaked with tears. Her hair has come loose, a jumble of chestnut streaked with gray. "You cannot shape her to fit your dreams of what's to come or cut her to fit you like a bit of cloth. Look at her! Can you not see she's bonny as she is?"

The crofthouse waits, patient as the dust motes that float toward the chimney, as Mither sobs and Fither caresses her tear-streaked face. "There, there, darling one. Don't cry. I cannot bear to see you cry."

This gentle treatment from Fither unleashes Mither's keening, an anguished sound more painful to me than the cutting has ever been. Mither rocks back and forth with the agony of it, her hands fluttering helplessly in the air.

I hear the others laughing, feel their rough hands pulling back my sleeves and the sharp sting of a stone hitting my back, watch a small child run away from me, hear furtive whispering. My life stretches out as jagged and lonely as the sea-battered cliffs of Hoy.

The knife lies on the floor undisturbed until a spark flies up from the fire, breathing momentary life into the cold blade. I reach for it, expecting someone to stop me, but no one does.

The knife feels good in my hand. A calm washes over me.

"I'll cut them myself!" I cry, and with one downward stroke, I slash the largest web. As the first wave of pain sears through me, Mither screams my name. She hastens to stanch the flow of blood. I look at the red droplets that fall on my apron and know that nothing will be the same from this day forward.

CHAPTER EIGHT

Mither leans over my wounded hand, pressing a blood-soaked towel on the wound to stop the bleeding. Hands clenched at his sides, Fither paces the floor of the crofthouse like a sentinel, searching for some small task to occupy his mind. Now and then, he makes some minor adjustment in the room, straightening the ladle that hangs over the hearth, tightening a latch on the cupboard door, as though performing these tasks will offer him some relief.

A numb feeling has crept over me. I allow Mither's ministrations without protest, waiting for Fither to leave for his nightly pint of ale in town. He is waiting to be sure his only child will not die from loss of blood, like the cut is that deep.

Will he never go? I'll survive. I have so far, haven't I?

After a time, Mither announces with relief that the bleeding has slowed. Fither mumbles a few words and strides out the door, as if he, too, cannot wait to be rid of us.

As the door clicks shut behind him, Mither pulls me to her,

but I am already wrapped in the smothering embrace of Fither's disappointment, and her cloying touch is more than I can bear.

I escape to the beach, where I can listen to the sea offer its constant greeting to the rocks below. Perched on Odin's Throne, I look back on the green meadow, where a spray of yellow wild-flowers lies sideways at the request of the wind, and the sturdier daisies shake their heads in agreement. I hear the plaintive bleat-ing of a lamb from the flock of sheep grazing peacefully in the field below. Nothing looks amiss. The sheep munch on the sweet summer grass contentedly. The lamb that complained seems to have solved its problem, and why not? What do sheep have to think about? All they do is eat and sleep and once a year give up their coats for a good cause.

My hand aches. Mither stopped the bleeding, but the gash opens and blood snakes out each time I move it. My lace sleeve is stained with blood. I had not meant to slice so deep.

Turning my face into the soothing rush of the wind, I close my eyes and am in Kirkwall town. Dressed in fine clothes, I have boarded the monthly ship to the mainland, where the others of-ten shop for the latest pretties from Aberdeen or even Edinburgh. I stroll casually through the cobbled streets, gazing in shop-windows, greeting passersby who have just returned from far-off ports like Amsterdam and London, exchanging pleasantries with scholars and merchants and ladies of fashion. My hands are en-cased in spotless white satin gloves decorated with pearl buttons. The gentlewomen gathered in the square exclaim to less fashion-able ladies, "You're not wearing satin gloves? Pity. They're all the rage in London this year."

Grandpa used to go regularly to Kirkwall when he was young to partake in singing and storytelling at the pubs and drink a pint as well. He took my grandmither, rumored to have been a great beauty, to the annual livestock sale and festival every year, but she died before I was born and he didn't care to go to the mainland alone. Mither never leaves the boundaries of the croft, and Fither, well, as far as I know, he has never left Shapinsay Island.

I have long since given up asking to go to the mainland. There's no point in it. The answer is always the same. "We have all we need here—fish from the sea, vegetables from the garden, and sheep to give us wool. Be grateful for what you have. What else would you be needing?"

It's not a matter of needing. It's a matter of wanting. Besides, are the two really so different?

The slender bodies of otters dive in and out of the sea, searching for herring for their suppers. Even at a task as serious as filling their stomachs, they go about it with a playful attitude. I long to join them in the sea. The salt water will take away the sting in my hand and heal the cut quicker.

I head down the path to the beach, still watching the otters, so I don't see him until I have nearly reached the water. Carrying a tin pail, Tam McCodrun searches beneath the rocks for limpets, hands deep in the watery sand.

I duck quickly behind a convenient rock before he sees me, but he is concentrating on the search. He drops a limpet unceremoniously into his bucket with a soft clunk. His dark hair ruffles in the wind, and it occurs to me that it needs cutting. I could do it for him. I have watched Mither cut Grandpa's hair and Fither's, too. A bit of shaping and he wouldn't look so menacing. A bath wouldn't hurt, either. I imagine the smoothness of his back, slippery with soap. Hidden behind the rocks, I could watch him all day and he'd not have the slightest notion of it, he is so engrossed in digging for limpets.

He's looking in all the wrong places. At this rate, it'll take him forever and a day to find enough shellfish for a decent meal. Fool! The limpets are farther out on the skerry. Everyone knows that. If the gypsies kept boats like the others, he wouldn't have to settle for gritty limpets for his supper, or better yet, he could sail to a richer harvest. Now he'll have to get his feet wet to find enough limpets to make a good stew. The gypsies are afraid of the water, even more than the others. Garn, I could find enough limpets for twelve hungry crofters before he's gathered a dozen.

The silence that follows these thoughts is disappointing, as though I expected an answer, but he is oblivious to me, digging madly in the sand. Ahead to my right is a group of large rocks, another hiding place closer to where he is digging. When Tam looks the other way, I gather up my skirts and pick my way cautiously toward him. Hunkering down behind the mound of rocks, I peer over the edge to watch him from this closer vantage point, but the beach is empty.

Where is he?

Crouching low, I creep around the rock to look in the other direction.

"Ahhh!"

A huge, dark bird looming over me obliterates the sun. I scramble backward on the damp sand but then see it is Tam, laughing as if he has seen the funniest sight in all of Orkney.

CHAPTER NINE

"Look what the sea washed up on the beach," Tam declares, pleased with his prank. "A young bit of skirly wheeter." He roams around me, taking in my sprawled, sand-decorated limbs.

I quickly pull my sleeves over my hands and compose the rest casual-like, skirts, hair, and finally, my apron.

"Are you following me, Selkie Girl?" Tam's mocking smile is infuriating. I feel a flush spreading across my face. The kiss that left me foolishly hopeful feels now like just another cruel joke.

I throw him a fierce look, but he continues to circle me. I am torn in half. Part of me will endure anything to be near him; another part wants to pummel him senseless.

"Don't look so stricken," he admonishes. "It was a joke. Have you no sense of humor?"

"Aye, when there's something funny." I am satisfied with the cleverness of this retort, but Tam's answer catches me off guard.

"You've a sharp tongue, then, haven't you?"

I have no reply to that. It's true, but I'll not admit it, certainly not to him.

"What're you doing here? Waiting for the King of the Sea to come courting you?"

"If he did, you'd likely bash in his head with a club, skin him alive on the beach, and sell his pelt."

"Fetch a pretty penny, too, more'n likely."

"How can you be so cruel to harmless creatures?"

"Harmless? Witches, they are, condemned for their sins to live in the sea. They was once people, but they was so evil St. Magnus banished them forever."

I've heard the stories the traveling people tell about the selkies and their punishment at the hands of St. Magnus. Some island folk believe it, too, especially the hunters. It makes the killing easier.

"That's not true. Selkies know nothing of witching—or of St. Magnus, for that matter," I protest.

"They're witches, sure enough. It's as true as the nose on your face. They sneak up on the land at night to steal the peedie bairns from their mithers and take them into the sea to drown."

"That's a lie! The selkies have done nothing but kindnesses for folk, saving them from drowning and the like. What about the stories of bravery and compassion they show toward those who hunt them? A kindness done for the seals will save your life in rough seas, you know that, and once you have met a selkie's gaze, you can never hunt them again."

Tam pauses, frowning at my reply. "You like the selkies so much, why don't you go live in the sea with them?" That mocking smile plays again on his lips.

A sharp retort lies in my mouth, but I swallow it.

"Cat got your tongue, then, Selkie Girl? Got nothing to say?"

"Aye. You'd best be looking for those limpets farther out on the skerry or you'll go hungry this night."

"Farther out, is it?" I look for signs that he is teasing me, but his face is serious.

"I'll show you," I venture, and take the lead. He follows me, stepping deftly on the slick rocks of the skerry.

"Here. Under these rocks you'll find the bigger ones."

Obediently, he reaches under the rocks, pries off a limpet, and holds it up proudly.

"Seems you know the limpets as well as the selkies." He flips a tangle of my hair, and I push his hand away. Will he never stop insulting me? I want to trust him, to bring him close, and yet I dread what might happen if I let him near me.

When I turn to look at him, I see hurt in his eyes. Then, as though it were never there, the hurt is replaced with anger. "You'd think I had the pox instead of a bit of honest dirt," he says.

"Honest dirt washes off. It's the dirty inside I'm thinking of."

His eyes narrow, and I regret having spoken.

"Miss High and Mighty," he hisses. "Keeping away from me like I'm lower than sheep filth. Because your fither has a bit of land and a byre doesn't make you so grand. You're no better than the rest of us."

I open my mouth to answer this tirade, but he cuts me off.

"You hate me because I'm a traveller, don't you, a wandering gypsy without a home. You're like all the others."

The others! Is that what he thinks, that I'm like the others? I close the distance between us, my cheeks burning. "I'm not like the others!" I say hotly, but Tam turns away.

"Ach, go on and leave me to gather my limpets in peace." He shoves his hands deep into the water. Lank hair falls into his eyes. He shoves it off his forehead.

Who does he think he is to order me about like a servant? Is it not enough that he mocks me to the point of tears? I could walk away, pretend he never existed, but I am not through with him yet. I stroll to a convenient rock and sit, carefully adjusting my skirts as if I plan to spend the afternoon contemplating the scenery.

"Are you still here?" he asks, without looking at me.

"I have a right to be here. This is my fither's croft."

"No one owns the sea. Or the beach. It belongs to us all, even if it borders your fine croft. So get off."

A menacing tone accompanies this order. I feel a tiny thrill of fear but refuse to yield. My pride will not allow it. "I'll not be bullied about by the likes of you."

Tam drops his bag of limpets and strides across the skerry, close enough to climb inside me as easily as he slides into his coat. "Get away before I run you off, or worse!" He takes hold of the soft skin of my arm and tries to lead me toward the beach.

I wrench my arm away. "I'll not give in to the likes of you, Dirty Tam McCodrun!"

Growling deep in his throat, Tam grabs me. His fingers dig into my arms as he shakes me. "Don't call me that! Don't ever call me that!"

I teeter backward, nearly falling into the sea, but I grab hold of his vest like a lifeline and manage to regain my balance, though not before Tam catches hold of my hands. The long sleeves of my dress have fallen back, and I see that the wound has opened and my left hand is red with blood. Tiny dots of crimson spatter Tam's shirt.

His face goes white with the shock of it, and I feel the ache of tears behind my eyes. He has seen the webs.

"Damn my ill-bisted temper," he says, cradling my bleeding hand in his own. "You're hurt."

My hands fly behind my back.

"I didn't mean to hurt you, only you called me that name. No one calls me Dirty Tam to my face. No one."

"I'm sorry. I . . ."

"What happened to your hand?"

"It's nothing."

Tam pulls a surprisingly clean cloth from his pocket. "Here. I'll bind it up for you. It's bleeding."

Could it be he didn't notice the webs? Or maybe he doesn't care. He seems concerned only with the blood.

"It's nothing," I repeat. My hands clench into fists behind my back, and warm liquid seeps down my hand. I thank St. Magnus he didn't see the webs.

"Garn. You mustn't be so stubborn," he says. His hand reaches for mine. His face is too close, the sea-sharp smell of him is too rich, his tone as sweet as treacle. Escape is impossible. I stand intoxicated as he finds my hand and gently opens my fist. "A kiss makes the healing quicker."

Before I can object, Tam brings my hand to his lips.

His eyes go wide when he sees the webs. The shock of it turns his face into a stranger's. Before he can taunt me, I try to run, but he holds me fast, staring at the webs.

I shove both hands in his face. One hand leaves a bloody smudge on his cheek like a birthmark. "Run and tell the others what you've seen," I manage to say, though my throat has tightened into a knot. "Tell them you've seen the webs! Green and slimy like seaweed, they are, with claws that tear the flesh of babies! Tell them she goes down to the beach to meet the King of the Sea behind the rocks. Tell them she's an unnatural thing, a freak! They'll think you're a fine one for knowing!"

Then I run.

The whine of the wind blends with Tam's voice behind me. "Wait!" he calls. "I'm sorry."

"I hate you, Tam McCodrun, and all the others!" I shout back at him.

59

"Selkie Girl! Wait. I said I'm sorry. Come back! Come back!"

His handkerchief still clutched in my bloody fist, I climb up the path until I reach the rise and collapse out of sight behind a rock. I can no longer hold back the tears.

"Selkie Girl!" I hear him call, but I do not answer. I am lost in the day's hurt, a gathering storm that fills me until there is no room for this new barrage of feelings. I want only to be alone.

Puffins and kittiwakes fly above me. Like the sheep, they are blissfully unaware of the drama unfolding below. They must think that such a commotion is an alarming waste of energy.

I chance a look down to the beach just in time to see Tam throw his tin pail onto the rocks with a crash. "Devil take you, then! Devil take any who call me Dirty Tam!" He kicks at the sand over and over, unleashing his fury until he flops down on the beach, arms outstretched as if offering himself as a sacrifice, and it occurs to me for the first time that he cares, maybe as much as I do.

"I didn't mean it," he calls into the wind. "I didn't mean to hurt you." But the only reply is the gentle kiss of the waves on the rocks.

CHAPTER TEN

The dream begins innocently enough. In it, I travel beneath the waves to the bottom of the sea. Endless plains of ruffling sediment define the ocean floor. On a huge hill, I marvel at a crystal-green forest below me, undulating in the tides. Emerald branches stretch upward as if compelled to the surface, but their watery roots anchor them deep in the sand, preventing their rise. Endless aquamarine arms, supple and soggy-barked, crowd the forest. A glow seeps through them like the dim light of the Midsummer sun. The crystalline arms of the thicket shift together, pointing their light toward the hill where I stand, and the ocean around me warms with their radiance.

I breathe easily in the water, enveloped in a sense of belonging the likes of which I have never known. Here I am safe.

A sudden shift in the dream finds me in a clearing in the middle of the iridescent ocean forest. There, around a blazing, watery fire, a selkie clan is gathered, mithers, fithers, sisters and brothers, aunts and uncles, children, too, and several graying elders who must be grandparents. Their fur ruffles softly in the tides. Their black eyes shine with knowing.

Illuminated by the sapphire firelight, each selkie takes a turn to speak. Solemnly, like a sermon delivered by church elders, the selkies chant, their animal faces alive and aware. I listen carefully, like a child watches a magic trick to puzzle out its mystery, but the selkies are speaking with such intimacy that only those gathered nearby can hear them, and I am too far away. I move closer and discover that they are speaking in the musical language of the seals, and that is the reason I cannot understand. There is a distinct cadence to their speech. Their heavy seal bodies sway with the rhythm. My body moves with them.

A wizened elder female, long white fur flowing about her body like a halo, floats apart from the clan. Near her is a black selkie huge as a draft horse, with a jagged scar slashed across his neck. The old female turns to me. On her face lies a hint of the young selkie she had once been. She smiles warmly, urging me closer to the firelit circle. "Look. She is here. The one foretold," the old one announces, and beckons to me.

I feel the heat of the fire, the kindly gaze of the family. Reaching out my hand, I move closer until I can feel the softness of the old one's fur.

Then sudden darkness engulfs me. An invisible arm yanks me upward. In the dream, I struggle but cannot break free. Through the watery layers, I am pulled, through the transparent tentacles of the forest, eyes blurring with the rush of water, salt stinging the back of my throat. Up and up, the sea foam smothering me, I am dragged toward the surface, until my lungs burn with the need for air. Panicked, I reach out for safety, but my hands come away empty. I am forced upward until my lungs fill and my mouth is locked in a watery scream. I break the surface, washed cold with northern air, but cannot take a breath. My heart lies still between my water-soaked lungs. I float on the surface, drowned.

I wake up, struggling for breath. My woolen dress clings damply to my skin. I wipe off the grass and dirt stuck to my cheek. A rock has burrowed into the skin of my arm, leaving an angry red dent.

This is not the first time this nightmare has invaded my sleep, but this time it felt real, not like a dream at all. This time I heard the words the old selkie said as clearly as if I had said them myself. *Look. She is here. The one foretold.*

And in this dream, I died.

I roll over in the scented field, my face pressed against the grass. Closing my eyes against the sun, I revisit the first watery gray and blue images of the dream, see the silver fish, the clever, darting otters, the underwater forest with its shimmering tentacles and seal fur rippling in the tides. I picture the old selkie and hear her speak to me.

What does it mean, this nightmare that has crept its way into my sleep, the images sharper and more detailed with each visitation? Is it a portent of some terrible future that waits for me? Who or what pulled me to the surface, leaving me drowned? I shiver, but it is not from the cold.

My back aches, and a stabbing sensation claws deep in my belly. I wish I were dead. I might as well be dead. Tam has seen the webs, and on the afternoon of Midsummer's Eve. How can I dance for the others now, even if Fither allows it?

The selkies sing their mournful, warbling song as if in sympathy.

Roooo. Roooo.

It's strange to hear them singing in the middle of the afternoon, before the sun dips into the horizon and the long day lopes toward its finish. But they know it is Midsummer's Eve. They know that today is different.

My hand throbs, although the bleeding has stopped. A corner of Tam's handkerchief is stuck to the cut. I peel it away, wincing, and stuff the cloth into the pocket of my apron.

When I stand up, there is stickiness between my thighs. My fingers come away wet with blood. My courses, today of all days! Another cramp sears inside me. I check the back of my skirts for telltale signs, but the blood has not soaked through. I am grateful for that at least.

For a moment, I concentrate on hating my body's betrayal. Before my courses came, I spent hours praying to St. Magnus to keep them away. Foolishly, I believed that I could deny the inevitability of womanhood, that enough prayer might prevent its arrival, but somehow the treachery happened anyway, even under my tidy vigilance.

Will this be my future, the pain of womanhood with none of the pleasure? What is the point of having my courses when no one will love me? I'll never have the joy of coupling, the fulfillment of children, the satisfaction of building a family.

Another stitch of pain claws at me, and I will it away. No wonder Mither's face is layered with sadness. If this pain is the mystery that women whisper about, children's ears large with the effort to hear, I wish I were a man.

CHAPTER ELEVEN

Mither tosses a pile of wilting weeds into her basket. Her garden is as orderly as the house; crisp spring leaves, dew-fresh even in the late afternoon, frame the black earth. Even the weeds have bent to Mither's will, growing neatly among the rows of vegetables.

Mither lays a hand on my back and rubs tiny circles. "Peedie Buddo," she croons. "Do you have much pain?"

"I can bear it well enough."

"That's my brave one. Did you find the rags?"

"Aye. It's a grand bother."

"But without it, there would be no children. Someday that will have greater meaning for you than it does now."

I think of Tam and am barraged with emotions jumbled together into a curious, gnawing sensation. I try to push the feeling away, but it clings to me like a lonely child. I recognize the anger embedded in it, and the familiar sense of longing, but something else, too, like the hardness of hatred, but with soft edges.

"Mither, how do you know if you're in love?"

"Love, is it?" She takes a deep breath and lays her garden tool aside. "Love is beyond us, grander and bolder than we are. It makes us behave in ways we never imagine, wonderful and terrible, too."

Wonderful and terrible. That's exactly how I feel. "Can you love someone you hate?" I ask.

"We do not choose who we love. It cannot be forced. You do or do not love someone." Mither's eyes shine, and I am suddenly afraid I have made her cry. I should not have asked, but now it is too late.

"Love is a gift, Peedie Buddo," she says. "And the gift of loving someone else is greater than the gift of being loved. It is rare and beautiful to love someone more than yourself. Some unfortunates never know that kind of loving. They remain always at the center of their world and can never move beyond it."

"Have you loved someone more than yourself?"

"I have loved you."

I try to keep the irritation from my voice. "That's not what I mean, Mither. It's another kind of love I'd be asking about."

"Aye, there was once one I loved." Mither lapses into one of her impenetrable reveries, but now that this tasty bit of information has been revealed, I cannot leave it unexplored. Why does she speak of it as though it is in the past?

"Mither . . . ?"

"Walk with me."

She rises, brushing off her skirts, and moves toward the house. The constant damp that accompanies life by the sea causes her hesitant, lopsided gait, Grandpa says. The limp and her gnarled joints give her the look of a grandmither, but the gray streaks that run through her chestnut hair frame a face as smooth and unlined as a bride's.

I follow Mither into the house, puzzling out ways to harvest more information. Who has Mither loved? I create an entire story, a lost love, handsome, accepting, calm-voiced. I imagine that he is my real fither waiting for us in some far-off land.

"I have a gift for you," says Mither.

A gift? Gifts in our family are rare and simple, given only at Christmastime and birthdays. I catch myself biting my fingernails and slide my hands deep into the pockets of my apron. "What is it? Tell me."

"I'll show you." Mither opens the ornate lid to her hope chest, a gift from Grandpa on her wedding day, made from rare hardwood from the mainland, a traditional gift that pledged his abiding affection and hope for her happiness. The intricate carvings must have taken Grandpa many hours of patient work.

A flash of aquamarine winks at me as Mither holds up a dress of the lightest fabric I have ever seen. Translucent green and blue mingle together in layers, and sunlight from the open window shines silver-bright through the cloth. So this is what I glimpsed in Mither's sewing basket.

"Oh, Mither," is all I can manage.

"Shall we see if it fits?"

I shrug out of my apron, then my woolen dress, and shiver in my shift until Mither lifts the gown over my head and expertly adjusts the fabric around my body. The dress falls mid-calf, its folds shaping perfectly to the curves of my waist and hips. A scooped neck reveals the creamy skin of my chest, and a generous hood blooms from the neckline that, when pulled up, covers my head.

Best of all are three golden rings glittering at the end of each voluminous sleeve. Mither slips them expertly on my thumbs and the first and third fingers of each hand. They slide easily onto my fingers to the webs, a perfect fit. The attached fabric falls around my hands. Concealed in the fullness of the layers lie the hated webs.

I wrap my arms around Mither's bony shoulders, trying not to hug her too tightly because I know she has pain in her neck and back. Buried in her sweet-smelling body, I ask, "How can I ever thank you?"

Her eyes, etched with tiny lines, savor this moment between us. "Dance, Elin Jean," she whispers, her voice filled with purpose. "You must not hide what is worthy in yourself."

CHAPTER TWELVE

In my box bed, waiting for this endless day to reach midnight, I fall asleep and dream again. Beneath the sea, in the translucent woods of the selkies, I sit astride the back of a huge selkie male, his back as wide as the massive draft horses that pull the wagons of wheat to market. My arms encircle his neck, and beneath my hands I feel the jagged swelling of the scar along his neck. He is the blackest selkie I have ever seen. The tribe surrounds me, gathered around the fire. Their fur ripples in the current. Their eyes shine in the watery light from the blaze at the center of the clearing.

"Tell the tale," the old one says to me, her white fur dancing in the tides, and the underwater language flows from me as easily as the songs I sang as a child. The tale is an ancient one, of humans and selkies living in harmony, sharing the harvest from the sea, of a time when fear sleeps and children play games with seal pups on the shore.

I am mid-sentence in the telling when the dream shifts and I am seated in my fither's house. I see through the smoky haze, half lit by the fire, that Tam McCodrun has come courting. He speaks humbly to Fither, and the two men share a cup of ale while we women busy ourselves, allowing the men privacy to discuss matters of my future. Tam speaks eloquently of his intentions. Fither nods his head in agreement.

The family sits down to a fine supper, Tam on Fither's right, the place of honor for a prospective son-in-law. We linger leisurely over the last morsels of a fine fish supper and another cup of ale. Then Fither stands, the signal for Mither to gather the bundling sheets.

Tam stands sheepishly in the center of the room as he is wrapped round and round in the bleached white sheets until he is mummified, and we carry him gently to my box bed, where only his head sticks out above the sea of fabric. When I lay my hand on his chest, I can feel his heart beating with anticipation through the layers of cloth. He will spend the night lying next to me, the bundling preventing him from exploring forbidden places but with our nearness filling us with thoughts of our lives together. In my nightdress, I climb into bed with my wrapped betrothed, suddenly too embarrassed to meet his gaze. I study the woven hangings that block the cold from seeping through the walls of the box bed.

"Come closer," he whispers. "I'll not bite you."

I inch nearer, the whole length of us touching through the layers of cloth, and when I meet his gaze, I see the longing in his eyes. My eyes close for a moment, and when I open them, Tam's smile distorts, swimming in brackish liquid. The walls of the box bed have closed in around us, and the bed is swimming in salt water. I claw at the sheets that engulf Tam but cannot unwrap the layers of fabric. He is trapped. I watch helplessly as he is drawn down and down into the water. I cling to him, and when he turns to me, his eyes are hooded, dark with hatred. His face stretches and distorts until it is unrecognizable. I begin to scream. Someone else's face hovers above mine, then swoops down like a carrion bird, eyes gleaming yellow-hot with fury, face split open in an empty, leering grin.

Fither!

I wake up. Trembling from the terrifying images of the dream, I am momentarily paralyzed by the effort to breathe. I had not meant to fall asleep, only to fool Fither into thinking I had. Then, when the chance presented itself, I would slip away to meet Grandpa at the foy. Tam would be there, with his black eyes and his multicolored vest.

Beneath my nightdress, the silken softness of Mither's gift lies promising against my skin. I run my fingertips through the impossibly light folds of the dress and wait for the panic to pass, listening to the selkies keen their Midsummer song. The night is cut in two with its sadness.

Roooooo. Rooooo.

Then I hear voices, two of them. Fither and Grandpa, I think, but I can't quite make out what they're saying. I draw back the curtains of the box bed, and Grandpa's voice rises, icy with conviction. "It's the bairns who pay for the wrongs of the ones gone before," he says. "Elin Jean'll be living with your sin for the rest of her life. I should have beat you with a stick until you came to your senses."

I hold my breath in the silence that follows, expecting Fither to meet Grandpa's intensity with his typical defiance.

"You shouldn't blame yourself," I hear Fither reply quietly. "It was my doing."

"I didn't stop you now, did I?" Grandpa queries. "That's my own wrong."

I hear the creaking of Grandpa's rocker as he rises out of it.

"I'll be trying to catch a bit of sleep before the foy," he says, the familiar sound of his pipe tap-tapping ashes into the fireplace. I yank the curtains back across my box bed. As I suspected, he shuffles toward me in the ben end of the house. Barely breathing, I listen as he draws the curtains and climbs into his box bed across the room.

Through the walls of the house, the moaning of the selkies beckons. *Roooo. Roooo.* But their song is broken by the rough sound of crockery smashing against the stone walls of the croft.

"Go back to the sea and leave us alone," Fither cries into the night, and the coldness of it echoes back to me like the warning of a ghost. "She belongs to me! Do you hear? She belongs to me!"

Fither's heavy boots clump across the dirt floor of the house, and the heavy front door slams shut like the sudden ending of a story.

I draw my feet up under my nightdress and hug myself against the night. What wrong happened before I was born? What sin will I have to live with the rest of my life? A melancholy feeling steals over me, strange and unsettling as the dream. What secrets have been kept from me? I could ask Mither, but she has gone down to the sea for her nightly walk after the washing up from dinner. She sleeps less and less these days, so it is unlikely that she will return until the others begin to gather for the foy. I shiver in my box bed, feeling like a stranger in my own home and more alone than I ever have in my life. I am afraid to know and even more afraid not to know.

But I will not give in to cowardice. I breathe slowly and palm the tears from my eyes. I climb out of bed, and as my bare feet touch the cold of the packed-dirt floor, the selkies' singing grows louder and more present. As I walk toward the main room of the crofthouse, it surrounds me, fills me, and I am calmed.

Such a lovely song. Different somehow. Mesmerizing. I feel my body move with the selkie crooning. *Roooo. Roooo.* I begin to sing with them. Somehow I know the melody, although I cannot recall ever having heard it before.

And strangely, with the song, the calling changes, and a harmony blends in the song, beckoning me, low and easy, like a parent croons to a sleepy child.

Elin Jeeeeeean! the selkies sing. *Elin Jeeeeeean!*

Clear as the broonie lights and no mistake, the selkies are calling my name.

Elin Jeeeeeeean! they sing. *Elin Jeeeeeean!*

Yes, I hear you. I'm coming. Wait for me.

Then I am dancing, my feet leaping over the crofthouse floor. I am alone in the room, and yet I feel as though hundreds of selkies are dancing with me. This sense of them beside me is so overpowering I stop for a moment to look for them. But I am alone, shards of broken dishes lining the walls of the room.

Selkie cries pummel the crofthouse, high-pitched and insistent. Glowing coals from the hearth cast shadows on the walls and the earthen floor. Wavering in the firelight, the images sharpen into focus until they are recognizable—ocean waves and nimble fish, sailing boats and the rocks of the skerry. Pictures of land and sea merge in a mural etched onto the walls of the house.

As I drink in the surprising sight, the unmistakable shapes of three selkies become visible on the floor at my feet. Their bodies form a rough circle, but they look away from each other, pointing in different directions—east, west, and south. The selkies are delicately rendered, with gently sloping snouts and tail flippers rich with detail; even their pelts look real. As I stare at the images, the selkie singing sweetens into a lullaby, and my name forms the lyrics. In the center of the circle, another image slowly emerges, the outline of a slender girl who points north.

Her hands are webbed.

Elin Jeeeean! The girl in the circle reaches out her arms to the selkies that surround her. *I'll watch over you,* she says. *I'll keep you safe.*

My name rolls like the waves until the house is fairly bursting with the sound of it. *Eeeelin Jeeeeean,* the selkies sing, and my arms are drawn toward the sea, languid in the warm night.

Find it, the selkies sing. *You must find it.*

Find what? Giddy God, what do the selkies want?

CHAPTER
THIRTEEN

Find it! Find it! the selkies insist.

"Find what?" I ask, close to tears, frantic for some sign, but the house has gone as silent as the grave. I study the images of the selkies on the floor for some clue, but they have not moved.

"Tell me what you want!" I beg, but there is no reply.

I begin to search, inside the chest of drawers, among the cooking utensils, lifting jars from shelves to unearth whatever might lurk behind them. With no idea what the selkies want me to find, I can only hope that instinct will lead me to it, and this blind belief keeps me searching. Holding up household objects in the undulating light of the fire, I pray for some portent to reveal the nature of my hunt. Nothing seems out of the ordinary or in any way distinctive. Under a torn fishing net huddled in the corner, in baskets of oily wool, in the cupboard filled with staples, in the flour bin, and in jars of dried herbs, I search, until I have pried and poked into every inch and random items tossed about in my desperate canvass litter the room. Finally, when I feel as though

I have examined every nook and cranny, I stop to scout for places I might have missed, but I have looked everywhere, in every corner, up and down.

The relentless keening of the seals begins again. *Elin Jeeeeean! Find it!* they sing, strident and unyielding, as if urging me not to give up.

"What do you want?" I shout into the night. "Tell me!" And the selkies respond in their beautiful, unearthly singing. *Find it! Find it!*

For lack of a better idea, I look up to the roof, packed tight with mud and straw to keep out the rain. Nowhere to hide anything up there. I reach above the windows and explore with my fingers, but I come away with nothing but dust and an old wooden button. I stand on tiptoes, stretching up into the aisins above the doorway. I am not quite tall enough to reach inside, so I jump, hanging by both arms from the door frame. I let go with one hand to try to explore inside, but still I cannot reach, so I drop to the floor, landing on cat feet. I drag a stool from the fireplace over to the doorway for additional height. Standing on it, I reach easily into the aisins. Feeling in the darkness of the narrow space, my hand grasps a bundle that gives in my hands.

Giddy God. Is it alive? I gain control of my fear and seize the thing firmly, dragging it out of its hiding place. Holding my breath, I lift the covering and see that the thing is an animal skin. I unwrap the skin. It is a brown-spotted selkie pelt. Relieved, I hold it to my trembling body, and the selkies instantly croon a different song, as if in response. Its former urgency gone, their singing spreads like a soothing quilt over the night. I bury my face in the pelt and breathe in its odor. It smells like the sea, like the Red and the Black and something else I can't quite name yet is as familiar to me as the sweet smell of bannock baking on the hearth. As I hold the pelt, my body rocks like a boat on the waves, and words of comfort fill the crofthouse. *It's fine. You're grand. Don't worry.*

A series of watery images rushes through me, the radiant forest of my dreams, emerald leaves dancing in the light, selkies on the beach, lifeless and bloody. I see my webbed hands parting the tides, furiously pulling me through the sea toward the beach where selkies lie weeping.

Cooing sounds float from my mouth and mingle with the singing that rides in from the sea. The two sounds blend, creating a harmony of land and sea. Held in thrall to it, I sway with the melody.

The stool tips, and with a yell and a great thump, I collide with the floor, my feet tangled in the rungs of the stool. On my way down, I manage to knock pots, pans, and other kitchen sundries to the ground in a great crash. The selkies' singing stops. Clutching the pelt, I stand and hastily brush the dirt from my nightdress.

Garn. That was enough noise to wake the dead.

"Jean!" says Grandpa from behind me. "What're you doing? I thought it was the bawkie man come to steal us away!"

Thank St. Magnus, it isn't Fither.

"Answer me. What're you doing?"

"I . . . I . . . couldn't sleep."

"Guilty conscience, eh?"

"No. I had a dream."

"What do you have there?"

I slide the pelt behind my back and face him.

"Nothing. I'm sorry I woke you. I'll be going back to bed now."

"Not just yet, Jean."

An impatient tone creeps into my voice. "What is it?" I ask. All I want is to be left alone with the pelt. I certainly don't want to waste precious time answering foolish questions.

"I asked you a question. It's still wanting an answer."

"What question?" Stalling is a lame tactic, but I try it for lack of a better plan.

Grandpa sighs. "I asked you what you're holding behind your back."

I make a great show of yawning. "Can we talk about this later? I'm tired."

"And I'm waiting, Jean. What is it?"

He won't let it go now. I might as well tell the truth.

"It's just an old selkie skin."

Grandpa takes a slow, ragged breath and blows it out evenly through his nose. "Where did you find such a thing, Jean?"

"It was stuffed up in the aisins."

"The aisins."

"Aye."

"What're you doing searching around in the aisins?" Grandpa asks in his barely-able-to-be-patient tone.

How can I answer him? I search madly for a plausible lie, but finding none, I decide to plow on with the truth. Grandpa clears his throat as a prompt, and I meet his gaze. "The selkies told me to find it."

"What a bulder of nonsense."

"The selkies wanted me to find the pelt, Grandpa. I know it."

"Sounds like a dream to me, Jean."

"I was dreaming, but then the selkies woke me. Didn't you hear them?"

"Hear them? You'd have to be stone-deaf or dead not to hear their bellowing."

How can I make him understand? "They were calling me, Grandpa, calling my name over and over."

"Selkies talking? Nonsense, lass."

"They wanted me to look in the aisins. They wanted me to find the pelt."

"You're dreaming, I tell you. And walking in your sleep by the look of it."

"This pelt is not a dream. It's as real as you or me. And look." I point to the magical images on the walls and floor.

Not a trace of them remains. They have disappeared, like spirals of smoke whisked out the chimney.

"But they were here. Pictures, Grandpa. There was a drawing of three selkies in a circle, and I was with them."

"Jean, Jean," Grandpa replies in his patient voice. "Sometimes dreams seem so real that we come to believe them."

"It wasn't a dream, I tell you. It was real, just like this pelt." I am shouting, but Grandpa seems not to care.

"Give me the pelt, Jean, and go back to bed."

"But it was stuffed up in the aisins. No one wants it." This argument makes enormous sense to me, but Grandpa dismisses it.

"It didn't get there by itself. Someone put it there, so that's where it's meant to be." Grandpa holds out his hand for the pelt, but I will not give it up.

"I'll be going down to the sea." I am halfway out the door before he stops me.

"Hold on, Jean," he bellows, and the desperation in his voice shocks me. Grandpa never shouts. "I'd think twice before doing that if I were you," he says more quietly, but a sharp edge surrounds the words. "You're asking for trouble. Return the pelt to where you found it." Grandpa's lined face is drawn tight with concern. "It doesn't belong to you, now does it?"

But it does. I know it. What is it about the pelt? What is it that caused him to raise his voice to me? It occurs to me that Grandpa has a stake in the pelt, that he knows more than he's revealing. If I ask him, will he tell me? I try another tactic.

"Who does it belong to, then?" I ask.

His face goes blank, and my question hangs in the dusty air.

"Why will no one answer my questions?"

"Leave off your whining. I'll hear no more talk of selkies this night," Grandpa orders, reaching for the pelt.

"I was meant to find it. I know it, Grandpa."

"Ach, Jean. Forget this nonsense. Come to the foy with your old grandpa and dance the music to life. That's what you're meant to do."

There is kindness in his eyes, but when I resist giving him the pelt, his voice goes cold as a winter storm. "Give me the pelt."

My fingers burrow deep into its fur. I will not give it up.

"I'll ask Mither. She'll know what to do about the pelt."

In an instant, Grandpa's face hovers inches from mine. His hand grips my arm with fierce strength. "Don't be bothering your mither. Talk of the selkies upsets her. You know that. Listen to me now and listen well." Grandpa's eyes bore into mine with dark, stinging purpose. "Forget you ever saw the pelt. No good can come of it. Do you hear me, Jean?"

My arm hurts from the force of his grip.

"Do you hear me?" he demands again.

"I hear you, Grandpa," I murmur.

"Then do as I tell you. Give me the pelt, go back to bed, and stay there until the foy."

Arguing is no use. Grandpa is like Fither in that respect. Stubborn. Once he has made up his mind, no amount of debate will move him. He will only grow angrier.

I hold out the pelt and he takes it, folding it once, twice. I am the good girl, the obedient girl. Or pretend to be. I head for the quiet of my box bed.

"Jean." Grandpa's voice is calm now that I have given in to him, the fierce energy of his anger spent. "Don't be mucking about with what you don't understand and cannot finish. Some things are better left alone. Someday you'll understand that."

He waits for an answer, but I have none to offer. The selkies are silent, as if they, too, have nothing to say.

"And not a word of this to anyone," Grandpa warns. "Do you hear me, Elin Jean?"

"I hear you."

"Then be off with you."

"I'm sorry I took the pelt." It is a lie, but I don't care. I need him to believe that I will do as he asks.

"Aye," he offers, his way of accepting the apology.

I pad my way to bed, leaving Grandpa alone near the fire. The moans of the selkies follow me into the dark with their melancholy longing. Through their lamentations, I hear Grandpa's voice. "Sleep. That's not likely for none this night."

I hear Grandpa throw another peat brick in the hearth to keep the blaze alive. The crofthouse suddenly feels stifling, even with the windows open to the night air. Pressed against the side of my box bed, I hear it all, Grandpa muttering, the fire crackling to life, and the sound I am waiting for, the sound of the door closing on an empty house.

Forget you ever saw the pelt, Grandpa warned, but with the selkies' cries drumming the bones of my ears, I can no more forget it than I can forget my own name. I remember the Red and the Black beside me on the skerry. I feel the sea run through my veins like seaweed is tossed by the tides, and pressed against the heavy curtains of my box bed, I am poised between two worlds: one defined by all that I have known, the other nothing more than a dream that promises an uncertain future. And in that instant, I know that I am lost to my family and their lonely world.

CHAPTER
FOURTEEN

I drag the stool back to the doorway. Climbing on it, I reach into the darkness of the aisins. Nothing. I reach deeper. Feel around. Still nothing. What if Grandpa took the pelt with him? What if he destroyed it or hid it where I'll never find it? *Please*, I pray silently to the selkies, *help me.*

As if reading my mind, a chorus of selkie moans rushes through the open window. *Find it. Find the pelt.*

My body lifts and moves weightless through the crofthouse, my feet barely touching the floor beneath me. I search near the washbasin, past the fireplace, and around the spinning wheel. Nothing. The selkies urge me on, but there is no danger of failure. As I look around the room, trying to decide where to focus my search, my eyes fall on Mither's hope chest. The ornately carved fish that decorate the hardwood lid feel smooth as feathers to my fingertips. At my touch, the lid opens as if welcoming me, and I peer inside, expecting to see the pelt, but only homespun sheets and woolen blankets rest there, alongside silvery crocheted doilies.

Plunging my hands deep into the chest, I feel along the smooth interior for the textured fur of the pelt until I reach the wooden bottom.

The selkies utter staccato barks, frantic with purpose. Without a thought for Mither's precious linens, I toss them on the floor one by one until the chest is empty.

The pelt is not there, but I know I am close by the forceful sounds the selkies send to me. I look toward the sea for further guidance, and I see the magical images—waves and fish, boats and rocks—reappear on the walls and floor, pictures of land and sea decorating the room again. The three selkies in the circle are turning inward now, and the image of the girl with webbed hands points to me. From her extended finger, a sliver of light reaches across the room and lands on the carved front of the chest. I explore the carvings with my fingers until I realize that the largest carving, a selkie mither and her pup, is loose. Reaching for a kitchen knife, I wiggle it into the slit around the carving, trying to dislodge it. I push the knife in farther without thought for nicking the wood, and the selkie carving pops out. A hidden drawer is cut into the chest. The drawer sticks when I pull on it, but I jiggle and rock it until it opens.

In the drawer lies the pelt.

I hug the softness of it to my body, and the selkie sounds shift again into a calming lullaby. No mistake, the pelt feels alive. I hold it close, huddling on the dirt floor, and wait for the selkies to tell me what to do.

The girl in the circle turns to me, and an invisible arm reaches around my body and propels me toward the heavy crofthouse door. It swings open by itself. The night rushes in, and the force of it knocks me from my feet. Although the night is warm and half lit by the persistent sun, I shiver under the dual layers of my dresses. My body feels reckless with power, as though a single leap from the doorway could land me on the beach, my feet carving deep imprints in the sand. The velvety folds of my new dress caress my body, and I laugh out loud with the pleasure of it. My heart beats hard in my chest. I can hear it speak to me. *The sea, the sea, the sea.*

Tucking the pelt securely under my arm, I begin a purposeful jog down the path. It shouldn't be hard to find Mither. As I run, I remember what Grandpa said, and a ripple of fear lodges in my heart. *Forget you ever saw the pelt. No good can come of it.*

Silvery shafts of northern light work their magic on the land, bathing the tall grass in deep violet-gold hues. The wind rushing in my ears mingles with the song of the selkies, and it sounds like the sea. The fog is thick, laying its silken covering over the landscape.

The moment my feet touch the beach, I look for Mither's familiar form, but she is nowhere in sight. Garn. If I travel too far in either direction, around the cliffs that house Odin's Throne or the other way toward town, I might miss her.

A final look around yields no results, so I jog through the damp sand until I reach the rough stones of the skerry. Holding up the hem of my nightdress, I pick my way along the stones until I find a comfortable perch on a flat rock. I'll wait here. Likely Mither will take the path back to the crofthouse that has brought me here. Besides, she often ventures out to the end of the skerry to be nearer to the North Sea.

The pelt lies warm and rich in my arms. I hold it up, and the folds fall open invitingly. It is longer and wider than I am, the inner skin pliable and soft, as though it still bears the warmth of its owner. I drape the pelt over my knees, and it surrounds my legs as if looking for a friend, warm and cool, all at the same time.

What could it hurt? I nestle myself into the length of the pelt, matching my feet into the narrow tail flippers. I stretch my arms into the front paws of the pelt. My hands fit perfectly. Holding the pelt in place over my shoulders, I hunch my face into the curved head, fitting the eyes and nose with my own.

Hunkered deep inside the pelt, the selkie songs caressing my ears, the nearness of the sea calming my heart, I sway like the seals who lie in the heady warmth of the sun. The seabirds are silent, as if they, too, are listening to the selkies sing. The whistle of the wind and the breaking waves add their harmony. In this peaceful harbor, the foy, Tam, the strange dreams, and even my search for Mither fade into the layers of fog.

CHAPTER FIFTEEN

Sharp cries jolt me from my reverie, the selkies barking furiously, the desperate squawks of birds. A dark mass stands over me, holding a raised club just above my head.

I duck and roll. "No! Don't strike me!"

The pelt peels from my shoulders. One of my hands is caught in the claws, so it drags behind me as I tumble down the rocks, nearly falling into the sea.

"Selkie Girl!"

I look up in time to see him startle as if struck by his own club. Giddy God! Tam's feet slip out from under him. His arms flail the air like the wings of some massive, terrified bird. In one suspended moment, he nearly steadies himself, but then, with a great splash, he falls backward into the white-capped sea.

"Help! Help me!" he yells, but I laugh at the sight of him, drenched and fighting the water.

"I hope you drown," I call to him.

His head disappears under the currents. Good. He deserves a dunking. He tried to kill me!

"You deserve to drown! Then no more selkies will die from the likes of Dirty Tam McCodrun!" But my shouting is met with an awful silence. I peer through the fog and see his head break the surface with a great sputtering for air and thrashing of arms.

"Swim, you fool!" I shout. "Or are you afraid they'll say you've a bit of selkie in you? I hope you sink straight down to hell!"

From the mouth of the voe, a cacophony of cries is unleashed by the selkies, and the song they sing sounds like a dirge. Forgetting my anger, I kneel on the rocks and reach out to Tam.

"Grab on to my hand," I call to him, but the current has carried him too far out to reach me. His wild eyes lock onto mine for a moment, and then he sinks beneath the surface.

Giddy God! He's drowning!

I peel off my nightdress, and dropping it on the rocks, I dive, cutting recklessly through the waves to Tam's still form. As my eyes adjust to the undulating half-light beneath the sea, I see him suspended in the water, lifeless. Positioning my body underneath his, I swim with him toward the skerry. Tam is heavy in the water. I am beginning to tire when the load lightens and I realize that I am not alone in my efforts to save Tam. The Red and the Black flank me, pushing Tam from either side.

Climbing onto the skerry, I grab under Tam's arms and, with the help of the two selkies, maneuver him to the safety of the rocks. I press hard on his chest to expel the water from his lungs as I have seen fishermen do when one of their own has fallen prey to the sea. Foam dribbles from his mouth. I wipe a string of seaweed from his face. "I'm sorry. I didn't mean it. I didn't want you to die!" The apology tumbles out of me. "Wake up! Please don't die."

He chokes, draws a single ragged breath, and lies still. I lay my ear on his chest. His heart beats steadily. I turn to the Red and the Black and, through my tears, see a wondrous vision. The Red and the Black loosen the fur that clings to them and begin to birth from their pelts. Their faces appear first, slick hair formed to their perfect human heads. First one arm and then the other become visible, reaching up and out into the cool summer air. Gently rounded breasts lead to curves of hips and slender legs that end in pale-veined feet. The pelts uncouple from the women, until they fall silently onto the skerry and the two stand naked before me. A sigh escapes from deep within them. They turn to each other and nod once in agreement, then look to me standing transfixed, not three feet away from where the metamorphosis has occurred.

The red-haired selkie woman shakes her head, and salt water flies from her wet hair. Her skin is creamy, unblemished from the sun and wind, like the skin of a newborn. Her eyes, set wide in her heart-shaped face, are green, flecked with gold.

My heart lifts, as if I might, at any moment, float up to the heavens.

"Hush your crying. He will not die." The Black dips her lovely head, and her long, peat-colored hair falls forward over her shining breasts. Her eyes are gray-blue, deep set in her angular face. Her skin is prison pale, tinged with lavender.

"You have saved him this night," she murmurs. " 'Tis the way of the selkies to save drowning men, even the killers."

"He'll wake soon enough with an aching head. None the worse for the baffin," declares the Red, and the two women dip their heads in unison. They reach out to me, and when I touch their hands, their skin is as fresh and pliable as new leaves.

"I heard you calling me," I manage to whisper. "But I didn't know you were human."

"Aye," said the Black. "One night of the year. Midsummer's

Eve, you call it, the time when the sun shines even in the night. Then we are as you see us." The Black strokes my cheek with her impossibly beautiful hand. "You have brought the pelt."

The pelt. I had forgotten it.

The Black gathers it up, folding it carefully. "You have the ears to listen this night . . ."

". . . and the heart to tell you what to listen for." The Red completes her sister's thought. "Look. She has her mither's eyes."

And the Black adds, "Green as the sea."

"You know Mither?" This thought leaves me as confounded as the presence of the selkie women before me.

"Aye. We know your mither, as we know the flow of the tides and the feel of the warm sun. As we know you."

Swollen with pleasure at the nearness of these beautiful creatures, my heart yawns to make room for this new delight.

"You're very like her, your mither," offers the Red.

"Give me your hands." The Black reaches gently for my hands, nestled in layers of dripping fabric and lace trim. Instinctively, I fold them deeper in the sleeves of my dress.

"They're ugly," I say.

The Black strokes my forehead with the back of her cool, lilac hand, and I am instantly quieted. Together the selkie women burrow in my sleeves for my hands, lift them into the light, and open them like flowers. Eyes kinder than ever before gaze on my hands.

"They are webbed. . . ."

". . . made for the sea." The Red enfolds me in her supple arms, and I sink willingly into her consoling embrace, thinking only to hold this moment forever, but her shoulders shake with sobs.

"Don't cry," I say, hoping to reassure her, just as I had done earlier when they lay beside me on the skerry. "I'll keep you safe. No hunters will find you. I will give my life to protect you."

The Black gathers us both in her arms. "She is not afraid. She weeps for one taken by a crofter sixteen years ago and kept from her home and family in the sea."

"Like in the stories?"

"A story as true as you're standing here." The Black looks again to the Red as if asking for permission. In the silence, the two women release me and stand together, the wind at their backs.

"The pelt belongs to your mither," says the Black.

"Our sister," finishes the Red.

For a moment, I feel nothing but the sea mist that rises from the rocks. I am suspended as the world whirls around me.

Mither is a selkie.

"But how can that be?" I ask when I find my voice. "You are young and Mither is old."

"Sixteen years kept from the sea has made her old," answers the Black. "The sea keeps us supple, heals our wounds, nurtures us. Your mither has lost her youth to the land and to the man who is your fither."

The Red lifts her radiant head. "Every year at Midsummer, we return to be with her. Seven children she had in the sea and we two sisters. There was once a mate, killed long ago by hunters."

I look down at my webbed hands with new eyes. Pride pools inside me for these graceful half humans who embrace me. The dreams, my need for the sea, Mither's strange ways—I understand all of it. "I'm one of the selkie folk," I say breathlessly.

"No, lass. You're part of your mither and part of your fither. Sea and land."

"The first of a kind."

"I don't want to be the first of a kind. I hate the land. I want to be with you in the sea."

In the distance, hundreds of selkies croon their song into the foggy night. The Red turns toward the North Sea, and her sister follows her as if they cannot be separated. The Black finally speaks. "Your mither belongs in the sea, but it is not your home."

A dark anger rises in me. It leaks through my skin like sweat, poisoning the joy I felt only moments ago. "I have no home," I say, my voice thick with disappointment. "I don't belong any-where."

The two women exchange a look.

"Belonging's not a place," offers the Red. "It's inside you."

"You will find the knowin' in time," says the Black.

More waiting. Always waiting. "I cannot wait any longer!" I cry, a storm rising inside me. "I will not!" My words echo until the mist swallows them.

For long moments, there is only the sound of the sea. Then the Black speaks. "Listen! There is a task you must undertake. And it begins tonight. You will give your mither back her pelt . . ."

". . . so she can return to her home in the sea," the Red adds quickly. "To swim again with us . . ."

". . . and begin to heal." The Black's earnest look tells me that this is why they have come. I feel a stab of guilt. The thought that the selkies had come because of Mither hadn't even occurred to me. I was thinking only of myself.

"Return to the sea?" I ask dumbly as the reality of their re-quest reaches me. I swat at my tears with the layered sleeves of my dress and summon the question that dwarfs all the others. I am so afraid of the answer. "But will she come back?"

A low moan comes from behind me, and the Red and the Black stiffen with fear.

Tam! He shudders once and begins a terrible retching.

"Quickly, the sea!" cries the Black, and the two women grab their pelts and slip into the safety of the water.

"Wait!" I call, torn between concern for Tam and wanting the answer to my question. "If I give Mither her pelt, will she come back to me? I need to know!"

But the two women expertly mold into their pelts, the fur melting onto them, smooth as candle wax. Half selkie, half human, rising in the rolling waves, they call, "Give her the pelt." The words float on the wind, and like with so much of this strange day, I am not quite sure they are real.

"Set her free."

"Give her back to the sea!"

I peer into the mist and see the Red and the Black one last time, weaving in and out of the waves. As I watch, they complete their transformation, human faces turning feral. The two seals dive together in perfect formation beneath the surface.

"Come back! Come back!" I scout the horizon for some sign of them, but they have vanished into the cavernous North Sea.

CHAPTER SIXTEEN

*B*ehind me, Tam groans. I kneel beside him, dabbing his face with the hem of my dress. His eyes flutter open, then close again, and he rolls away from me. He moans again, louder this time, but I roll him over and see that the bluish tint has faded from his sunbrowned face. I can feel the steady rise and fall of his chest. *Thank you, St. Magnus.*

Why doesn't he move? Is he hurt?

"Wake up, please wake up. I didn't want you to drown. Just not to hurt me."

Cool arms surround me. Warm lips cover mine. They are surprisingly soft. I push against his chest, but he does not let go. His mouth moves on mine, and I sink into him. He releases me suddenly and laughs. "A kiss from the Selkie Girl. Almost worth drowning for."

"I hate you, Tam McCodrun!"

"What, for a kiss?"

"You tried to kill me!"

"I was after the pelt. How was I to know you were darned down in it?"

"Killing was all you were after. I'll never understand it as long as I live. And that might not be long if you have any say in it."

Tam laughs as if I've made a huge joke, but I fail to see the humor. "You should be ashamed of yourself," I accuse. "What kind of man clubs an innocent selkie?"

Tam sinks down on his haunches and studies the silvery rocks of the skerry. "The hungry kind."

"The night of the Johnsmas Foy? There'll be plenty to eat. You could eat to bursting and still have a full belly in a week's time."

"That's true."

I have him there. Well done, me.

He turns his black eyes on me. "But there's other kinds of hunger than in the stomach."

"What other kinds?"

"Did you never feel fairly silted to have something? Wanting it so much you cannot think of naught but that?" Tam picks up a loose rock and expertly skips it through the waves. Then he looks back at me. "The wanting is with you first thing when you wake up and last thing before you close your eyes at night. You'd do anything to have it. Anything."

In the tone of his voice, I recognize the sweet ache. I know the longing intimately. "Aye. Waiting for it to happen. Deathly afraid it never will."

"That's the feeling."

A question hangs in my thoughts, and although I argue with myself about the wisdom of asking it, I cannot stop myself. "What are you silted for?" Waiting for his answer, I concentrate on memorizing the curve of his jaw where it meets his ear. I see the grime nestled there and want to touch it.

"To wake up every day in the same place, to have a home. That would be the end of the longing for me."

"A place to belong?"

"Aye. Even the feast at the foy cannot fill up that yawning hole."

"I understand. I want to belong, too."

Tam makes a short, barking sound. "You? You have a home, a fine croft with a byre full of sheep and ponies, too. What would you know of it?"

Struggling against the impulse to fling a handful of loose rocks in his face, I answer him. "What good is a fine croft if there's no one to share it with? What good is it if none of the others want to be with me?"

At this declaration, Tam looks toward the land, then back at me, his face serious as church. "I do," he says quietly. "I want to be with you."

A yielding sensation sears through me. I think of the rags stuffed between my legs to catch my courses. My face reddens and I turn away from him, as though he might read my thoughts. "But you're always teasing and calling me Selkie Girl," I answer.

"There's no meaning in it," he scoffs. Tam shoves his hands deep in the pockets of his trousers, then yanks them out again, as if they are too restless to stay there. Finally, he folds his arms across his chest like a barrier. "If you ask me, I'll not be making sport of you ever again."

A part of me leaps to believe it, but I hesitate at the risk of trusting him. "Why should I believe you?"

"You saved my miserable life, did you not? I owe you that at least."

My heart drops to my feet. That explains it. This isn't about his feelings for me at all. I did him a good turn, so he is beholden to me. How could I be such a fool? "Aye. I saved your life," I fire back at him. "More's the pity."

"You're a hard one, Selkie Girl," he declares, and picks up a stone, tossing it playfully at me. It bounces gently off my foot. "If you ask me, I'll never make sport of you again." Tam leans closer. If he reached out, he could catch me in his arms like a fish in a net and I would not stop him. "Ask me," he demands.

The sincerity in his voice is richer to me than gold. I search his face. Is it possible that I might feel safe? Could I give up my exhausting watchful ways? I am weak at the prospect. "I'll ask you, then," I venture, squaring my chin for effect. "Don't be calling me names."

"Never again."

"Swear it to me."

"Swearin', is it?" This amuses him, but I am deadly serious. In Orkney, an oath is not taken lightly. It is a matter of honor for Orcadians and gypsies alike. A broken oath brands a man as a villain and a liar. I wait to see what he will do.

Tam raises a damp hand and covers his heart. His other hand reaches out and covers the place where my heart lies in my chest, trembling like a frightened animal under the layers of my dress.

"I swear it," he whispers. "I swear I'll never make sport of you again."

"And swear to me you'll never raise a hand to hurt the selkies as long as you live."

Tam's hands fly up. "I've done enough swearing for one day."

"It's only one more promise I'm asking for."

"Do you know the price that's paid out for a single selkie pelt?"

"Aye, but there's other ways than killing to earn your keep."

"Earn my keep? Is that what you think I'm about? I've some

plans, and by God, I'm going to see them through. Hunting selkies is the means to an end for me." Tam paces, his bare feet silent as a prayer on the rocks. When he speaks again, the words pour out of him treacle-sweet. "I'm saving up for something. Land, if you must know it, Selkie Girl. A home."

So this is it. He wants to leave behind the traveller ways. He wants to settle down in one place and build a life. The passion in his declaration makes me bolder than I've ever been. "Is there something else you'd be wanting, Tam McCodrun?"

"Aye." A slow grin splits his face wide as the sea. "There is. A lass to love me as brave and true as yourself."

"Are you saying that because I saved your miserable life?"

Tam selects another rock and throws it out to sea. "Ach, better you let me die."

"Never say such a thing," I admonish. "It might come true. Did your mither never tell you not to tempt the Fates?"

"She's long dead. The day I was born. It was my birth that killed her."

A jagged place inside me is released and made smooth.

"I'm sorry," I say. "I cannot imagine life without Mither." But this is exactly what the selkies have asked of me, to give my mither the means to leave me.

"Ach, who wants all that fussing over?" Tam answers, but he is lying, I can tell, and I want to know the place inside his heart where his mither might have lived. I lean my body into his and feel a small shiver bind us together. We stand still as jackrabbits, as if the smallest movement might be dangerous. Our breathing gradually slows, and the night air surrounds us like the walls of a room. On the slender finger of the skerry, where the calm of the voe meets the wild North Sea, we are the only two people in the world.

CHAPTER
SEVENTEEN

Tam sighs, and I feel his warm breath on my cheek.

"I'll content myself with this spotty pelt," he whispers.

I push away from him. "No. The pelt belongs to me. You cannot have it."

"I can take this pelt if I want," he replies with mock belligerence. "And maybe if I take it, you'll follow me, like in the stories."

"I'll not follow a thief."

Tam laughs. "Don't fret, Selkie Girl. I'll not take your precious pelt—if you'll dance with me at the foy this night."

In that moment, the future feels as if it might be worth living. Dance with Tam at the foy. That'd make the others stand up and take notice. Tam McCodrun dancing with the Selkie Girl. He has gone mad, they will think. But such a welcome madness!

I bite a tiny chunk off my fingernail and look at him carefully for signs of deception. "You want to dance with me? At the foy?"

"Aye. That's the trade. The pelt for a dance."

"I'll dance with you, then," I say. But feeling too bold, I add, "If that's what you want."

"I said it, did I not?"

Tam takes me about the waist with one lanky arm and whirls me around. My hair billows out behind me, and I laugh at the sheer pleasure of it, until the inevitable happens. Tam loses his footing on the slick rocks and we fall, tangled together like puppies. Tam holds my hand in his own. I try to hide it, but he brings it to his lips.

"They're beautiful, your hands," he says, and I go soft with contentment.

"Promise me you'll stop killing the selkies," I breathe.

Tam shakes his head. "Why must you ask me for the one thing I cannot do?"

"I'll dance with you and only you if you'll promise me this."

His eyes, velvet-soft, gaze at me. He sighs. "It's a hard bargain you're asking for, lass."

"Aye. But I will not dance with a killer."

It all hinges on this promise. I send a silent prayer to St. Magnus that this will be the first of many promises he will make to me and that keeping them will be as sacred as the saints who lie buried in the cathedral.

"Done?" I ask, so close that only a sliver of night air separates us.

"Done," he agrees, and my lips meet his. The pelt drops on the skerry as Tam pulls me to him. His body is hard and soft all at the same time, and I allow a momentary loss of reality.

Then I remember what the Red and the Black have told me I must do. Mither might arrive at any moment, and Tam mustn't be here. I bundle the pelt in my arms.

"Thank you, Tam McCodrun, for your promise."

A tiny, sad pull tugs the corner of Tam's mouth. "You'll be the ruin of me for sure."

"I have something important to do," I say, mustering up as much authority as I can. "Be off with you now until the foy."

"What's making you so foreswifted to be rid of me?" he asks.

Although I would like nothing better than to share the burden of this secret with him, I know that I cannot. "I have something to do, and I must do it alone," I tell him. "Get on with you now and leave me to myself."

"You're mighty mysterious. What are you about?" he asks, studying me.

He'll not likely be satisfied until I give him an answer. That's certain. I cast about for some reasonable excuse. The lie must be believable. Anything less will never fool him.

My dress, still wet from the sea, clings damply to my legs, and I seize the opportunity. "Well now," I reply, summoning up as much haughtiness as I can under the circumstances, "I cannot go to the foy all far-flung-like, then, can I?"

Tam looks down at his grimy hands and wipes them on his ragged vest. "Oh. I'm thinking I have something to do, too," he says, looking in the direction of the gypsy camp. "I won't be long."

"Nor will I."

"When the music starts, you'll find me here. Ready for the dancing."

He turns to go, but my voice stops him. "Tam McCodrun."

"My name," he answers. "Say it again. I like it when you say my name."

"Tam McCodrun."

"Aye. That's it."

"Don't forget your promise about the selkies."

"I swore it, did I not?"

"Swear it again."

"I swear I'll not hurt the selkies."

"Never, never forget your promise."

Tam leans in to me. "I'll not forget. I am pledged this night and forever."

I turn my face to meet his kiss. One last look passes between us.

"Run!" I tell him. "Don't come back until midnight!"

"Until the foy!" Tam shouts, and with a great roar, he vaults over the jagged rocks, his legs propelling him toward the beach.

I watch him until he disappears over the rise, headed for the gypsy camp along the road. Even out of sight, I can feel the nearness of him. *Is there something else you'd be wanting, Tam McCodrun?* I asked, and he answered, *A lass to love me as brave and true as yourself.* Aye, I'll dance with you, Tam, dance with you through the night.

Holding the pelt firmly under my arm, I pick my way back to the beach as fast as my legs will carry me, and when my feet touch the yielding sand, I begin to dance. "I'll dance at the foy!" I shout into the wind, feet kicking up the sand.

Panting, I fall onto the cool beach, the pelt pooling at my feet in a small puddle.

A solitary figure walks toward me. The hesitant gait, the drop of her shoulders are unmistakable.

" 'Tis good to see you smiling, Peedie Buddo."

Kneeling, I wrap myself around Mither's slender waist.

"I'll be dancing at the foy this night. With Tam."

"A smart lad, that Tam. And lucky, too."

For a moment, I am filled with gratitude for Mither's constant understanding. I need Mither on my side about the foy. I know what Fither thinks of the travelers and their wandering ways.

I look up at her face, her cheeks reddened by the wind, her hair half blown out of its knot at the back of her neck. She looks like a girl in the evening light, and I remember what her sisters said to me. *Your mither has lost her youth to the land and to the man who is your fither.* Is that why she walks by the sea each night, to be near its healing salt water?

I remember what I must do, and there is a rending inside me like the cliffs of Hoy splintering in two, sliding into the bottomless chasm of the sea. I will away the tears and slowly lift the pelt from the sand.

"Mither, look."

I offer the selkie skin to Mither, a reluctant gift. "I found your pelt hidden up in the aisins," I tell her.

She shudders, then her knees buckle and she falls to the beach. I lay the pelt gently in her outstretched arms. She moans at the first touch of the pelt and utters a sound made all the more astonishing because it has been so long since I have heard it. Mither laughs. She laughs with abandon, with utter joy, and I know that this thing I have done is good.

Mither runs her hands over the folds of the pelt, as if memorizing it, pressing its softness to her. Like the pelts of the Red and the Black, her pelt is the exact color of her hair, easily fitting each curve of her body.

"Peedie Buddo," she whispers. "You've given me back my life."

Pride pours through me until I feel as if I will burst with the force of it. I have felt so useless in the face of Mither's melancholy state, but now I have made her smile. She laughs into the midnight sun, and it sounds like church bells celebrating a holy day. I look at my webbed hands and remember the words of the Red and the Black. *You will give your mither back her pelt. Give her back to the sea.*

"Your sisters said you'd leave me for the sea."

The wind makes ragged halos of her hair, the sea wild and dark behind her. She takes my hand and leads me to the edge of the water, where the waves gently wash our feet. Tiny fish scurry away to safer depths.

Mither lifts her voice over the wind. "Sixteen years I have been captive on the land. In that time, I have grown old and stiff. My skin is dry and cracked for want of the sea. My bones are as brittle as the driftwood lying on the shore. I can no longer survive on the land. It is my time to return home."

I cannot imagine life without Mither. I said it to Tam, and it is true. I want to beg her not to leave me. I want to keep her with me, now more than ever. I think of Fither's anger rising like a storm and the disdain on his face as he looked at my webbed hands. How can I face the future without the one person who understands? Who will stand between Fither's mad determination and my willfulness?

"Mither, don't leave me," I beg.

The waves pounding the skerry punctuate Mither's words like a drumbeat. "Leave you? Never, Peedie Buddo." She points out to the endless ocean. "Look to the sea and you'll see me there, in the waves breaking on the rocks, the sun glittering on the sea foam. Precious shells will wash up on the beach. Fish will leap into your nets, and the selkies will guide you safely through the tides in the sea. I will always be with you." Mither kisses each of my sea-moist cheeks, and I cannot stop the tears.

"You are a woman now, Peedie Buddo. There is no end to what you can and must do. You will find your way to the knowin'."

Mither wades into the frigid water. It curls around her legs like a lover. I feel the pull of the sea, inviting me to lie in its embrace.

Mither looks back toward the crofthouse. Is she thinking of

her life with us and all its complications? I wish desperately that I could change it all, find a way to keep her with us, but I know she cannot wait for a miracle, even if I could summon one. She walks deeper into the waves, throwing the pelt around her shoulders.

"Take me with you." I wade into the sea beside her. "Please. I hate the land. I want to be in the sea."

"Are you not afraid?"

"Aye. Afraid of being left behind among the others."

I expect her to argue, to pummel me with reasons why I must stay on land, but she hugs me, then pushes me away and studies my face. "Listen well, then, brave one. I will give you the gift of the wind to travel beneath the tides."

CHAPTER
EIGHTEEN

Mither's eyes bore into mine, green as emeralds. The calm water of the voe laps against my legs. She takes my hand in hers and leads me back onto the beach. She lays her pelt reverently on the sand and faces me. "Only do as I do and you will have the way to find the knowin'," she tells me, and taking my other hand in hers, she leads me in a dance of the sea.

I follow her movements, mirroring her motions as closely as I can, and soon I climb out of myself. Like in the crofthouse only hours before, I float, lighter than the night mist. There is nothing else in the world, just the sound of Mither's breathing, and I match my own to its rhythm.

We glide along the beach, twin figures, arms, legs, necks, and backs; we mirror each other in a graceful promenade. Mither painstakingly moves her twisted limbs in an ancient dance of the sea, and I follow her, as though we are choreographing the dance together. Images form on the soft surface of the beach where our feet have fallen, impressions in the sand that tell a story of primal tribes and family bonds, of life and death, killing and survival. Embedded in the sand are the now-familiar shapes of the three selkies in a circle and the slender girl with webbed hands.

As I dance among the images, a cool rush of wind covers my face, my mouth opens, and the sea enters me, filling my lungs with its pungent smell. I taste seaweed, salty-sweet and slippery. Minuscule sea creatures swim through my body. How odd to be filled up with liquid but have no sense of drowning! I am buoyant. I no longer need to breathe. I move easily on the land, infused with an endless expanse of the sea, suspended, neither in the sea nor on land.

The rush of cool wind whisks over me again, and I breathe the metallic air of land. The comforting presence of Mither is nearby, but she appears changed, someone different, as if I am seeing her for the first time. Her skin shines in the Midsummer light, damp from sea spray. Her eyes are as vibrant green as the seaweed that washes up on the beach.

" 'Tis a fearful thing to enter the sea," she says.

"I am not afraid," I answer, and am surprised that it is true.

"Listen to your instincts and follow their path. There is more beneath the sea than you can dream of."

"Tell me, Mither. I want to know."

A look of melancholy passes over her face. "Know this. I would face any danger for you, but I cannot tell you the knowin' you seek."

Mither kisses me once, and before my astonished eyes, she slips out of her clothes, dropping them in the shallow water near the shore, and walks naked into the sea with her pelt. When the water covers her hips, she turns back. "My heart is turned inside out with the pain of leaving you," she says. "But it is my time to go." She shifts her body into the pelt and rebirths into the selkie she once was.

I hold my breath as I watch her metamorphosis, hair and skin and crippled bone becoming sleek animal flesh. Then, like in the ending of a story, the selkie that was my mither nods once in my direction and dives beneath the sea. She resurfaces farther out, blowing air from her nose. Her green eyes glint briefly back at me from her cunning seal face, and she swims quickly through the waters of the voe toward the North Sea.

I fly sure-footed over the rocks, keeping Mither in sight. When I reach the end of the skerry, I call out to her. "Mither! Wait! Wait for me! Don't leave me behind."

My pleas are met with a profound silence, not a single cry from the selkies. Even the birds have gone quiet, as if in mourning. All I can hear is the sound of the relentless waves ending their lives on the unforgiving rocks of the skerry.

I lift my arms to dive into the sea but am stopped by a callused hand that seizes my arm.

"Elin Jean!" Grandpa's coat thrashes about him in the wind, and I see his pipe dashed to pieces on the rocks at his feet. He knows. How he knows, I cannot imagine, but suddenly I realize that my family has kept this secret from me. It is a grand conspiracy, and I have been a fool.

"Hover you now, lass," he shouts, and I struggle to free myself from his iron grip. "You cannot follow her. Stay and dance for your old grandpa at the foy."

Even as he pleads, the foy, which only a moment ago was everything to me, becomes trivial compared to the future that waits. The selkies have summoned me. Their prescription has reached inside me and lodged its authority there. *Join us. Know us. Help us.* And although Grandpa's fervent pleas touch my heart, the pounding sea, the selkies chanting my name like a prayer, fill me with purpose, and Grandpa's request fades to a place as far away as my childhood.

As if they have read my thoughts, the selkies call my name. *Eeeelin Jeeeeean.*

"Elin Jean!" Grandpa shakes me, and I meet his gray eyes with my own. "You cannot follow her!"

"Do you hear the selkies calling me?" I ask. "I cannot stay on land."

"Listen to me! The tides will draw you under and you will drown." He trembles with fear for my safety.

"Don't be afraid for me, Grandpa. I was meant to find the pelt."

Grandpa presses his face to mine, holding me so tight the breath is knocked out of me. "No, I forbid it. I will not let you go."

I think of Mither, held against her will, withering year after year for want of the sea, and in that moment, the chance that he can stop me is nothing more than a child's wish flung willy-nilly into the air.

Grandpa clutches me against him, like a mither memorizes her newborn babe. All the days of my life have led up to this moment, and some small part of me has always known it.

There is no time to explain. "Don't try to stop me. If you hold me here, I'll hate you forever."

Is he thinking of Mither, too? Does he realize that I have already been a captive like her? "Let me go," I beg. "Let me go, Grandpa."

He holds me fast to him, his face buried in my hair. When he faces me, his eyes are wet with tears and his face has lost its desperate look, as though he has let go of a great weight. "Go, then," he says, releasing me. "Go where you must and St. Magnus be with you. I'll not hold you here. Quickly! Duncan'll be coming up the beach for the foy."

I return Grandpa's fierce hug with all the love I hold in my heart for him. I know what it costs him to let me go.

"I love you, Grandpa. I'll love you forever."

He looks at me and smiles, tears streaking his wrinkled cheeks. "Go on with you, then," he encourages, giving me a small push, then turns away as though he cannot bear to watch.

"Don't be afraid for me, Grandpa. I'll find the knowin'."

I imagine the weight of the sea cushioning me in its embrace. My toes feel for sure footing on the rocks. My arms lift to dive.

"Selkie Girl!"

On the beach stands Tam McCodrun, waving wildly. He has changed into his Sunday trousers and a clean shirt. In his outstretched hand is a hastily picked bunch of wildflowers.

"I've come for my dance," he calls buoyantly as he navigates the rocks toward us.

My heart moves in my chest. He looks sweet with his wilting wildflowers, face scrubbed like a schoolboy's. Earlier tonight he was all I wanted. Now it is too late. Tam McCodrun belongs to another life. I pull Tam's bloodstained handkerchief from my pocket and drop it on the sparkling rocks of the skerry. I have no choice but to leave him behind with the others. "Keep your promise, Tam McCodrun! Never harm the selkies, no matter what comes. Don't ever forget!"

The wind blows my hair into my eyes, blocking Tam from my sight as if he were already gone. I push the curls away and glimpse him one last time, running recklessly along the skerry.

I meet Grandpa's eyes and silently ask him to be kind to Tam. Then I dive into the sea, cutting through the waves as easily as a knife slices through butter, and as the ocean embraces me, I know I will never see either of them again.

Part Two

THE SEA

CHAPTER
NINETEEN

'll find it, I'll find the knowin'. The words pinwheel round and round in my mind as the cool hands of the sea enfold me and my water-blurred eyes search for some trace of the path Mither has taken. No markers offer clues to aid me in this task, and although I continually scan the sea around me, I see no disturbance of any kind, nothing but the vast, endless ocean.

For a moment, panic stops me. Tiny multicolored fish peer curiously as if to ask, *Who is this stranger who dives so recklessly into our midst?* One bright purple fish with protruding eyes looks at me quizzically, nose to nose, and offers a sympathetic smile before it darts away. Its pity emboldens me. I swim west toward the great North Sea, staying near the surface for easy access to the air above. I will not be deterred in my search for Mither. Finding her will be the beginning.

The sea-green dress, lighter than a breeze on land, is heavy in the water, slowing my progress. I am reluctant to leave it behind, but wearing it is a foolish waste of energy. It is even more voluminous in the sea than on land, swirling about me. It seems thicker, as if it has grown new layers. I gather up the tiers of fabric, intending to pull the dress over my head, but my hands slide down the cloth. Even when I manage to grab a fistful, it disentangles from my grip as though I never held it. When I try to lift my arms through the sleeves, the dress swirls about me, alive with resistance. I struggle, frantically trying to free myself, but my grasping hands slide through the layers as though they are drenched in slick seal oil. Helplessly entangled in its folds, I feel the dress lift, swirl upward, and cover my face, snaking through my arms and legs, until I am blind and paralyzed in its cocoon.

St. Magnus, help me! What is happening?

Wrapped tight in its layers, my chest compresses, forcing the remaining air from my lungs. I fight savagely to be rid of it, and when my trembling hands finally gain a hold on the bodice, I pull with all my strength, but the fabric clings to me, as if fused to my skin. I try again and again, desperate to breathe, but my flesh has become pliable, stretching with the cloth. I am rendered helpless as the currents pull me down to the ocean floor.

There is a great rending sensation in my chest. My lungs burn for want of air, until I know I must surface or die. For a single moment, I think of Tam and Grandpa on the skerry, how glad they would be to see me again, and I imagine their arms surrounding me, a safe harbor.

"St. Magnus, save me!" I cry out, and the sea, welcomed by my open mouth, spills into me.

I give myself up to a dark, watery grave.

But when I touch the silt of the ocean floor, there is a shift in the deepest part of my belly. The sensation expands, traveling through my body, reaching every inch of me. My nostrils shrink inward and my throat closes to protect my lungs from the liquid rush. Arrows of pain shoot through my arms and legs, feet and hands. My legs melt together, hot and boneless, arms retreating into my body, becoming short and flat. When I feel my face re-molding itself, malleable as clay, I begin to scream, but the only sound is a bubbly eruption, like a burp after a satisfying meal.

Why does it take so long to die? I always thought drowning would be quick. One intake of the sea, a small struggle, and it would be finished. But this death is as endless and lonely as the land.

I wait for oblivion, but instead, an odd sense of comfort washes over me as I lie on the silky bottom of the sea, swaddled tight in the dress. The purple fish still hovers nearby, gazing at me with a look of sympathy, its rotund body shimmering with violet hues. Tiny herring dart past but solemnly refuse to approach. Shells lying around me on the ocean floor burn with an unnatural brightness, lit from inside by an orange-gold glow. A thousand sea creatures appear with new clarity, their colors profoundly richer than any I have ever seen. The fish, slender and quick, radiate light from within as though they have swallowed tiny seal-oil lamps. How can this be? The creatures that inhabit this sunless world seem to have the means to light the darkest sea by themselves. Even through the layers of current, I can see farther than I ever thought possible. The soft breathing of multitudes of fish, gills opening and closing like the rustling of grass, soothes my ears. I can hear vegetation swaying in the tides, accompanied by a soft, shushing noise whose source I cannot locate.

I risk a small movement, and the salt water parts to invite me in, my slightest movement answered by the rolling sea. Is this death? If this velvet embrace is oblivion, it is nothing like I imagined. The need for air is gone, and my earlier panic is replaced with a rabbit-still quiet and an odd sense of belonging that pulses in the deepest part of me. The shushing noise has taken on a slow rhythm, like the sound of the wind as it moves over the land.

Exhausted, I close my eyes. I'll lie here on the ocean floor, fall into a dreamless sleep, and never wake up. No more troubles, no more pain. Releasing all the muscles in my body, I roll down the mushy silt of an incline, down and down, until a slight depression in the sand stops me.

I lie in the embrace of the sea, my eyes closed tight. That's when I realize the source of the shushing sound. It surrounds me. It *is* me. I silently offer a prayer to St. Magnus and open my eyes. Playing among the currents is feathery brown fur, and in that moment, I know I am a selkie.

CHAPTER TWENTY

*R*apture floods through me as my selkie body tumbles effortlessly in the tides. My animal muscles, powerful and lithe, are strong beyond human capability. The smallest effort propels me like quicksilver through the dense sea. Tightening my body, I swim with a new speed that leaves me reeling, like leaning far out over the crashing sea on the towering cliffs of Hoy, giddy with the danger of it. The salt water lies with me like a trusted friend. Gone is the tension in my shoulders and neck, replaced with a sense of joy, and I am a willing hostage to it all.

Allowing animal instinct to lead me, I tunnel furiously into the ocean with renewed hope of finding the path Mither has taken. The deeper water is smoother, requiring less effort to navigate. I travel straight as a furrow, plowing the sea. Even with no sense of a final destination, I feel a surprising lack of fear, only an eagerness to find Mither and her sisters, the Red and the Black.

Ahead, the vast, nearly flat plain of the deepest ocean stretches before me. Here and there, rock plates stack up one upon the other, creating low, rolling hills. Occasionally, deep trenches break the monotony of the terrain, but even they slope gradually into acres of flat, sandy tundra.

My animal-sharp eyes easily pierce the currents ahead, but random gatherings of tiny, luminescent fish are the only creatures I see. Then three dark shapes flash in the distance—at least I think there are three. I can't see them clearly. I narrow my eyes, scanning the area where they appeared. Nothing. But as I swim forward, they dart past me, closer this time, the unmistakable outlines of seals. I am not alone! I swim toward them but stop when the selkies glide directly in my path, blocking my progress. They reel past again, bumping into me. I tumble in the tides from the force of their bodies. Is this some kind of game? I tread water, waiting anxiously for them.

They reappear as suddenly as they vanished, and I am face to face with three brown-spotted selkies like me. Still as stones, they stare with an expression of such intensity that the fur stands up on my broad seal back. I form my face into something I hope resembles a smile and nod my head at them, imitating the Red and the Black.

They do not respond.

Garn. I'm a fool and half again a fool. I should say something. Can I speak under the sea? If I can, will they understand me? But before I decide what to say, the selkies scatter. One swims in front; the other two take positions on either side of me. I am surrounded. I stare from one selkie to the other, looking for some sign of what they want. They watch me, their faces blank and flat as plates, three pairs of eyes blinking in the eerie glow of the sea. I cautiously approach the nearest selkie, but he quickly darts out of reach. I face the other two, and the third selkie repositions himself. They peer at me with animal eyes through the watery light of the deepest ocean.

Then a bizarre sensation takes hold of me, entirely new, but at the same time familiar. I feel the need to breathe. I nod again to the selkies and quickly point my body up to the surface. I'll breathe, then return to deal with the selkies. Maybe they will follow me. Above the water, I can speak to them, and even if they cannot understand the words, at least they'll hear the friendly tone in my voice.

As though they sense my need to breathe, the three seals swim above me, creating a barrier with their bodies. I try to swim past them, but in military formation, they block my path to the surface. Their muscular tails churn the sea until it is whipped into a thick foam, and the force of the currents they create begins to pull me back down.

They are trying to drown me.

I push forward with all my strength, trying to escape their hostile blockade, but I am not a strong enough swimmer to break through their churning animal mass. My body sinks inward with the need to breathe. Recklessly, I charge at them, thinking only of the sweet air above. The selkies pummel me with their hind flippers, and I am driven back. I charge again, knowing that if I fail to break through soon and fill my lungs with air, I will drown.

I feint to the right and, when they follow, dart quickly to the left, distracting them long enough to glide past their barricade in a dash to the surface. They may be determined, but I am smarter. And certainly more afraid.

My head breaks out of the ocean with a great splash, water streaming down my seal face, and as my eyes clear, I feel the strange sensation of my nose and throat yawning open to receive life-giving air. I breathe once, then duck quickly under the water to see if the selkies have followed me. The dim outlines of their bodies are far below, swimming restlessly through the currents. They are waiting for me.

I bob on the surface, waves lapping against my fur, trying to decide on a possible course of action. As the prospects race through my mind, I discover the rhythm of breathing as a selkie. A single breath takes longer to inhale, then is held for a time before the equally slow process of release, as though the ability to remain underwater for longer periods of time requires more preparation. I breathe until I am sated, but I linger on the surface. It feels safer here in the crisp air. Perhaps the selkies will tire of waiting for me and leave me alone.

Why would they try to kill me? Have I blundered into some sacred territory? Does the stink of land still cling to me, frightening them? But that wouldn't explain their hostility. Can it be that the selkies are even crueler than the others? This thought is too discouraging, so I push it away, and as brief as the sun in winter, it is gone.

Faint fiddle music floats in and out, and I recognize a lilting melody I have known since I was a bairn. But in my animal ears, it sounds so fresh and new that it is as if I am hearing it for the first time. I never knew music could be so impossibly beautiful, joy and melancholy mingled together in the same melody. The tiny, far-off shapes of the others dance on the beach. In spite of the events of the day, the Johnsmas Foy continues, without anyone caring that I am lost to the sea. Perhaps they don't even know.

I haul out onto a nearby cluster of rocks that rise above the sea and peer through the mist, but even with my new selkie eyes, I cannot recognize the one I seek among the others. Is Tam dancing with another lass? Is she pretty? Does he care that I broke my promise to dance with him?

Dark thoughts take hold of me and will not leave. I have made a mistake. I will never be able to go back to being human.

I will never walk on the beach or go to the foy. I am altered forever. And even if I could return, it must be on Midsummer's Eve, at the seventh tide of the seventh tide, a whole year from this night. I will have to wait to feel Tam's arms around me, to dance at the foy, to be the girl I used to be. Waiting, always waiting. And now the waiting must be endured in the unknown world of the sea.

I can almost hear Grandpa saying, *You have made your bed, now you must lie in it.*

CHAPTER
TWENTY-ONE

The dream that steals into my selkie sleep is maddeningly familiar and yet entirely new. I am standing on the beach. It is summer, because the air is warm, and the clouds are whisked about by the wind like Mither sweeps the dust from the floor of the croft. The shushing of the sea lapping the beach, the selkies singing, the sea grasses that line the shore bending with the breeze—all these are customary for this time of year, but something is strangely different, heavy and foreboding.

When I look up, the sun is erased by a sudden storm. The wind howls as it assaults the land, whipping the sand on the beach into a squall of its own. I am in the midst of it, the sky black with thunderheads, the roar of the sea pounding my ears and the rain stinging my face. I fall on the beach from the force of the gale. The insistent wind competes with the cadence of the sea, whispering wild mysteries, until I think I will go mad with the barrage of sound. I clap my hands over my ears against the onslaught.

Then silence. The storm is gone as suddenly as it arrived. Even the seabirds are quiet.

A young crofter sprints down the beach. Slung about his neck is a net to troll for herring. He is well made, a slender, sinewy man, and I can tell by his clothes that he is prosperous.

As he lays out his net, dark shapes swim through the fog toward the beach. Are they sea trows come to snatch the crofter away?

Then I hear the strange, mournful cries of the selkies. The crofter must hear them, too, because he hides behind the rocks so as not to frighten them away.

Three small selkies swim up to the beach and haul out on the shore. The moment their bodies touch the beach, they roll, and as I watch, astonished, they shed their skins to reveal three glorious women. One is fair-skinned, golden-red hair haloed about her head. The second has shining black locks, dark as the Orkney winters, flowing down her back. And the last selkie girl's chestnut hair is a mass of tangled curls like mine. She walks toward me until she is standing so close I can reach out and touch her shimmering skin. It is as cool and smooth as stones beaten flat by the sea. I am in thrall to her beauty. The selkie girl dips her head and smiles at me. "Know this," she says. "There are mysteries in this life that you can only dream of."

Then the selkie girls are dancing, dancing on the land like waves on the sea, a wild, primitive dance. They dance like Mither did, once upon a time. They dance like me.

The crofter rises up from behind the rocks, staring at the beautiful, naked limbs of the selkie girls. His gaze shifts to the pile of pelts fallen near the place where the sea caresses the land, and I know his intent. I shout a warning, but although my mouth opens and my lips form the words, no sound emerges.

The crofter runs forward and, quick with purpose, snatches up one of the pelts.

Tiny, malevolent ghosts appear out of nowhere. Like puffs of clouds, they are, wisps of spectral spirits that snarl and nip at his shoulders with their jagged teeth, but the crofter ignores them. He cares for nothing but the pelt that lies draped in his arms. The tiny wraiths surround the crofter, buzzing with agitation, and as they close in, I think he will drop the pelt, but he is determined, never taking his eyes from the curly-haired selkie girl.

The black-haired girl cries out a warning, and she and her red-haired companion snatch up their pelts, escaping into the churning safety of the sea. Like a frightened animal, the third selkie shivers at the frank stare of the man before her. Her eyes beg him to return her precious skin, but the crofter tucks the pelt firmly under his arm, and the selkie girl falls onto the beach, weeping bitterly. As sure as the fish flounders in the net, she is caught. Without her pelt, she cannot return to the sea but must follow him wherever he might lead her.

The crofter gently lifts her small hand and kisses it tenderly. He helps her to her feet, and she follows him without a struggle. The tiny ghosts buzz above his head and snap at his bare heels.

The moaning of the two selkies is carried inland on the wind. The selkie girl looks back at them, and my heart cracks open at the longing in her eyes. I reach out to her but am rooted to where my feet touch the beach. I cannot move. Tears fall down my face, cooled by the wind.

"It's the bairns who pay for the wrongs of the ones gone before," says a voice from above me. I look up, and a craggy face parts the swirling clouds above me.

Grandpa!

Has he been there all along? Was he a witness to the

crofter's theft? Tears trail into the crevasses that define his weathered smile. He has watched it with me. He mourns with me. My eyes follow his gaze to the man and woman walking up the hill. They are not much older than I am now, but I recognize them still, and I know the sorrow they carry with them because it is mine.

Grandpa's face distorts, melts into the clouds. I look again to the crofter and the selkie girl, but they are gone.

A cold wave from the rising tide slaps my face, and I am awake. The sea that surrounds me and the land in the distance blur into one, and I understand my beginnings.

CHAPTER
TWENTY-TWO

The torches on the beach have blazed through their short lives, glowing with a last, dim light. To the east the first hint of day peels back the layer of night. The music is done, but I can still hear a few shouts from determined revelers on the beach, and one couple whirls wildly about despite the absence of music.

A family of otters has joined me on the rocks, searching for limpets and mollusks for their breakfast. They grin at me sheepishly, their teeth flashing white in the sun, as they use their tiny hands to break the shellfish on the rocks.

A jumble of emotions washes through me, a wave of anger mixed with the overripe fruit of self-pity. Everyone knew. The taking of my mither had begun it all, her captivity, my unnatural birth, the others' fears. And no one told me. I have been an outcast in my family, too. I am weighted down with this knowledge, the layers of complications and meanings.

My life could have been so much easier. If only I had known. The truth would have comforted me, at least a little. We could have shared it all. Instead, they kept the truth to themselves, selfishly guarding their secret. Were they protecting me? Did they convince themselves that it was for my own good?

.For my own good. *It's the bairns who pay.*

The indulgence of self-pity vanishes, replaced with a determined fury. They may have treated me like a child, but I am no child now. Mither has given me the means to find my birthright, and find it I will. Nothing and no one will stand in my way. My tail beats on the rocks, and I allow myself a low bellow of anger. The otters scatter, clutching their shellfish.

I dive into the sea and turn hard to the right to avoid the three selkies who attacked me. How hopeful I was at the sight of them. Now I know I must avoid them or risk another near-fatal encounter. My tears are whisked away in the current, as if the sea refuses to acknowledge them. There is no time for crying now.

I navigate forward until I travel through a series of currents, flowing horizontally in multiple directions. I plow through the push and pull of the random tides, and the sea takes on a new clarity, the water aqua-bright. I reckon I have traveled in the right direction, far beyond the voe into the North Sea. I can feel the subtle variations in water pressure as I slide between the tides. Buffeted by the intensity of the directional shifts, I swim forward through it all, navigating into the end of the world.

Ahead is darkness. I slow up a bit, figuring caution to be the best choice, and there, directly in front of me, lies the shining blackness of a sheer wall, rising like a great sea mountain. Black as tar, unforgiving, and I cannot see the end of it. So it is the end of the world after all, or at least an end to this part of it. I explore its craggy expanse and see that it is built of thousands of layers of thin shale, stacked like plates, sheer and impenetrable.

Wait. There. A small opening, as if someone has burrowed a

hole in the wall. I swim closer to the opening and see dim light reflected from the other side. I push my seal face into the portal. It opens into a narrow tunnel, so long I cannot be sure there is an end to it. But there must be. The light is coming from somewhere. Further inspection reveals other illuminated openings in the wall. Perhaps the light is glowing from the wall itself or from something at the end of the tunnel.

My instincts quicken as I sense danger behind me. I twist around and see three shapes swimming purposefully in my direction. Giddy God! The three selkies have followed me. I cannot believe how rapidly they are approaching. With sheer rock before me and the enemy selkies behind, I have little choice. I slither into the mouth of the largest portal, praying that I can escape to the other side before I run out of air.

In the passageway, the unforgiving rock walls scrape my sides. Warding off the sense of gloom that pervades the tunnel, I swim as quickly as the narrow passageway will allow, making small, purposeful movements forward. I lengthen my round body into a slender projectile and am making good progress when the tunnel narrows unexpectedly, and I feel my sides ripped by the sharp rock walls. I ignore the pain and push forward in my effort to be out of the narrow prison of the passageway.

Then I find myself wedged so tightly I cannot move. A sense of dread washes over me. What if I cannot fit through the tunnel? There is certainly not enough space to turn around and retreat. The thought of being trapped in this dark place terrifies me. I have no sense of how long I can remain underwater before the need to breathe must send me desperately to the surface.

Please, St. Magnus, don't let me die here alone in the dark.

I paddle my hind flippers in small, forceful motions and am rewarded with faint forward progress. Ahead, a tiny light glows and, with it, the unreasonable hope of safety. I inch forward, my flippers nearly pinned at my sides. I am tiring, but the light beckons, inviting a renewed belief in the possibility of survival, so I push harder, until suddenly a rush of current pulls me out of the portal into a huge cavern.

I shake out my sore muscles, rolling joyfully in the freedom of the sea around me. The interior of the cave is lighter than the tunnel, the rock walls glowing with spectral brilliance. Weak with relief, I scan the waters of the cave but see nothing of concern. My only companions are tiny rainbow fish darting along the ledges of rock.

The three selkies have not followed me.

I stretch my cramped muscles and inspect the cuts and scrapes on my sides. None of them seems serious, and they have stopped bleeding in the healing salt water. I offer a prayer to St. Magnus. *Thank you, thank you, for freeing me from that deadly, stifling tunnel.*

Around me the rock walls gleam silver-bright, and drawn to their unnatural light, I see reflected in the flat, mirror-like surface the clear image of a young selkie. Like all selkies, her snout slopes down from a flat forehead framed by unexpectedly tiny ears. Her cylindrical body curves in the water, ending in hind flippers that rotate both forward and backward, to navigate both land and sea. Whiskers sprout from her forehead down to her cheeks. Her round eyes shine black as coal. Her fur coat, though brown in color, has spotted patterns of dun and ivory running up and down its back and sides.

Inspecting my reflection in the walls of the cave, I cannot puzzle out why the selkies would attack me. What horrible part of me do they see? I am formed like all the young females, whether black or brown, red or gray. I am in every way like an ordinary selkie, like hundreds I have watched haul out on the skerry to bathe in the midday sun. A bit smaller perhaps, and my face is more angular than round, but why should that matter?

The school of rainbow fish shoots back and forth, keeping a uniform distance. Even they shun me. As if reading my thoughts, the fish duck, then slide past, engaged in a game of follow the leader. Each time their gills open to breathe, they light up the water around them like miniature lanterns.

I watch their antics for a moment, then swim back to where the portal led me into the cave. All well and good for them to play, but I need to find my way to the surface to breathe. I scan along the layers of rock. Where is the opening? Solid rock, onyx and oozing, is all I can see.

Not possible. The portal must be here. It was, only a moment ago. Trying not to panic, I begin a painstaking search for the passageway. I look for landmarks to be sure this is the area where I entered the cave, but no matter where I look, I cannot find an opening. I navigate the circular walls of the cave once and then again, forcing myself to swim slowly, but I cannot see even the tiniest pinpoint of light. It is as though once within the cave, the openings are obliterated.

There must be a way out. There must be.

Swimming to the top of the cavern, I find it covered with sharp, razor-like stalactites, hanging down like icicles. A greenish liquid oozes from between the pointed spikes. Tendrils of the fluid mingle with the sea and are slowly sucked into the atmosphere of the cave. I search between the spikes for some passage out but encounter only unforgiving rock and the pointed stalactites, sharp as knives.

How much longer until I must breathe? A minute, an hour? I know that it must be soon. I swim along the sandy bottom of the cave, but it, too, yields no exit. I must stay calm. Think. Swimming back and forth, I concentrate on formulating a plan while praying for a miracle. Knowing it is foolish, I pray anyway. *St. Magnus, make an opening appear.* But when, as I expect, no portal is revealed, despair, dark-winged and determined, comes knocking and I am powerless to stop it.

I sink to the floor of the cave.

As I lie there, sunk into myself, a sudden movement flutters along the wall, as though the edges of the cave are undulating in an underwater jig. There is motion on my left, my right, then all around me, and I see them, horrible and unyielding, moving through the water toward me.

Sea trows! Covered in seaweed hair, the stocky little men slide through the water, their stubby webbed hands and feet churning the sea at terrifying speed. Smaller than the trolls of Norse legend, these equally devious creatures have human-like characteristics but are not human at all. Hawk-beaked noses dwarf their faces, and their tongues make strange clicking noises as they swim. Their gnarled monkey faces lap greedily at me, their tiny eyes flashing gold in the dim light. The sea trows are every bit as terrifying as I have heard them described—the ugliest creatures on earth or in hell. Murmuring in their guttural language, their knobby bodies surround me, short spears curled in their webbed fists. My heart goes cold in my chest as the trows smack their sea-wrinkled lips in anticipation, and I realize their plan is to eat me!

Frantically, I try to recall the little I know about the trows. Too lazy to fish for herring themselves, they steal the day's catch from unsuspecting fishermen's nets, leaving the surprised men to rail at the uncaring sea for their loss. Their thickheaded brains are slow to reason, limiting their thinking skills to solving simple problems.

I dart swiftly to the left, avoiding the spear the sea trow leader suddenly flings at me. I am faster, but I can't elude them forever in this contained place, and no matter how limited their reasoning, I am outnumbered. They will eventually figure out a way to capture me, trapped as I am in this cave.

As they renew their pursuit, I swerve to the right and swim to the top of the cave. The trows follow me, shaking their scaly fists and grasping my tail in an effort to drag me into their midst. Ahead of me I see a narrow opening between the spikes that hang down from the ceiling of the cave and I swim into it, barely missing a huge swordlike spike in my path. I hover there, momentarily out of reach, trying to ignore the green ooze.

I watch the trows gather, chattering with anger at their inability to capture me. They confer, their heads nodding solemnly as if agreeing on an important decision. For long moments, they mumble together. My mind races for some escape plan, but I am too frightened to think clearly. One of the trows begins to shout in anger, and within moments, they are all yelling simultaneously, embroiled in an argument of some sort, none of them listening to the other in the chaos of so many voices echoing off the walls of the cave.

Their anger will either make them stupider or more cunning. I'm not sure which is worse. Perhaps they are so disorganized they will give up and leave me alone. Even as I think it, I know it is futile. They mean to make me their morning meal.

The trows shout and argue until one particularly monstrous trow, whose nose reaches all the way down to his chin, gives out a huge roar and the others fall silent.

"Spread out!" he grunts into the quiet of the cave. The fact that I actually understand the trow leader's command terrifies me even more than being trapped among them, but I reach a new level of fear as more of the little men appear out of nowhere and layer themselves from wall to wall until their bodies completely cover the floor of the cave. They cheer up at me in anticipation of their forthcoming victory and shake the spears in their leathery hands, readying themselves for the final attack.

I imagine the spears entering my body, cutting through animal flesh, tearing the smooth skin of my underbelly. I dart back and forth but know the effort is useless. They are too many, and I will soon tire from the chase. I am powerless. Then I recognize the familiar shape of a selkie sliding into the cave through an invisible portal. A huge, Roman-nosed selkie male, his thick neck pounding rapidly through the water, swims toward me, until he positions himself between me and the drooling trows below like a protective wall. An angry scar slashes across his wide face, curving down his neck, the map of an earlier battle.

"You are safe now," he whispers to me. "I am with you."

Then he turns to my attackers. "Listen well, trows," he shouts, and embedded in the deep musical tones of his seal voice is the knife edge of fury. "Find your catch elsewhere."

The trows grumble and smack their lips, gaping at each other with their tiny, bulging eyes. Their long-nosed leader utters a rubbery, chortling sound, and soon all the trows are shaking with what I realize is laughter. The cave fills with the sounds of their glee, and I am sure that despite my selkie friend, the trows will have us for their breakfast. The snickering stops as suddenly as it began as the ugly trow organizer shouts orders to his companions in their guttural language. Shaking their spears and chanting predictions of their coming victory, they gather in a tight circle for a renewed attack.

"Two are better than one," the trow leader cries. "We will all have full bellies tonight!"

I am frozen with fear, but my protector is unruffled by this threat. "This young one is not for you," he calls. "She has lived among humans."

His declaration is met with a collective gasp from the trows. They scatter stupidly, bumping into each other in their terror and confusion.

"Attack them!" orders the trow leader, but his minions are too busy chattering about the news to hear him.

"Idiots!" he shouts, and in his fury, he throws a spear at the nearest available trow. The spear embeds itself deep in the un-suspecting trow's thigh, and he yelps in pain and surprise. The trows turn to their leader, trembling with the possibility that he might kill them all, one by one. The wounded trow still screams in pain, but the leader ignores him, mumbles to the companions nearest him, and leads them toward us.

"Follow me." The Roman-nosed selkie deftly herds me along the rock wall away from the approaching trows in the direction of the opening where he entered the cave. I pray he has better luck than I have had in finding it again.

"Faster!" he calls back to me. "Swim faster!"

The trows behind me nip at my hindquarters with their sharp-clawed hands. I slam my tail through the water as hard as I can. Out of my peripheral vision, I see several trows flung to the side and smile at my victory, but in that same instant, I feel others digging their spears into my already-wounded sides.

"Quickly. This way," my rescuer orders, and following the di-rection of his pointed fore flipper, I slip past him into an imper-ceptible opening in the rock wall. The trows are dragged off me, shouting with rage at the loss of their prey. I cannot turn to look back at the oppressive prison of the cave, but I can hear the fury of the trows and know that it is aimed at my protector, left be-hind at their ravenous mercy.

Pushing with all my strength, I struggle through the tunnel that leads to the safety of the open sea, and when I finally break free of the passageway, I swim with powerful strokes to the surface for desperately needed air.

Breathe and release, breathe and release; the cool air fills my lungs again and again. I remember Mither's lesson on the beach and replay it in my mind. *Are you not afraid?* she asked me.

Oh, yes, Mither, I am afraid.

I take in the sweet air slowly to lengthen my time beneath the sea. Then, sated and more determined than ever, I dive down and down, because at this moment, I am most afraid that my huge selkie defender has sacrificed his life for mine.

Plunging deeper, I travel until I am face to face with the black rock wall. I search for the opening but am not surprised that it has disappeared. Peering through the dim light of the sea around me, I realize that I am entirely alone. Even the rainbow fish have deserted me. I shiver, but it is not from the cold.

Where is he? *Dear God, let him live.*

Long moments go by, and still there is nothing but the vast emptiness of the sea. Can the trows swim through the portals? Of course they can. They are much smaller than selkies, and besides, how else would they enter the cave? I lie in the sea expecting at any moment to see them swim through the invisible tunnels and overtake me. I should swim away from this place, but I cannot. I will not leave him behind. Not even if it means that I am in danger.

Devil take the trows straight down to hell!

A storm rages inside me, but the sea is quiet. I search again for a portal. Navigating along the wall, my eyes scanning the crags and fissures, I realize the search is futile. What can I do, even if I find a portal? Swim into the cave to rescue my defender, only to find myself trapped again? Foolish, foolish girl. My selkie savior has been overpowered by the trows. I know it. Their pointed teeth are tearing the soft flesh of his body. He fights them off as best he can with his powerful tail, but he is not equipped to fight off attackers. He has only his courage.

Please, St. Magnus, spare his life. Let him be saved from the trows.

Tears gather in my eyes and mingle with the sea. He gave his life for mine, and I don't even know his name.

"Elin Jean." I turn and see my protector floating behind me, his mouth drawn up in a selkie smile.

"Did you think those devious little demons got the better of me?" His great shoulders shake, and the sea is filled with the rich sound of his laughter, pure, joyful exaltation at his dominion over the trows. His gentle eyes look through me, all the way to my grateful heart. "I am Arnfin," he offers in a voice as rough as sandpaper. "I will keep you from harm. As long as I am with you, you are safe."

Thank you, Arnfin, I say with my eyes, but the giant selkie is already swimming away.

"Come," he demands, and I follow him without question into the dark ocean.

CHAPTER
TWENTY-THREE

*E*ndless schools of fish, some tiny as minnows, others large as dolphins, float in and out of the tides. Mysterious creatures, sleek and self-satisfied, dart around us, long and sensuous as snakes. Several of these eel-like fish swim with us, their open mouths pouring light from deep within their bodies, illuminating the sea ahead of us. Enthralled by the unfamiliar sea life, I nearly cut myself on the sharp, bonelike reefs that rise on the ocean floor like steeples, but Arnfin steers me away. "Be careful. The reefs are elegant but sharp-toothed and waiting," he warns. "Follow me closely." I stare at the opalescent pink and yellow blooms dancing in partnership with palest blue and lavender spines among the reefs. I am stunned by the beauty and danger that surround me in this new world.

We journey through the endless sea until there is movement ahead, and I see the Red and the Black swim into view. Together they slide gently along my sides in a greeting, touching the length of me as they pass. They turn and approach me again, grazing me lovingly on either side. Their touch soothes the wounds on my flanks.

Arnfin touches his nose to the face of the Black, then the Red. He dips his head once to me and leads us to the surface for air, the Red and the Black swimming beside me. I am weak with relief to be in this fine company.

As we break the surface, I look toward the land, but even with my keen selkie eyes, I cannot see a hint of the world I left behind. The flat line of the horizon is broken only by waves that skip above the tides. We must be far out to sea. The sky spreads above us, an unbroken slate of charcoal gray. How long has it been—a day, a week?

Breathing the cool northern air, I risk an attempt to speak. A small bark is all I can manage, and my selkie aunts grin at the effort. Arnfin floats nearby, but he is busy scanning the sea, ever watchful for danger.

"Where?" I croak, and then I feel my voice open, mingling with the air that rushes into my lungs. "Where is she? Where is my mither?" The beauty of my voice, musical and sonorous, takes me by surprise. I cannot believe the ease of the selkie language. It is as though I have always known it. There is so much I want to say, so much I want to know, the words tumble out in a great rush, but the Red and the Black hush my curiosity.

"Not now," admonishes the Black. "Breathe. We must dive again." She senses my disappointment in her refusal to respond, and her voice turns gentler. "All we have asked, you have done," she says, brushing my face with her own, and the Red finishes her thought. "Your journey begins here."

I can only think that this journey already feels like a lifetime and the last few hours feel like forever, but I keep that thought to myself.

"Come," says the Black. "The Arl Teller, who knows the past and the future, waits for us." Her loving face quiets my fears, and I follow the selkies as they dive, one dark, the other red as the sunset. I watch amazed as the currents clear a path for us into the deepest part of the sea, the Red and the Black on either side of me, Arnfin leading. Inside this loving triangle, I finally feel safe.

My eyes have adjusted to the dim ocean light, and a powerful sense of ease washes me clean of fear. I have always felt at home in the sea, an expert swimmer among nonswimmers, but I could never have imagined the speed that shoots us through the currents. Tensing my seal body, I easily move ahead of the Red and the Black, circling them, but they firmly herd me back into formation. Arnfin moves closer, tightening the triangle.

A sound roars by like the tumbling of gypsy wagon wheels on the rocky roads of Shapinsay. We swerve sharply left to avoid a collision with enormous hulks of dark flesh cleaving the tides. A great pod of blue-gray whales marches past, their graceful bodies cutting through the water, tails waving in a giant arc. We roll in their wake. The whales acknowledge us as they pass with a polite dip of their giant oval heads. We nod back at them. The currents churn the sea where they pass, leaving us bobbing with the force of their drift. Long after they have disappeared, the tides rustle softly like hands clapping in polite appreciation.

The Red and the Black point their bodies down until we rest on the silt carpet of the ocean floor. The selkies lead me forward along the cloudy bottom. Then, poised on a precipice, they point their noses down into the void, and there, stretched out below us, is the sparkling forest of my dreams.

The sight fills me with wonder. I had hoped to someday find

this place, but now that it shimmers before me, I am stunned with gratitude that it is real.

Below us, a giant kelp patch surrounds the emerald forest in an uneven hug, stretching on slender stems toward the surface as if desperate for sunlight. The plants stand at attention, but firmly anchored in the sandy silt, the waving jade stems barely touch us, hovering above them on the precipice.

My selkie friends lead us downward through the canopy of giant kelp to where a cleared path etches its way into the woods. I have never seen trees the likes of these. The few trees left on Shapinsay Island are scraggly and stunted by the wind. The trees that surround us now are more filled with life than most people I have known.

As we weave like serpents through the shining, transparent forest, the barkless branches part as if guiding us to our destination. Inside the branches, veins pump a life-giving indigo liquid so brightly hued that it looks like the trees might speak to us. One of the supple branches sweeps by my face, and I see that the veins within it pulse with life. Their trunks, anchored in the silt, are as translucent as their pliable arms, the layers of each year's growth clearly visible, pastel-colored, robin's egg blue, buttercup yellow, and seashell pink. I reach out and touch my nose to one of the branches. It is yielding and warm as it slides down my face.

I am amazed to see the floor of the forest carpeted with shells. Broken into small fragments, they seem to reflect the light that glows from the branches of the trees. But when I look more closely, I see that it is not the trees that illuminate them. Thousands of miniature eyes twinkle underneath the shells. Later I discover that the blinking eyes of thousands of sea snakes that burrow beneath the shells, foraging for the minuscule creatures that live there, are illuminating the ocean floor. The effect of this blanketing is an odd sense of another society visible just beneath us. On land, this could never be. Hundreds of stomping feet would crush any life that dared live so near the surface of the earth. But here there is no danger. We float above them. And if we do rest on the lively flooring, our bodies are still buoyant from the salt water, so they have little weight. Perhaps these creatures are afraid to venture into the vast world of the sea and that is why they live below the surface. This life is not safe for any of us, no matter how big or small. I am sure of that.

A gentle nudge from behind startles me. Arnfin urges me forward, and I hurry to keep up with the two selkies who lead me down the path.

Is that a light ahead? It shimmers in the tides, and as we move closer, weaving in and out of the embrace of the supple branches of the forest, it illuminates our fur with an emerald glow. The sparkling arms of the trees crowd together to point the way, blue liquid light pulsing through their sheer arteries. Their limbs part gently as we pass, until suddenly the young saplings in front of us bend down until they touch the ocean floor, and before us, just as I dreamed it, in all its opulent expanse, is the clearing. And there, gathered around the sea-green fire, the blaze crackling in the shifting tides, are the selkie folk. Mithers and fithers, siblings and grandparents, kind and stern, young and old, each one as distinct and individual as any human.

I scan the group for Mither, but she is not among them. I turn to the Red and the Black to ask them why she is not here, but a sudden disturbance interrupts my question. Some signal has caused a mass movement of the clan. Together they float upright in the tides, their tails sweeping the ocean floor, their faces pointing north.

At the far end of the clearing, I see what has captured their attention. The old one, her face lit by the dancing firelight, stands before the fire exactly as I dreamed her. Taller than the other selkies, she is covered in a lush robe of dappled gray and white fur. Her supple whiskers curve down the length of her body, and her eyes blink intelligently on nearly opposite sides of her head. Encircling her entire upper body and neck is a great ivory ruff that undulates slowly in the tides. She is even more magnificent than I imagined.

The old one lifts her fore flippers like arms in a benediction, and at her signal, the clan begins a low hum deep in their animal throats. The humming swells until the force of it fills the sea with pounding vibrations. It reaches its pinnacle, then slowly fades, the echo hovering in the clearing for long moments until all is silent.

"Listen to the Arl Teller . . . ," the selkies chant in their musical language, and the sounds pour honey-smooth through the water, ". . . the Keeper of the Stories."

"She knows the old ways . . ."

". . . and the new."

"The past and the future."

"When we are in need, we go to her."

"She chooses a tale to point the way."

"Ask her."

"Listen to her . . ."

". . . and you will know what you must do."

"Where is my mither?" I whisper over the Black's shoulder.

"Hush," the Black hisses. "Listen to the Arl Teller and you will soon know more than you do now."

And so, reprimanded, I float quietly in the clearing behind the Red and the Black, collecting the questions that tumble my thoughts. Jumpy and eager, I try to concentrate on the Arl Teller's story.

CHAPTER
TWENTY-FOUR

"Once, at the beginning of time," the Arl Teller begins, "there was an Orkney laird who had a daughter named Britta, taller than most men and fairer than any to be found on the islands. She had hair that fell in ringlets to her ankles, her eyes shone like pearls, and her skin felt as soft as the belly of a newborn lamb. Now, Britta was a great friend to the seals, refusing to use our oil for lamps or fur for coverings and would eat none of our flesh.

"Suitors journeyed from the far corners of the Orkneys to court her, even from Norway and Wales, but Britta had her own mind. She would choose for herself or have no husband at all, so she set the suitors aside, one after the other, finding fault with each of them, until, at last, there were none at all.

"Now, her fither, the laird, needed a husband for his only daughter in order to create a line of heirs to the throne. It was his sworn duty to protect his land and his daughter's birthright to it. So do not judge him too harshly for his actions."

At this admonition, the selkies interrupt the story, whispering fervently to one another, as though they are arguing about the laird's actions. They seem to know the story and hold differing opinions about its characters. Why have I never heard of Britta? Perhaps no one on land knows these stories. In this moment, among these wise creatures, I feel as small and young as I ever have. I glance at the Arl Teller, who swims back and forth in small circles, waiting patiently for the clan to quiet. Her pure white whiskers play in the tides. She raises her body upright, and the clan quiets so she can resume the story.

"So the laird searched the lands far and away to find a man equal to his daughter's willful nature. At last he found just the man, Ronald, the seal hunter of the Faroe Isles, with blood-red hair and a chest the width and breadth of a Viking ship. Handsome, he was, and determined to have Britta for his own. He courted her with hearty persistence and was not dissuaded by her cold response. Britta cried and moaned that she could never love a seal killer, but her fither insisted, and they were married in a ceremony the likes of which the Orkney Islands had never seen before, with five days of feasting on the richest food and endless tankards of ale.

"The morning after the wedding night, the guests assembled again for further merrymaking, but everyone saw that Britta was sullen and silent. A veil hid her face, and she ate none of the feast nor the sweet ale offered her. The laird questioned Ronald, who replied that his wife was changed forever now and had grown thoughtful and quiet contemplating her duties as the wife of a powerful man. Britta's fither agreed with the logic in this and joined the other guests in their reveling.

"On the fifth and last night of the marriage celebration, Britta waited until the guests, and particularly her new husband, had fallen where they feasted into a drunken slumber and slipped silently out of the great hall. Barefoot, she ran blindly until she reached the seal caves at Nettle Gee. There she hung her head and sobbed, crying seven tears into the tide, and straightaway out of the sea came a seal, eyes chocolate brown and moist with sympathy because he knew Britta to be a constant friend to his kind.

" 'How can I serve you, O Lovely One?' he asked her.

"And Britta cried through her tears, 'Seal in the sea, seal in the sea, come forth from the tides to salvage me.'

"The seal hauled out on the rocks near the crying girl. The veil fell to her feet, and he spied the purple and yellow bruises that spotted her fair face with sorrow and the swelling that caused the corners of her mouth to turn downward."

Great moaning sobs arise from the clan, who weep openly for Britta's sadness. Even though they know the story, they are moved by her sad circumstance. I am amazed at this organized expression of sympathy. On land, only funerals allow for public displays of emotion. And even then, there is a sense of shame connected to this kind of public display. Women, who do most of the mourning, keen and moan indoors, never in the open air. But these creatures unleash their sadness at Britta's misuse with abandon, encouraging each other's grief. Even the Arl Teller's tears mingle with the sea. The Red and the Black touch noses with each other and those around them. They seem to have forgotten I am here. No one takes any notice of me; they are so caught up in the story.

The Arl Teller floats upright again, and when the selkie clan has taken her lead, she continues. "Do not despair, selkies, for you know there is more to come. Listen and learn!"

The selkie folk nod in affirmation.

"Dane, for that was the seal's name, caressed Britta's face," intones the Arl Teller. " 'Return you here on the seventh tide of the seventh tide,' says Dane to Britta, and quick as a minnow, he disappeared into the sea.

"Britta did as she was told. She bore her cruel life with Ronald until the seventh tide of the seventh tide, and early that morning, lighthearted with hope, she made her way to the seal cave at Nettle Gee to wait for her savior. But the sea remained quiet, and soon she lost all hope as the minutes became hours and still there was no sign of him.

"Then, when the sun was at its highest peak and Britta had shed her woolen cloak to enjoy its warmth on her bare arms, she saw the sleek body of a seal swimming in to shore.

" 'I have come for you, Fair One,' the great male said to her, for he had told his kind, and as was their way, they would not turn away one who asked for their help.

" 'Join me in the sea and we will make a life the likes of which has never been known by human or animal. We will have a love as wide as the two oceans and as high as the hawks that fly up to the sun.'

"Although Britta was terrified of the sea, like all the island folk, she fixed her eyes on his and believed the promise blazing there. She removed her wedding ring and threw it as far as she could into the sea. Dropping her gown onto the rocks, she walked naked into the water, into Dane's embrace, and together they dived deep into the sea and down, down into the waters below."

A cheer rises from the gathering, and the Arl Teller's smile falls on us like quiet morning rain. "And during their journey," she continues, "a miracle transformed them both. Britta became part seal and Dane became part human, each sharing half of the other, so that they understood each other's nature as none ever had before. Her need was the catalyst and his love the impetus for the wonder that occurred.

"Britta loved her mate with her whole self, and when they touched, it was with a tenderness that healed all she had suffered at the hands of her human husband. Britta bore her chosen husband many children, each as lovely as the sea anemones that hover in the ocean's radiant glow.

"Then, in the seventh year of their union, Britta's skin began to grow thick and rough. Her fur fell out in patches, and she grew listless and disinterested in feasting on the schools of succulent herring. Healers were brought together at the ebb tide, the time of greatest portent, and they prescribed the only cure. Britta must go back to the land."

The selkies around the sea fire grow agitated and cry their protest at this suggestion. I hear the Red call into the sea, "Do not go! Stay with us!"

I stroke her face with my own and am surprised when, in the midst of her frantic pleas, she flashes me a broad smile. I look around at the selkies settling in after their outburst and realize that these responses are all part of the ritual. Like at a church service, the selkie clan is performing the reading and response. But it is so real, so heartfelt, that I did not realize its true nature until this moment.

"At first Dane refused to let her go," resumes the Arl Teller when the clan has settled. "For he feared that if she returned to the land, he would lose her forever. But the healers insisted it was the only way to save her. If she remained in the sea, she would die.

"So Dane, the seal, took his wife and propelled them both up to the surface, swimming to the cave at Nettle Gee where they had first met, their children paddling hopefully behind. Carrying her limp body on his back, Dane hauled out on the beach and laid Britta gently on the sand. The moment her soft underbelly touched the land, Britta shuddered once, then transformed before her husband's startled eyes into the elegant woman she had been so long ago. Her skin shone with health, and she was filled suddenly with hunger. Britta looked down at her pelt and saw the patches of fur that had fallen out had grown back, as full and soft as ever. The land that had given her birth had healed her.

"A great moan escaped the seal man, and Britta saw that her beloved was in misery, so fearful was he that she was lost to him. To reassure him of her love, she laid her human body on his, fitting herself to the length of him, as he had once done for her.

" 'My only love,' she declared. And Dane's great body shuddered until his pelt lay beside him and he stood upright, as powerful and well formed as ever a man has been. Britta embraced her husband, filled with the wonder of it. Standing together on the beach, Britta and Dane watched in delight as, one by one, their children came ashore, shed their skins, and became humans, with eyes set far apart like hers and skin as pale and velvety as stones pounded smooth by the sea.

"But above them, a fisherman spied movement on the beach. He looked down on the family and, recognizing Britta, ran straight to Ronald, the seal hunter, hoping the delivery of this news would garner him some reward. But without a word, Ronald drew his sword, leaped on his horse, and rode directly to the caves at Nettle Gee. There he confronted his rival, demanding Britta's return.

"Dane took up a piece of driftwood, holding it like a club. Now that he had the means, Dane would slay his beloved's tormentor, Ronald, and keep his children safe from the seal hunter of the Faroe Islands."

The selkie folk lean toward the Arl Teller, and I lean with them.

"So great was Ronald's fury, he slashed at Britta's seal man, hoping to kill him with a single thrust of his sword. But Dane dodged Ronald's blow. Ronald slashed at Dane again and again, but Dane was quick and patient. When Ronald was exhausted from wild thrusts and slashes of his sword, Dane attacked and, with one giant blow, slew Ronald, then watched the beach turn red with his enemy's blood. Dane held up the bloody club he had used to kill Ronald, bellowing his victory, and Britta's family rejoiced for all the seals who would be spared the harpoon and the net at the hands of the killer.

"Fitting the pelts around their shoulders, Britta and her family entered the sea, and as they glided through the voe, their skins fused to their bodies and they became selkies again. And from that day forward, at Midsummer's Eve, Britta and her family returned to the beach at the seal caves at Nettle Gee to draw strength from the land that was her first home, so that they would thrive and prosper.

"They were the first of the selkie folk, living in the sea but returning to the land one night each year on the seventh tide of the seventh tide. And ever since, the selkies repeat the ritual. We go to the land each year on Midsummer's Eve, shed our skins, and dance, to celebrate the birth of our kind."

A cry of joy rises from the selkies so deafening that the tides churn in response and the watery fire dances, as if it, too, is celebrating the happy ending. The Arl Teller shifts her body until she is looking directly at me. Her mouth slants upward in a benevolent, feral smile. Her white fur ripples in the aquamarine firelight as she holds my gaze, and in that moment, her eyes penetrate the deepest part of my soul.

CHAPTER
TWENTY-FIVE

"Arl Teller. Arl Teller. Arl Teller," the selkies chant tenderly, and the ancient selkie dips her white head in response. The selkies file past their leader, and she nods to each of them, taking in all who are gathered with her warmth. The selkies sing her name as they pay homage to her, and she acknowledges their fealty with the graciousness of a queen.

When all the selkies in the clearing have been recognized and have returned to their places around the fire, the Arl Teller's eyes fall again on me, and she beckons me inside the circle. A hundred eyes shift to look at me. I am a shadow behind the barrier of the Red and the Black.

"Selkies!" the Arl Teller calls out to the gathering, her voice echoing through the sea. "Look. She is here. The one foretold."

Giddy God! The Arl Teller has uttered the exact words of my dream, in the same voice, just as I imagined it. *The one foretold.* But what does it mean? That I was meant to give Mither back her pelt? I've already done that, and Mither isn't even here. A small shiver of fear runs through my body. What am I meant to do? I am alone among strangers in a foreign place. I am completely vulnerable. It must be a mistake. How can I be the one foretold? In this moment, all I want is to be safe in my box bed at home, hearing the faint sound of Mither singing her songs of the sea.

The Arl Teller gently commands me forward again. This time the Red and the Black dip their heads in encouragement, herding me past them until I can feel the heat of the watery fire on my face. Heart beating hard in my chest, I feel the selkies' eyes staring at me. As I have done so many times on land, I make myself as small as possible, floating still and silent in the clearing.

A lifetime goes by. Why don't they say something, do something? Tell me! What does it mean to be the one foretold? Why is it a secret? Angry words crowd my thoughts. If I am a part of the clan, then tell me. Don't make me stay in this dark place of confusion. If I am the one foretold, then I deserve to know.

A young selkie breaks from the group. "Killer!" he shouts. "She is a killer!" And a cry rises from the clan until the mighty ocean shakes like thunder, as if it is as intimidated as I am. The selkies break from the circle, scattering into the depths of the undulating forest.

"Wait!" My seal voice breaks with the effort to be heard over the din. "I am a selkie. I am a selkie like you."

Arnfin comes to my defense, shouting, "She is not a killer!" And even though he follows the selkies, demanding hoarsely that they return to the clearing, his words are lost in the panic.

The Arl Teller is silent, watching the selkie clan disappear into the crystal forest, one by one, until only the Red and the Black remain with me near the fire. They are staring at me, their eyes wide and pitying.

What is it? What are they staring at? I look down, searching my body, and am sick at the sight. Embedded in the cartilaginous extensions of my selkie flippers are five perfectly formed human fingers, pale and rounded, one species blended into another. I am a freak of nature. No wonder the selkies called me a killer. No wonder they hate and fear me. Now I know why the three selkies attacked me. I am as much a monster in the sea as I am on the land. Instinctively, I try to hide the ugly appendages, but now I have no folds of fabric to cover them. Part animal, part human, they hang like mortal enemies at my sides, exposed for all to see.

Liquid fire rips through me, and then I am screaming. "Cut them! Cut them off! I hate them!" As though from a great distance, I hear myself howling but cannot stop. Great wrenching sobs tear through me, but still I shout, though my voice is already hoarse and raw. "Cut them! Cut them off!"

The Red and the Black flank me, stroking me with their bodies until I can scream no more. Tears flood my face. Through my sobs, I hear the Arl Teller speak to me from across the clearing. "They are part of you. Sea and land."

I look to the Arl Teller. "I hate the land," I manage to choke out. "I must belong in the sea or I have nowhere else to go."

The Black is nearest to me, so I beseech her. "I am the daughter of a selkie. Tell them. Then they will understand."

The Arl Teller's eyes rest kindly on me. "You are come from the land. The lesson of fear is the first we learn, and it is the one that keeps us alive. They are afraid of you."

"But I would never hurt a selkie. Never!"

"I believe you," the Arl Teller says in her silken voice. "But they are afraid of humans, even one who lives in the body of a selkie."

Something gives inside me, and I let go of it. "Then I am lost."

"We are all lost until we find the knowin' we seek."

"There is no such thing as the knowin'! The knowin' is a lie."
I instantly regret this outburst, but the words are out and I cannot take them back. I wait for the Arl Teller to respond to my angry challenge, but she is silent.

"Where is my mither?" I plead. "I need to find her."

"Your mither is not among us," the Black answers solemnly.

"Nor can we tell you where to look for her," finishes the Red.

I look to the Arl Teller for help, but her face remains inscrutable.

"You cannot find her until she finds you," says the Black.

"Is she looking for me? Does she even care that I am here?"
The Black ducks my question. "You are not alone."

"We are here," the Red agrees, and touches her nose to mine.

The Arl Teller swims the circumference of the clearing, parting the sea with her flowing ivory ruff, before returning to my side. "You have made a brave choice to enter the vast sea."

"I heard you calling me, telling me to come."

"The voice you heard was not mine. Nor any of those gathered here today."

"But it was the selkies who called me. I know it as sure as I know that the sun will rise and set in a single day."

"Perhaps it was fate that called you."

The Red and the Black swim close, sliding along my body in a loving gesture, a cool hand placed on a child's feverish cheek.

"Live among us. Learn our ways. The selkies will come to learn your true nature, and we shall see what the future holds."

The Arl Teller raises her tail and, with a single mighty thrust, dives among the transparent trees and is gone.

CHAPTER
TWENTY-SIX

And so I learn the ways of the selkies. As life in the sea unfolds before me, I watch it all. I am shot through with homesickness, a feeling entirely new, since I have never been parted from my family before. It leaves me weak with melancholy, and there are days when I wish only for something, anything, to happen that will take away this awful loneliness. I know that I am marking time.

I discover that I am considered to be a near-grown selkie. On their search for the knowin', the near-grown selkies go through a solitary year called the solus. During this time, the young selkies are separated from their family and assigned an advisor to teach them. I often see the young selkies swimming with their guides, who speak to them in solemn, hushed tones. This year has great significance, for now the near grown learn the finer points of survival, mating, and the complicated ethics of the clan. I can instantly spot those selkies who are in their solus year. They emanate a confidence and pride the younger selkies have not yet earned.

Since I am without a family, except for the Red and the Black, I hope that one of them will be assigned to be my guide, but instead, Arnfin becomes my advisor. This is a surprise but not a disappointment to me. I am drawn to this hulking selkie, with his wizened face and sloe eyes, who saved my life. It is as if I have known him forever, so easy is our time together. Ever careful that no harm comes to me, Arnfin is my constant companion, and although I am not sure why, it is him I come to rely on.

The selkie clan avoids me, swimming away if I approach them. "Freak," the young ones whisper as they pass by. "Unnatural thing." A part of me is grateful that they no longer run from me, but I am well aware of their mistrust. I can only hope that time will convince them that I am not a killer.

Occasionally, a curious selkie draws near to inspect me, and my heart leaps with anticipation for some simple, friendly interaction, but if I speak, the selkie darts away. And even though they never try to do me harm, their shunning is even worse than the taunts of the others on land.

Patiently, Arnfin teaches me to feed. Together we stalk the schools of herring, swallowing them raw and whole. The sweetest herring lie beyond the crystal forest, so we often venture out of the safety of the trees to hunt for food. If necessary, the rainbow fish that reside in the forest can be eaten, but they are difficult to catch and, I discover, bitter-tasting.

Feeding is a skill that takes practice, darting openmouthed between the currents, catching the herring with scooping motions. It requires concentration to keep my selkie gullet open to swallow the fish while the airway beside it remains tightly closed. The first time I attempt to feed, I nearly choke to death on the double rush of fish and water, and I hurry to the surface to clear my lungs and breathe again.

"Let us stay here so that you can practice without drowning yourself," Arnfin teases, and we float near the surface for some much-needed rehearsal.

As if the physical challenge isn't enough, another, more difficult mental maneuver is required to catch supper. Anticipating the direction the schools of herring will take is crucial, so I learn to plan ahead.

Swimming as quietly as I can through the currents, I am careful not to signal my proximity to the herring. I choose a likely school of fish and watch them, memorizing their swimming patterns, making imperceptible movements with my tail to keep me hovering in place. Once I am confident of their pattern, I quickly position myself where they will swim next. Now I am ready to make my move.

Yes, I have guessed their route. I open my mouth to receive them, and in they march, unsuspecting and delicious. Chewing is unnecessary. The herring are small enough to be consumed whole. Eating has never been so difficult and so much fun. I do miss the satisfying feeling of chewing—the crunch of an oatcake or the soft mush of a hot potato—but I love the puzzle of eating in the sea and feel some satisfaction that I can manage my own sustenance.

For the first time, I become aware that I am consuming food that has a life. I ate lamb and fish on land but never really gave thought to its life before it died to feed us. I wonder about the herring. Do they have a society like the selkies'? I resolve to eat as few fish as possible and learn to enjoy the plentiful seaweed and other ocean plants. The texture reminds me of spinach, but the taste is unlike any vegetable I have ever eaten, smoky and rich, with a hint of bitterness. If I swallow the vegetation whole, there is no taste at all.

I feel less guilty but am still aware of the aliveness of what I am eating. I think of the killers. If they hunted the selkies only for food, I might understand, but few on land eat selkie meat. The selkies are hunted for their lush fur and oil, the meat left to rot in the sun.

The herring and plants are plentiful, but I discover how easy it is to lose track of my internal compass in the vastness of the ocean. It is dangerous to enter unprotected areas where fishermen, with their unyielding nets, stalk the seas. Once caught in a net, a selkie will die, either dragged on land to be bludgeoned and skinned or drowned from lack of air.

"Never swim near where the killers fish," Arnfin admonishes me until I am rubbed raw with his endless warnings. "Never follow the herring too far. Stay ever alert to where you are in the sea."

The Red and the Black teach me to clean the fine fur of my pelt with sand and sea flowers growing on the ocean floor. Arnfin will take no part in this activity. "Sea-bathing! Nothing but female beautifying," he scoffs dismissively. "A waste of time and effort." He hovers nearby, watching over me as usual, as I slide the sleekness of my body along the sand-soft ocean floor, cleaning away particles of seaweed and plankton embedded in my pelt. Once my fur lies smooth, trained with the combing to remain in a single direction, I glide smoothly through the supple gardens of scented purple and blue-green flowers that undulate in the currents. The flowers rub gently against my flanks, belly, and back, the sweet smell of pollen lingering for hours. The sea-bathing leaves my spirits temporarily lifted and my body relaxed.

I swim near Arnfin and wave my fore flipper at him so that he can smell the sea flowers that perfume my pelt. "A selkie should smell like herself," he complains. "Not like flowers." But

I like the smell the blooms leave behind in my fur, and I suspect that gruff old Arnfin is merely embarrassed by female pastimes.

And so I fall reluctantly into the rhythm of life beneath the sea, learning the daily necessities that form the selkie world. Eyes closed, I glide sightless through the tides, muscles loose and formless, practicing the art of swim-sleeping. The selkie folk sleep for short periods in the sea and wake when they feel the need to breathe. I learn to doze among the currents, but I miss the deeper sleep of the land.

Swim-sleeping offers a brief respite from my troubled thoughts, but there is danger in it. When the need to rest claims me, I pray to St. Magnus, *Make me dreamless, keep the dreams away.*

I am terrified of the images that visit me, but the nightmares come in spite of my pleas, horrible fantasies crowded with images of seals, broken and bloody on the beach. I wake shaken and restless, unable to remember how or why the terrible events occurred. Nothing remains but random images, vivid and terrifying.

I often wake from these dreams sobbing, my body shaking uncontrollably. And even though I know the nightmares didn't actually happen, I remember that my dreams on land foreshadowed the future, and the thought that they might be a portent of things to come fills me with foreboding. So I stay awake until a desperate need for sleep claims me and I fall into an edgy reverie, hoping to avoid the terrible dreams that might slip into my rest. I become irritable and listless from lack of sleep.

One day when I have stayed awake so long I have forgotten the pleasant sense of feeling rested and refreshed, I am coasting among the embracing arms of the forest, Arnfin tailing me. My eyes grow heavy and heavier still until they become tiny slits and I drift into unconsciousness.

Then I am being dragged forward by a giant pull of water. I hear Arnfin yelling, "Swim backward! Get out of the way!"

Directly in front of me is a gigantic gush of water shooting up from a hole in the ocean floor. The geyser rises higher than I can see, and the power of its thrust unsettles the sea into churning layers of current. I am being sucked into its whirling mass and am powerless in its grip. The whirlpool spins me round and round, pulling me toward its center. Shaking off the dullness of sleep, I try to heft myself away from it. Behind me, I can hear Arnfin shouting, but the force of water pounding my ears turns it into nothing more than a garbled mess. I swim with all my strength to escape, but I am buffeted back even farther into the circle of water.

And then I notice that the water near the center of the whirlpool is warmer. Giddy God! I am being drawn into the center of an ocean vent, vast holes that spew boiling-hot water. Terror gives me renewed strength, and I turn my nose away from the circle's center and paddle with my powerful tail to escape its grasp. But it is no use. I am sucked back into the whirlpool.

The hot liquid scorches my flesh.

There is only one way I might break through. If I swim directly through the center, I might find a break in its force. But it is risky. I could be horribly burned by the hot water or spewed up to the surface only to fall back down hundreds of feet, plunging to my death.

I feel myself tiring, fighting the force of the whirling water. I must decide on a course of action soon, or the choice will be made for me.

Then I feel something swim beneath me. Arnfin has entered the vent and is lifting me up with his powerful body. I mold my body to his, and together we struggle to escape the pull of the crater. I feel the heat of the center burning me. I cry out with the pain. Arnfin pulls us through the edge of the whirlpool's center, and with a last mighty push, we break free.

We swim until the vent is far in the distance. Tears sting my eyes and are washed away in the sea while Arnfin swims nervous circles around me.

"This is my fault," he says. "I was not vigilant."

"No, Arnfin. You saved my life. You have saved it twice."

"And I would save it a hundred times. I would do anything to keep you safe. But today I failed."

"How can you say that when I am here before you, unharmed?"

"You are not hurt? No burns?"

"Just a few."

"From now on, I will be twice as careful, and you must be, too. Promise me."

"I promise."

"You are the one foretold. You must never forget that."

"I do not forget, Arnfin." How can I forget when every waking moment, I am trying to understand why I am here? "Why am I the one foretold?" I ask. "Tell me."

Arnfin shifts his eyes away. "Do you think if I knew the answer I would keep it from you? The legend says that a girl from the land will come among us. That is all I know."

"Tell me the legend."

"That is not my task. Only the Arl Teller can choose the story. And only when she believes the time is right."

I frown at this response. "There are more rules and barriers to the knowin' in the sea than on the land."

Arnfin is kind enough not to find my impatience amusing. I love him for accepting my faults and for his reluctance to point them out to me.

"The selkies find their own way," he says. "To offer our answers to others' questions is to insult their powers of reasoning."

"But what if I make the wrong choice? What if I never find the knowin'? What then?"

"It is easier to be told what to do, I do not deny it, but there is a satisfaction in the discovery of the knowin' that is beyond imagining. None of us would cheat you of that."

"I can't see how a little help along the way would hurt," I say glumly.

Arnfin touches his nose to mine. "Trust is the greatest respect we can offer each other. That is the way of the selkies."

There is finality in this last statement, so I swallow the questions that lie tasteless in my mouth. "If no one will help me, then I am truly alone."

"No more than the rest of us." Arnfin smiles, sad and knowing. "Come," he says. "I will show you what I can." And Arnfin leads me in and out of the cool pockets of tides that layer the sea until we surface and I recognize the west side of Shapinsay Island.

Ahead of us is a gathering of huge boulders, sparkling with ocean spray. Alongside this craggy array lies the beach, made smooth by the constant tides. Beyond the beach is the entrance to the caves at Nettle Gee. Arnfin has brought me to the place where the selkie folk began.

After a quick look around to be sure no humans are in sight, Arnfin and I swim in and haul out on the beach. Above us, seabirds complain to each other as they dive among the rocks. I wonder, *Do they have questions about the knowin' like we do? Do they care about more than a mate and a full belly? Do they worry about the choices they make and the cruel expectations others have of them?*

I look to Arnfin, but his attention is elsewhere. Rocking our bodies forward, we painstakingly navigate the land until we reach the curved entrance to the caves. The sand is smooth on our bellies, warm from the sun. I realize how much I have missed being on the beach.

Inside the cave, it is dark, and I can hear drops of water plink on the sand from the ceiling above us.

"Wait here," Arnfin orders, and rocks his body across the cave. Then, unexpectedly, he is climbing up a narrow ledge that leads to the top of the cave.

"Be careful," I call to him.

He looks back at me with amusement. "I have climbed higher places than this, Selkie Girl."

I am afraid of heights but keep that fact to myself. I watch my friend climb until he arrives at a small platform at the top of the cave. He reaches his head into a crevasse above him. It disappears and his heavy body is all I can see.

What is he doing? Whatever it is, I'm not at all sure I like it. I look behind me to be sure we are alone.

"Arnfin?" I call, and he offers me a garbled answer. "Arnfin?"

Silence.

I am about to forget my fear of heights and follow him up the ramp when suddenly the cave is flooded with light from above where a now-illuminated Arnfin smiles down at me.

"Trapdoor," he chuckles, and positioning his body at the top of the ramp, he rolls down, tumbling over and over until the momentum of his fall lands him at the sandy bottom of the cave.

"Is there no end to what you can do?" I say proudly.

"None that I can find."

"Can I try?"

"Of course, but first, look around you."

And as my eyes skim over the illuminated walls of the cave, I gasp. There, etched into the rock, are the images that appeared to me on the crofthouse walls the night I found the pelt. Ocean waves and nimble fish, sailing boats and the rocks of the skerry, pictures of land and sea are etched onto the walls of the cave.

I feel Arnfin at my side. He points his flipper straight ahead at the carved rock wall in front of us. There the unmistakable shapes of three selkies form a rough circle, and just like in my dream, they point in different directions—east, west, and south. In the center of the circle is the outline of a slender girl with webbed hands who points north.

CHAPTER
TWENTY-SEVEN

Since the day at Nettle Gee, I am sure that there is a reason I am here. I resolve to be patient and wait for the moment of knowin' to tell me the path my life will take. I wonder how my life will be different. I wonder if I will feel whole, if I will finally have a sense of belonging. It is strange, this waiting, and my restless nature is not suited to it. And although Arnfin stays near me, I am hollowed out with an emptiness that even he cannot fill.

Each time my head shatters the mirror of the surface to breathe, I gaze toward the land, thinking of those I left behind. Is Grandpa's troublesome back hurting him? Did Fither bring in a good catch for market today? I wonder if they miss me, if they mourn my loss. Do they think of me the way I think of them? Perhaps they are glad I am gone, one less problem to manage. I imagine their lives are somehow easier without me. The hiding, the shame of my hands, the worry about my future and who might take me to wife must be gone now, one less concern in the endless cycle of challenges that trouble their lives.

They must be glad to be rid of me.

I think most often of Tam, long legs striding the beach in trousers ballooned by the wind. I replay the look of him that last night, remembering his black eyes, the pressure of his mouth on mine, the curve of his shoulders, the easy way he whirled me around in his arms. And I hear the echo of his promise. *Never hurt the selkies,* I asked of him, and he swore to St. Magnus he never would. Now that I am gone, will he keep his promise? I pray he will stay true, but I know that it is unfair to expect him to hold fast to his promise when I threw mine so carelessly away, and though I nurture the hope that a miracle might happen, I know it is unlikely I will ever see Tam again.

The gypsies have long since packed up their caravans, hitched their sturdy ponies to the harnesses, and moved on to another part of the island, telling fortunes, selling their wares, digging for limpets along the way. The travelers never stay in one place for long.

Tam will have found another lass to dance with him. I can picture the girl's blond hair curling softly around her face, one cool hand reaching up to tuck a lock behind her ears. And when she reaches out to touch her dancing partner, her hands are perfectly formed, slender fingers fitting into Tam's hand like a glove. She makes a pretty partner for him, flirtatious and laughing.

During these days of unrest and dark thoughts, I think often of death. The manner of my death, oddly, is of little concern to me. I only hope it will come quickly to numb the pain of this cruel trick that has left me with constant reminders of my tie to the killers. Hoping to find a home, I have found instead a new meaning for loneliness.

The selkie folk meet often in the clearing in the crystal forest, habit and instinct calling them to assemble. I discover that death and couplings, too, bring us together, for the selkie folk mate for life. The stories define the selkies' lives, reminding us of the hard-won lessons of history and, most importantly, providing healing through understanding.

Since light does not define day from night beneath the sea, the telling of stories occurs at any time, initiated by one or another selkie to help a family member or remind a straying youth of the strict code of conduct. Not infrequently, the Arl Teller chooses a story that kindly illustrates the petitioner's own faults. Unlike the prideful crofter families on land, the selkie society freely admits its flaws, without shame or embarrassment. Often I catch family members muttering a tale to remind them of a particular lesson or belief. I have even seen Arnfin repeating a tale as he guards me from a distance.

The selkie clan tolerates my presence at the gatherings, although they keep their distance and so do I. I feel the sting of jealousy when the Arl Teller accepts a request for help from a troubled selkie, her attention focused on finding an appropriate tale to suit the situation. As the words spill out of her, I am transfixed by the beauty and wisdom she brings to the task of helping her kind. Directly descended from Britta and her selkie husband, the Arl Teller assures the continuation and protection of the most sacred stories, those that are based on an ancient code of truth, passed down through the generations.

When the telling is finished, the Arl Teller gazes deeply into the eager face of the petitioner and asks the same question. "Do you know what you must do?" Now it falls to the selkie who requested help to find the connection between the tale and the situation.

I have made many requests for the Arl Teller's guidance, but the answer is always the same. "Not yet. Wait. Your time will come." I try not to be angry at the Arl Teller's refusal to help me, but I am. If I am the one foretold, then why must I wait and still wait?

I often catch the Arl Teller staring at me, and I wonder what she is thinking. I stare back, but her face is inscrutable, washed clean of emotion. Sometimes I feel eyes on my back and discover the Arl Teller gazing at me through the supple branches of the clearing. And for a moment, she wears a look of sadness on her perfectly formed face. What draws her to me? I find myself drawn to her, too, and I long to ask her a hundred questions. But I am not allowed to approach her without permission.

And then, when I least expect it, an audience with her is granted. I hadn't planned to blurt out my questions. I had intended to present a carefully demure attitude to show my maturity. I would wait for her to take the lead, quietly respectful. But when the moment arrives, I am so excited I cannot bear to wait another moment.

"Where is my mither?" I ask. Then, not waiting for an answer, "If she loved me, she would be here."

"She is with you even though she is not here," replies the Arl Teller, dipping her graceful head.

"But why can't she be here?"

"She is healing, and that takes time," replies the Arl Teller.

"She has abandoned me," I reply haughtily. "I would never abandon my child."

"But you are not a child." The Arl Teller's eyes bore into mine, and I am silenced. I hunch away from her. This is not the answer I want. Disappointment lies in my heart like a stone.

"Your mither has given you a gift, the most precious gift she could give you," the Arl Teller continues.

What gift? Mither has left me alone in the sea with no hint

of when or if she will ever return. She might be dead for all I know, lying bloated on the ocean floor or eaten by greedy trows.

"She has given you the means to find the knowin'," the Arl Teller says softly. "And she waits for you to find it. It is not easy to be near grown, but all of us look back on our solus year with affection and gratitude."

Affection and gratitude! I feel only frustration. Waiting and wondering, the knowin' still out of reach. I am doubtful I will ever find it.

The duet of our fur coats ruffles in the tides, making velvet seal music. The Arl Teller settles her fore flippers alongside her body, a resting pose she assumes before beginning a tale.

When I meet her gaze, she begins. "Once there was a girl who was melancholy because of a terrible wrong between her fither and her mither, a wrong that happened before she was born. Now, the girl wanted happiness for her family. She had a generous heart and wished contentment for all the world, and though no one has the power to accomplish that, the girl did all she could to make it so. But the world was not content, and neither was her family.

"Her mither fell into a deep despair, and the girl knew she had failed. She was filled with hatred for herself because she believed her family's joyless existence was her fault. But the wrong had happened before she was born, so the blame was not hers. What she didn't know was that a task awaited her, a sparkling future lying veiled, like the herring hide from the danger of the nets."

Coiled near the Arl Teller, every part of my body is alive with anticipation as I wait for her to continue. She draws closer, her black eyes penetrating mine. "Now, there came a time when the girl felt a renewal, a stirring inside her that she could not name, and a chance to right the great wrong was presented to her, but like all chances, it came with a price. She might solve the riddle of her mither's unhappiness, but it would alter precious parts of her life forever. So the girl made her choice, and because she was brave, she chose to right the wrong at great sacrifice to herself."

I look into the Arl Teller's onyx eyes. "This is my story."

"So it is."

I wait, trembling, for her to continue.

"The girl was willing to risk her life for those she loved. That kind of courage can change the world. But there is always sacrifice." The Arl Teller dips her huge white head and falls silent.

"Tell me the ending!" I demand, desperation cracking my voice. An emotional response to the Arl Teller's story is considered vain and rude, but I cannot stop myself. "Does the girl lose her mither? Is that the sacrifice?"

"The ending of the story is yet to be told. It waits for the girl to finish it." The Arl Teller strokes my face with her fore flipper, drops her eyes, and signals an end to the meeting. "Do you know what you must do?"

I replay the story over and over until I think I will go mad, looking for some clue that will tell me what I must do.

Still, I cannot find an answer to the Arl Teller's question. I found the pelt and gave it back to Mither, just as the Red and the Black instructed me. Even the Black agreed I have done all they asked. Now they ask nothing of me, and I am left with the hardest task of all—waiting.

And so, my curiosity dragging behind me through the crystal forest, I wait to find the knowin'. I am teased by my own gnawing guilt. *Do you know what you must do?* The question beckons over and over, and the answer is always the same. *I do not know.*

Arnfin takes on the task of tutoring me in the sacred stories, to distract me, I suppose, from these distressing thoughts. Day after day, he tells me the stories of the selkie folk, and I learn their rich history.

One day we swim among the clear, bending branches of the sparkling forest until Arnfin is satisfied he has found a suitable spot. The indigo arms of the trees part for us as we settle. I hover near Arnfin, waiting. He grunts and shoots a stream of water from his mouth, as he always does before beginning the tale.

"Once, long, long ago, before you were born," he intones, "there was a selkie named Taghd. He had eaten his ration of herring for the day, and as he was swimming back to the forest, he heard a strange cry."

"I know this story," I interrupt. "Taghd saves the baby left on the rocks by two careless fishermen. Mither used to tell it to me when I was a bairn."

Arnfin fans his huge ruff in a gesture of impatience. "If you know the story, then I suppose you have no need of the telling." He is clearly annoyed.

"I want to hear the story," I reassure him.

"Don't try to mollify me," he says. "You have no further need of ugly old Arnfin. I am nothing but a bother to you."

Oh no. I didn't mean to hurt his feelings.

"I was only expressing my enthusiasm," I say defensively. "You're not a bother—"

But Arnfin cuts me off. "You needn't explain," he says in a hurt tone. "I'm sure there are other selkies who need me."

"No. You are my protector, always. I need you." His back is to me, so I cannot read his face. He makes a small sound. Is he crying?

Arnfin's huge fore flipper swipes through the sea, and the

force of it sends me reeling. When I look up, I see his body shaking with laughter.

"The look on your face!"

I hate teasing, but his amusement is infectious, and soon I am laughing, too.

Arnfin pushes me gently with his tail. "It is time for you to tell me the stories. And I will listen."

And so I begin to learn the art of storytelling. At first I am awkward. The sound of my voice is unpleasant to my ears, shallow and thin as a reed, and I am as shy in the sea as I was on land. When the Arl Teller speaks the tales, her voice is soothing and her choice of words poetic, filled with clarity and truth. So it is her voice I hear as I practice with Arnfin every day, listening to myself form the sentences of the tale, but they are too long or too short or, worse, boring. I beg Arnfin to let me memorize his words and make them my own, but he rails against this idea. "It is one thing to know the events. But that is not enough. You must mold the story into a meaningful experience for the listener. Each of us finds our own style, our own method of telling. Words and rhythm, cadence and repetition—all these are choices that make the story your own."

"But who will hear my stories? The selkies do not come near me, much less let me tell them a story."

"They have much to learn, like you."

I am certain that even if the clan would listen to me, they would judge me and find my storytelling as inadequate as I do.

"My voice sounds grotesque," I complain.

Arnfin nods slightly, and the water around him ripples. "You must not listen to the sound of your own voice," he advises. "The important thing is the tales. If you are listening to yourself, then you are not thinking about the telling. It is less about you, more about the stories."

With this advice giving me direction, I lose myself in the tales, distancing myself from my own voice, so that it feels as though someone else is telling the stories. I practice until the vibrations of my voice resonate deep in my chest and my face buzzes with sound. And as it becomes a familiar and comforting sensation, I begin to love the telling. It becomes a passion, the single distraction that saves me from thoughts of death and gives me a reason to feel alive. And when Arnfin nods his head approvingly at my efforts, I am filled with a sense of pride. In those moments, my body floats as light as the sea flowers that undulate on the ocean floor.

CHAPTER
TWENTY-EIGHT

What is worse than feeling trapped? The sense that no matter what you do, you cannot shape the world into even a tiny facsimile of your hopes for the future. Enfolded into life in the sea, I have learned the lessons of survival and even mastered the art of storytelling. But what good is it? I have learned it all, and yet I feel as if I know nothing.

Arnfin is endlessly kind even when I snap at him for some small infraction. I grow silent and watchful, secretive. I no longer have the will to tell the stories to Arnfin; in fact, I rarely speak, and when I do, it is from necessity rather than from the desire to share conversation or reveal my thoughts. The dreams come more frequently, the images increasingly real, but I tell no one about them.

I miss Grandpa, with his kind manner and loving smile. I miss the smell of rich soup simmering over the fire and the oily feel of wool between my fingers. I imagine I can hear Grandpa's fiddle playing an island jig. Mither sings the words in her husky voice. Even Fither, with his demanding ways, lingers in my thoughts.

In this state of discouragement, I am sullen and snappish.

"Must you follow me everywhere?" I complain to Arnfin, and when he replies that it is for my safety, I resent his vigil even more, although I know he does it for love of me. I am nagged with the thought that he doesn't trust me. I am tired of being treated like a child, an elder always at my shoulder. It seems that nothing I do assures him of my competence.

I am determined to have some freedom. "Will you never trust me?"

"You know it is not a question of trust."

"If you trusted me, you wouldn't crowd me every living minute of the day and night."

"It is important that you be safe."

"How will I ever be safe if I never have a chance to take care of myself?"

But Arnfin will not relax his watchful ways, and so I am lodged in the prison of his protection. I complain to the Red and the Black one particularly cranky day when I feel the whole world heavy and oppressive around me.

"You are fortunate to have such a protector," the Black admonishes me.

"And to be so loved," adds the Red. "The Arl Teller has given you her most fierce and loyal guardian."

"Be glad of it," the Black says sharply, and that is the end of the discussion.

I know what they say is true, but I cannot take comfort in it. My restless nature wants only to push forward into the next adventure. Haven't I had enough happen already? Do I love danger so much that I court it? Why am I never content with what I have? Perhaps it is that I know there is more to come and am jumpy and anxious until I face it and call it by name.

Through it all, I am less angry with Arnfin than disgruntled by the constant sight of the other young selkies swimming together, testing their speed in the currents, challenging each other in games of skill and strength. The elder seals are polite to me in a cool sort of way, but not a single young one will come near me, let alone call me friend. I hear them laughing, whispering in their musical seal language, but whenever I swim toward them, they quickly dart away, pretending not to have seen my approach.

And so, with Arnfin floating at a respectful distance, I create my own vigil. I study the young selkies, their movements and the patterns of their games. I choose one particular tightly knit group to follow. Athletic and self-assured, they bind themselves together, a tribe of the most accomplished. I study how they gather and where they feed. I memorize their habits. Other young selkies attempt to join this inner circle, but they are turned away for one reason or another, not quite making the grade. No excuses are made for this rejection. It is simply clear that interlopers are not wanted, as if the young tribe has all they need and want in each other.

I never attempt to approach them.

"Killer," they whisper as they pass by, and when the elders chastise them for their rudeness, they nimbly display another countenance—meek, apologetic. "Greetings. Have you fed well today?" When the elders are out of sight, they sneer at me, as if they blame me for causing them trouble. Then they ruthlessly redouble their efforts to humiliate me, laughing as they disperse.

I know what to expect if I try to talk to them. I have seen how they hurl ridicule at the young ones who seek acknowledgment, but I find an odd satisfaction in following them, and as I learn their habits, I imagine myself one of their society. Out of their sight, I practice their rituals, the way the females slide their bodies suggestively and the young males nod their sleek heads to show approval, their cheek-to-cheek greetings, and the intricate patterns of their swimming.

Truth be told, I hate them and, more than anything, long to be one of them. This contradiction lodges itself in my heart like a stone wedge, cold and unforgiving. Just as I was on land, I am an outcast in the sea.

Interminable waiting defines my days, and although vague ideas of action visit me now and then, they are too indistinct and frightening to be acted upon with any certainty. So I wait, knowing that the strongest heart cannot endure such circumstances for long, knowing that I must take action soon if I am to survive.

I watch the young selkies swim sleekly through the water, daring each other to go faster, turn quicker, stay under longer. I have learned the rules of these games from my vigil, and although I have never played them, I love their daring and long to take part.

One selkie challenges another to stay below the surface beyond the safe zone, forcing their lungs to go longer and longer without air. The group might have a race through a prearranged obstacle course. Some days the young seals make a show of strength, trying to move huge rocks with their muscled bodies. Often they perform the demanding move of sliding sideways through the tides in a sleek line without disturbing their flow. If only they'd give me a chance, I could show them my courage and perhaps I could be one of them. But I know they'll never invite me into their circle.

So I watch and wait. Until one day when I finally see my chance. I am hovering at a safe distance, like always, Arnfin behind me. The young crowd is huddled together in a buzz of excitement. I am too far away to hear their plan, but it must be something exciting from the look of them and the sound of their chatter. At a signal from the light-coated selkie who is the challenger, they swim off in formation. I watch them go and am filled with regret that I am left behind again.

An annoying group of otters slides by in the water, nattering on over some argument about a mollusk they've found. Two otters have hold of it, each trying to pull it away from the other. The other otters have taken sides, supporting one or the other depending on which one they think might be more likely to share the feast.

"I found it," one of the otters whines.

"But I broke my tooth opening it. It should be mine," another argues.

The disagreement escalates as they pass me, and some of them have begun to punch and kick each other. The two opponents snap their teeth, one bites another, and in a moment it will heighten into a full-scale otter battle, teeth gnashing, fur flying. Most probably, the mollusk will be lost in the fray.

The otters are headed directly toward Arnfin, who has not noticed their antics. His eyes are closed, and I suspect he has fallen into a light swim-sleep, as he sometimes does on long afternoons. I see the collision coming and smile. This should be amusing. I see it unfolding, the crazed otters and sleepy Arnfin crashing together. The otters will regret not paying more attention when they taste Arnfin's wrath.

At the exact moment when the otters and Arnfin collide, I act.

Without a backward glance, I follow the path the young selkies have taken. I know that by the time Arnfin realizes that I am gone, the bubbling wake I leave behind will have disappeared and he will not be able to follow me.

CHAPTER
TWENTY-NINE

I catch up to the young selkies soon enough when they stop momentarily, their heads pressed close together in an intimate discussion. They turn sharply left and are off again. I am surprised. This is a route they have not taken before. I stay far enough away to avoid their notice but close enough to keep sight of their movements.

The ocean is filled with glowing neon fish that allow me to track the selkies. My heart beats faster when I realize that they are headed in the direction of the fishermen's boats, where nets are spread along the ocean floor to catch unsuspecting herring.

I hear Arnfin's warning replayed in my mind. *Never swim near where the killers fish. Stay ever alert to where you are in the sea.*

These waters are forbidden. The young selkies know the danger. What are they thinking? Perhaps they have grown bored with their regular games. Perhaps these pastimes have grown too familiar, too easy, and they are looking for a different thrill.

Ahead of me, the sound of their laughter travels through the tides. I still my senses and listen. The challenger dares the other selkies to swim through the fishermen's nets. He proposes a race where they dart above the nets to see who will be the first to reach the reefs just beyond where the fishing boats lie anchored above.

I want to shout a warning, anything to stop them. *It's too dangerous! You'll be killed!* But they won't listen. They would laugh at my warnings. They would never trust me. So I keep silent, a small pebble of satisfaction lying warm inside me. Why should I interfere? They are so sure of themselves. Let them play their dangerous games. Why should I care what happens?

I know I shouldn't stay another moment in these dangerous waters, but I cannot tear myself away. I float quietly behind a stand of opal sea grass, listening to the unfortunate followers as they are coerced into agreement by the challenger. I hear them negotiate the instructions for the game. The challenger is quite a bully. He encourages their ideas, and even allows one of his friends to make a decision, but if a suggestion contradicts his intent, he manipulates the others with threats until they take his side. His young companions are oblivious to this conniving, enthralled with his daring leadership. I wonder if he will take the dare himself. Probably not. He will keep himself safe. He's so obvious. Why can't they see it?

I circle around the hazardous area, catching up to the others when they reach the reefs, but when I hear the shout that signals the beginning of the race, I cannot stop myself from following. Staying close to the perimeter of the area so I will not be seen, I peer through the dense currents, looking out for the thick, knotted rope of the nets. It is darker now, the neon fish being too aware of the nets that lie in wait to take part in this risky game.

For long minutes, the young selkies traverse the area, slipping in and out of the nets without incident, and I begin to think that my fears are unfounded. Then, without warning, one of the nets is pulled shut, and the selkies are trapped. I hear a sharp cry followed by the deep selkie wail that indicates danger. I wait to hear the answering cry that signals a quick response from the clan, but no answer reassures me that help is coming. Of course not. We are too far away from the crystal forest, too far removed from the safe waters of the clan.

In the silence, I realize that even if the selkies heard their cries for help, there is little they can do. Once a selkie is caught in the net, the clan is powerless to save them. Drowned, unable to surface for air, skinned while the others watch helplessly—that will be their fate.

Ahead, the bellowing of the selkies escalates. I cringe at the eerie sound of it. Swimming carefully nearer to the danger area, I can see them tangled in the net. The selkies thrash desperately, trying to free themselves. The cocky challenger, who is not trapped, swims away from the net, then powers with all his might into the ropes that hold his friends. This assault has little effect, except to further terrify those enmeshed in the trap. He swims away for another try, but it is a useless effort. The ropes are swollen tight from the salty sea.

"Help us," mourn the young selkies, the strangled sound of their voices indicating an already-desperate need to breathe. The leader charges again, and although he stretches the ropes that circle his friends, the knots hold fast. The selkies will die if they are not released soon. Their cries echo through the ocean tides, constant and desperate.

I look at the fingers embedded in my flippers. If my fingers were free of the webs that bind them together, I might be able to loosen the knots. I dash toward the jagged reefs ahead and glide my flippers along the sharp ridges of rock until I find what I need—a narrow ledge that juts out from the rest, sharp enough for cutting.

St. Magnus, help me!

I lay my right flipper along the sharp edge, positioning it carefully between the thumb and first finger, and thrust downward with all my strength. The rock cleaves the webbed cartilage in two. Tendrils of blood scatter red in the currents. The sharp rock has made a clean slice, freeing my thumb and finger from the web that connected them. Squinting against the pain, I move my thumb and discover it has nearly as much freedom of movement as it had on land.

I reposition my mangled flipper between the first and second fingers, close my eyes, and push down again. Blood swirls into my eyes, blinding me, and I wave my other flipper to clear my vision. The rock has pierced the web, but only part of the way through; my fingers are still held together by the web between them. Dizzy from the pain, I place my hand above the protruding reef again and slice through the remainder of the cartilage.

I will not faint. I will not. Now a wiggling thumb and first finger give me good range of movement in my right hand. I plow through the sea to where the selkies are trapped, a thin line of blood trailing behind me. Using my left flipper for leverage, I maneuver my fingers into one of the knots and begin to work it loose. Thank God I know these knots well, having watched Fither tie them hundreds of times.

The trapped selkies crowd in wide-eyed, trying to help by pulling the net taut with their bodies. I feel the young challenger at my side but do not acknowledge him. My own need to breathe is increasing rapidly. I haven't much time before my reserve of air is gone. The captured selkies are young and strong, giving them a decided advantage for longer survival without air, but eventually, we will all drown. My fingers burn, but I think that if I can only untie just one knot, the others might be unraveled.

"Hurry," the challenger hisses nearby, setting off another chorus of moans from the netted selkies. I want to shout at him to be quiet but force myself to concentrate on loosening the knots. Fresh blood seeps from my wounds as I manipulate the twisted rope. Then I feel a small give in the knot, so I grip the edges of it as hard as I can with my mangled fingers, twisting it back and forth until I feel the knot give again and begin to unravel. It falls apart in my hands, leaving a ragged hole in the net.

Immediately, the selkies dive for the opening, crowding each other, pushing and shoving, preventing even one prisoner from escaping the net.

"Don't crowd," the challenger orders. "One at a time." I feel his burly weight push me aside as he takes command of the situation. "All of you!" he shouts. "Move aside!"

The selkies, intimidated by his manner, miraculously shift to allow the smallest selkie to squeeze through the opening. She wiggles her lithe body through the net and flings herself toward the surface, without so much as a backward glance.

"You next!" he yells, pointing to another selkie.

The pressure in my lungs pushes up to my throat and I want to break for the surface like the first freed selkie, but the challenger stares at me with an "I dare you" look, so I hold his gaze until only one large male remains in the net. He tries to maneuver his body to follow the selkie in front of him, but he cannot quite slide his rounded middle through the tear in the net. The challenger signals to me, and we flank the entangled selkie and, grabbing his fore flippers, try to pull him through the hole. With one huge yank, the selkie slips through the opening and, dragging the net behind him, bolts for the surface. A mighty slap of his tail shakes him free of the net.

I charge to the surface alongside the challenger. There we bob breathless, snuffing water from our noses while drawing in the fresh, clean air. The fishermen's boats, a cruel reminder of our misadventure, nod in the water nearby. The fishermen point at us, surprised to see selkies swimming so close to their boats.

The challenger stares at me. I stare back, sending daggers at him. This was his foolish idea. If he hadn't dared the selkies, they never would have taken on such a foolhardy escapade. My fore flipper throbs, blood still seeping from the wounds. I wonder if the webs will grow back like they did on land.

The challenger is still staring at me. Now the group knows I have been watching them, or they suspect it at least. All I want now is to go back to the forest and rest.

The challenger barks a series of short commands, and his companions draw near.

"How will we repay the one foretold?" he asks the young selkies, and all eyes turn to him. He is swimming close enough to touch me, closer than any of them have ever been. "She has saved your lives."

"I ask for nothing," I reply. "And expect nothing."

The challenger smiles, his whiskers standing at attention in the cool air.

"What say you, friends? Do we repay those who save our lives with nothing?"

A cheer rises from the young selkies, and they swim around me, taking turns sliding along my sides, laughing and shouting in triumph, the leader's voice loudest of them all as he begins the chant. "El-in Jean! El-in Jean! El-in Jean!"

CHAPTER THIRTY

"El-in Jean! El-in Jean! El-in Jean!" the young ones chant and I feel like I will burst with satisfaction. My heart leaps in my chest as they swim around me, splashing their flippers until the water is rich with foam. I remember my first encounter with the selkies, how they tried to drown me, churning the sea to stop my progress to the surface. But this time the commotion is a celebration, and the selkies, openmouthed with delight, are not running away.

In the distance, fishing boats loll in the water. Close by lie the skerry, the beach, and Fither's croft. How I wish Grandpa could be here to share this moment! I imagine his face lit with pride, smoke from his ever-present pipe curling in windblown wisps. Mither would wash my cuts with water warmed by the fire and wrap the wounds in clean bandages. Fither would prowl the crofthouse, eyes hooded with concern, stopping at the window to gaze at his domain, the land and sea that earn him his living, then look back at the family that defines his life.

Would Fither be proud of me now?

The challenger lies alongside me in the sea and touches my nose with his. His light-spotted coat ruffles in the tides.

"You are a brave one," he whispers to me in the musical seal language. "You saved their lives." He grins and calls to the gathering. "Many would have fled, but this female stayed. She has shown us courage this day and proved again the bravery of our kind!"

A satisfied cheer rises from his followers. I have heard the selkies bark like this when I was on the land but never imagined that it was a celebration. Closing my eyes for a moment, I allow the warmth of belonging to burrow into my heart. It rests there, and I am filled up with contentment. I have earned this moment, but it has come too late. I cannot pretend to have forgotten the days I have spent among them as an outcast.

I wait until the shouting subsides. "You speak of the bravery of the selkies," I say. "And yet if I had needed your help, what would you have done? I have seen you turn away those who only want to belong. Would you be willing to risk your lives for them?"

"I would risk my life for you, Elin Jean," the challenger shouts, and the selkies murmur their approval of his courting technique.

"Save your own life," I reply. "I will look out for mine."

A shadow of anger crosses the young challenger's face at this snub, and I fear that my forthright response will create enemies I can ill afford. But I no longer care for that.

The young male quickly rallies. "This female wants none of us. The land that lives in her has made her as sour as the killers. So be it. Let us waste no more precious sunlight arguing. Come! We will rest on the beach!"

Another cheer greets this audacious suggestion. The group swims into formation and, like a wedge, drives forward to the skerry.

I watch their sleek bodies grow smaller and smaller and remember the night I left the land behind forever. How determined I was to find Mither. And how sure I was that I would find the knowin'. It seems so long ago I hardly remember the girl I once was.

My fingers ache, but the salt water will heal the wounds quickly. Already the bleeding has stopped and the flaps of the webs are beginning to fuse together. My body has a mind of its own and is no more obedient to my wishes than I am to what others expect of me. Is it wrong of me to ignore what others want in favor of my own choice? I am nothing but a foolish, stubborn girl.

The selkies are far in the distance now. I want to call out to them, *Wait! I want to be one of you. I want to belong.* But I do not call out. I will not be a part of their cruel ways, ever.

I would rather be alone.

Ahead, the young selkies haul out on the beach. Their bodies, so sleek in the water, lumber awkwardly on the land, sand flying, fur matted with salty water. I swim to the skerry and haul out onto the rocks at the pointed tip farthest from the beach. Here my keen animal eyes have a fine view of the selkies basking on the beach, close enough to watch their movements but not too close for them to notice me.

The selkies cruise about on the warm sand, rolling over one another, bawling and moaning their land song, uncaring that they have finally received the shunning they so casually apply to others. They don't even know they've been rejected.

The challenger rolls languidly, demonstrating for his followers the power of his muscled body. He lifts his head, bellowing a song of his maleness into the crisp sea air.

I watch them until my eyes grow heavy from the radiant sun

that filters through the low-lying clouds. My mouth opens in a great yawn, and I lay my head on the convenient smoothness of a rock.

The thunderous sound of selkie bellowing wakes me. Shaking off the haze of sleep, I turn toward the beach. The young selkies hulk awkwardly about, moving in ungainly circles as though they are taking part in some strange race with no finish line. Their mouths, split open in the damp midday air, bawl their rage and frustration.

Then I see the reason why. Men are climbing over the rise to the beach. Five of them, I reckon, and they are carrying clubs. Their running can only mean one thing. Hunters. But what are hunters doing here? It is the wrong time of the year for the cull; the pups haven't even been born yet. They must be on the beach for some other reason. My mind races for an explanation, but when I see the first club raised high in the air, there is no doubt why the men have come.

The selkies, realizing along with me the fate that has befallen them, bellow a warning and lumber toward the sea, their powerful bodies lurching forward, kicking sprays of rocks and sand behind them. But the men are faster. Again and again, their clubs fall on the heads of the young ones until the beach is red and still with death.

I watch the slaughter from beginning to end, tears running down my face, heart pounding with revulsion at the carnage. The men grow animated with the killing, their clubs rising and falling over and over. I cannot see their expressions from this distance, but an odd enthusiasm in their voices indicates their pleasure in the event. One killer is especially fearsome in the fray. His long hair flies about his head, his club flailing through the air with terrifying rhythm. He cries out, his mouth open to the sky, but I cannot hear the words he repeats like a prayer.

Toward the end of the struggle, the maddened killer collapses on the sand, watching the other men finish the massacre. The killers chase the remaining selkies to the water's edge, where they follow a few unfortunates into the shallow water, striking them there. With no means of retaliation, the animals are helpless. Their only alternative is flight. Two selkies manage to escape into the sea. They swim by but take no notice of me as I lie still on the skerry, trembling with hatred for a place that spawns such killers. I look for the challenger but do not see him. I imagine his fine young body dead on the beach.

I dive into the sea, following the two who have escaped. The selkies ahead of me moan their grief, and the eerie sound of it pummels in their wake like the driving rain bends the tender shoots of barley. I swim close and quiet, moving swiftly beside them as we head toward the crystal forest.

As we approach the clearing, the Arl Teller floats in her usual spot by the watery fire, deep in conversation with several selkies who hover near her, listening.

"Massacre!" cry the two survivors as we reach the clearing.

The clan gathers instantly, sliding through the transparent emerald trees to join the frightened young ones. In halting speech, riddled with gasps and cries, the selkie survivors pour out their loss.

I listen to them tell it, filled with shame. I am alive and they are dead. If only I had gone to the beach with them. If only I had followed them, I might have stopped the killing. I should have been there. But I was prideful. I chose to mock them even when they were kind to me. I chose arrogance instead of generosity. My vengeful heart was as cruel to them as they were to me. They called me brave, but I am a coward, and now St. Magnus has brought this disaster. In this moment, I hate myself, and I only wish that I could disappear.

"Mourn, selkies," wails the Arl Teller. "Mourn your song into the sea. Grieve for those lost and love those who remain."

The lamentations beckon more selkies to the clearing until hundreds are grouped around the fire, summoned from the farthest reaches of the North Sea. Together they keen their loss, wailing their pain.

I sing my sorrow with them. *I'm sorry. I'm so sorry. St. Magnus, forgive me.*

"Death is a part of life," intones the Arl Teller. "Some must die so that others can be born."

The selkies nod their assent and call out in a single voice. *Roooo. Roooo.* And the macabre sound of their melancholy song fills the clearing.

The two selkies who managed to escape the slaughter haltingly recount the names of those who died, and the Arl Teller repeats them in her sonorous voice. As the names are intoned, one by one, the families of the dead are enfolded in the embrace of those nearest them until the seals have surrounded each other, comfort pouring from their mouths.

I can stand it no longer. Knowing that what I am about to do is against the ways of the selkies, I do it anyway. I swim into the circle and confront the Arl Teller without permission.

"Arl Teller!" I shout in my loudest voice. "I saw it all from the end of the skerry."

Instantly, the Red and the Black swim to me, and I draw strength from the nearness of them.

"I saw it and did nothing."

The Red and the Black stroke my sides, but I am not comforted.

"And what could you have done?" asks the Arl Teller. "Reliving the past is useless, and thoughts of what we should have done leave us sick at heart. We look forward, never back. What matters is what you do now." The Arl Teller strokes one of the survivors with eyes round as the full moon.

"A dark one led the killers," she sobs, trembling at the memory of the slaughter, and I hear the sound of clubs crunching against bone.

"The tallest one, he was," she continues, her voice shaking with emotion. "Thin like the reeds that grow near shore."

The other survivor, a male with a blunt, freckled snout, speaks. "Maddened, he was, just from the sight of us. He urged the men to kill until all were dead. He spoke of revenge."

"Revenge?" murmurs the Arl Teller.

A tiny rock of fear lodges in my heart.

"A man so cruel and depraved his heart has flown out of his body and the seabirds have eaten it," says the freckled male. "He looked at our faces careful-like, as though he might recognize us."

My heart pounds in my chest.

"Aye," says the round-eyed female. "They called him Duncan. And he was looking for a selkie he called Margaret."

CHAPTER
THIRTY-ONE

Since the slaughter, my sleep, agitated and uneasy, leaves me exhausted and annoyed. I am plagued by images of the bloodshed on the beach. Thoughts of the carnage are bad enough when I am awake. But sleeping leaves me vulnerable, and the dreams invite themselves, the most unwelcome of guests. No matter how desperately I will the visitations away, no respite arrives, and I am weak and lethargic from lack of sleep.

During the time when the dreaming holds me captive to its dark visions, I am drawn to the land. The survivors do not blame me for what happened—in fact, no one speaks of it to me—but I know it was my fault. The brash challenger, his skinned body moldering on land, may have made the choice to lead the selkies to the beach, but the killer so cruel the birds flew away with his heart is Fither, and his unrelenting anger has been given life because of me. Now the danger to Mither, wherever she might be, is real.

The dreams begin innocently enough. I am a selkie, hauled

out on the skerry at the widest point, where it meets the beach. The warm sun has dried my mottled fur to velvet, bristling in the sharp Orkney wind. My face is turned up to the sun, eyes blinded yellow underneath closed lids.

In my dream, Mither is the young woman she once was, lovely and whole, running toward me on the beach. Her feet chuff through the sand, toes kicking up a spray of fine grit behind her. I am human again, my legs planted firmly in the sand. Above us on the bluff, I see Odin's Throne, its smooth surface winking slyly through the damp ocean spray. I stretch my arms with joy at the sight of Mither, remembering her calm voice and tender touch. I am overcome with a desire to run to her, but my feet will not move. With every fiber of my being, I try to run, but I am paralyzed, as if I am made of stone.

Mither's eyes meet mine, and a look of horror crowds her familiar features until they melt into someone else's face. Mither's features transform into the faces of the others who hate and fear us. One moment she is old Mrs. Muir, wizened and gray. Then her face shifts until it is the brash selkie challenger who died on the beach. Her face sharpens, and weathered lines etch into the sides of a thin, cruel mouth. Her eyes narrow into familiar black slits, and I am looking at the seething face of Fither.

I hear a strange whirring sound behind me and turn just in time to see Tam smiling lovingly at me as the club he wields crunches into my skull, splitting it open like a ripe pumpkin. Wildflowers of blood scatter around me on the sand. I glimpse the horrified look on Mither's face as she reaches down on the sand to retrieve a piece of my skull, lying hot and pulsing at my feet. As her hand touches the bloody bone, it transforms into the fore flipper of a selkie severed from its body, and the image of wounded seal pups bleeding out their lives on the beach is all I can see.

Then Fither's tortured face hangs near my own. "Forgive me," he pleads in a voice filled with such sadness that I reach out to him.

I fall, and the descent wakes me.

Shuddering, I blink my eyes, trying to orient myself. Where am I? For a moment, I am not sure. Was it a dream? It seemed so real. Too real. It was a dream, I know, but in my heart, I am afraid this hope is a lie. Hadn't I heard the selkies calling me in the dream? Hadn't I seen the image of the Arl Teller around the fire, the selkies gathered around her? The slaughter on the beach was foreshadowed, and the image that has haunted me since childhood pummels my dreams until I think I will go mad with it, the helpless white bodies of infant seals dying on the beach.

Arnfin swims nearby, cleaving the sea with the wake of his huge tail. Since the massacre, he is aloof, not speaking to me unless I speak to him. But the distance between us hurts more than any angry words he might fling at me. I want him to admonish me. I feel as if no punishment can be enough for what has happened and my part in it. Even worse, Arnfin suffers with me. I can tell by the look on his face and the way his body is humped in on itself. He has tightened his vigil, refusing to sleep, his eyes ringed with lines, his face swollen with concern.

I can stand it no longer. But my attempt to find relief from my own awful guilt becomes an attack on my beloved protector. "I only wanted to be one of them," I say to him sharply.

Arnfin's face darkens, and he snuffs the sea from his nose. "It is bad enough I must watch you day and night to the detriment of peace, quiet, and sleep. But to have you jeopardize your own safety, well, that is more trouble than even I deserve."

"I'm sorry," I snap, but there is no real apology in it. I am too angry to be apologetic.

"Save your apologies, Selkie Girl," Arnfin growls. "You may have greater need of them later." His huge body ripples into a more comfortable position. "You know you are chosen. You are here for a reason and it is more than playing foolish games."

I want to defend myself, to say that I did not take part in the reckless games, that I never have, but I choke back the impulse, knowing that Arnfin is in no mood to be contradicted. I should not have gone off without him. It was a foolish and dangerous thing to do.

"I'm sorry," I say in a gentler tone.

Arnfin tosses his ruff and pierces me with a withering look. "You're sorry. What of the apology you must make when you fail to fulfill your destiny? Sorry will be useless when you are dead."

My destiny. At this moment, I care nothing for it. All the talk of being the one foretold. I thought that meant I was special, in some way chosen, but I still feel like an outcast. If it is true that I am the one, and I am not at all sure of it, then why am I still so far from the knowin'? If I have a destiny at all, it feels so far away I will never find it.

Arnfin stares at me as if he wants to take back his angry words. "Anger is good," he declares, a bit too loudly, and I wonder who he is trying to convince. "Anger is just the other side of love." He touches his nose to mine. "The challenge is to identify the object of our anger."

"You are angry with me," I reply.

"Yes, but I am also angry at myself."

His words comfort me. I feel better just being near him but cannot say why. We float together without speaking, and in that moment, I decide to tell him.

"Arnfin."

He turns to me, and I see that his muzzle has begun to turn gray with age.

"I need your help."

"And you have it. You know that."

"I must go to the land."

I expect a flurry of protest or a curt refusal, but Arnfin surprises me again. "I understand," he says, and at that moment, I love him more than I did even a moment ago.

"You must follow your instincts," he continues. "They will lead you to the knowin'." He places his flipper on my head and draws it down, stroking my face. "I will go with you."

And I realize that Arnfin has filled an empty space inside me, more a fither to me than my real fither has ever been. I reach out to him, but he is already pointing his nose toward the land.

Silently, we navigate the sea to the narrow tip of the skerry. I stare at the shore for some glimpse of those I left behind. On the horizon is Malcolm Seatter, a fisherman Grandpa often sails with, throwing out his nets for a day's catch. I call out to him as his boat bobs calmly in the voe. The man looks briefly at the selkie who yelped at him, then turns back to his nets. To him, the sound is nothing more than another small selkie howling in the wind. I wish I could tell Grandpa where I am. But even if I could, even if I poured my heart on the sand where he stood, he would not understand the only language I can speak.

I haul out on the skerry, Arnfin following, staring at the beach until it floats like a mirage. The sun struggles through the clouds, heating my back, and I am momentarily grateful for some warmth in my barren heart. Arnfin's eyes droop to half-mast.

"Sleep, my friend," I say. "I will keep safe."

Arnfin mumbles, "Not that trick again. I will not be sleeping. One eye will remain open, watching you."

I rise up on my hindquarters for a better view of the beach. Nothing. Not a soul. On the rise ahead, several goats cling to the steep hill, grazing on the grass that seeps through the sprinkling of rocks. I might lie here for hours and not see any people. I suppose they are all going about their chores or at school. Perhaps later they will come down to the beach to harvest fish in the evening tides.

I settle down to wait. To keep myself awake, I sweep my eyes over the horizon from one end of the beach to the other, back and forth. Above me, seabirds swoop down to catch surprised herring. My eyes grow heavy.

Then, up near Odin's Throne, I spot a flash of red. I am instantly alert. Someone is sitting there. I have always thought of Odin's Throne as mine, but this is wishful thinking. Of course others have discovered it, but I have never seen anyone there before.

Swift as a cat, I slip into the water, swimming closer to determine who the interloper might be. A splash behind me tells me that Arnfin's one eye is ever vigilant and he is following me into the voe. I am grateful for his presence.

Nearer to the beach, I look up again, blinking the sea from my eyes until they are clear.

Giddy God! On the ridge above the beach, Tam McCodrun sits on Odin's Throne looking out to sea. He wears the clothes of a prosperous crofter, including a fine fitted wool vest. Its violent red color has drawn me to him.

Recklessly, I swim to the beach, but I hesitate. Once on land, I am vulnerable, and although I want more than anything to be near Tam, I dare not go too far inland for fear of the hunters. An image of the recent attack flashes in my mind. I look back at Arnfin. A part of me wants him to follow; another yearns to be alone with Tam, no matter what the danger might be. I open my mouth to explain, but Arnfin makes the choice for me.

"You know this human?"

"I used to."

"Can he be trusted?"

I look up again at Tam. Has he broken his promise? Has he prospered from the sale of pelts and seal oil? Do his fine clothes mean that he is still a killer? I cannot bear the thought.

"He made a promise to me once, but I'm not sure he has kept it."

"I will stay close, just in case. I hope this human is honorable."

I touch my nose to Arnfin's grizzled face, and he gives me a slow, sad smile. "Do not go beyond where the rocks of the skerry meet the beach," he warns. "Close enough for flight."

"Thank you, Arnfin," I say, but it is too little to express the gratitude in my heart.

He nods his great head and hauls out on a convenient rock to keep watch. Then I am gone. Quickly reaching the widest part of the skerry, where the rocks are anchored to the beach, I haul out on a mostly flat rock and wait. In my seal body, I can easily be mistaken for one of the rocks that form the promontory. How will Tam know I am here? I bob my head up and down. At least he will know I am not a rock. I watch him scanning the sea. What is he looking for? The set of his body is easy, as though he plans to spend the afternoon watching the clouds as they meander by.

St. Magnus, let him see me.

I imagine his eyes resting on other island girls with comely faces circled by the white-blond tresses of the Norse people who settled here. He watches them walk, graceful as stalks of grain moving in the wind. His heart stirs with their beauty. Does he even remember me? Am I pale and wanting in comparison? I feel him near me, so close that I might reach out to him. I would bend under his eager touch.

"Rrrrooooo," I call in the low moan of the selkies. "Rrrroooo."

Never taking my eyes from him, I float my command on the wind. "Rrrroooo."

I am here. I am Elin Jean. Come to me.

He looks toward me. I can tell he has heard me by the set of his body. I wail again, as loud as I can in my seal voice. He peers down at me.

Now my cries become thankful. I am small, but my voice gathers strength from the hope that pulses inside me. Tam picks his way down the rocks toward the beach. I notice with relief that his hands swing freely at his sides. He has no club.

I smile wide, showing my small, even teeth, as he approaches. He will expect me to slip into the safety of the sea and swim out a safe distance, as seals always do when they are confronted with humans. When I remain still, staring at him, he moves more cautiously, trying not to frighten me with sudden movement. Carefully, he inches closer, astonished that I have not fled. When he is within ten feet of me, he lowers himself on his haunches and waits.

When I continue staring at him, he speaks. "What are you doing here, little one?" he asks. "Why aren't you with your family? Do you need help?"

My heart swells with tenderness for him. I form my lips into the mysterious smile that makes the seals seem human. Tam grins back, amused. "Go on now," he croons, making shooing motions with his hands. "It's not safe for you here. Go back to the sea where you belong."

If only you knew. If only I could tell you.

I roll my body forward onto the sand as far as I dare, and the waves creep onto the shore with me, working their way toward high tide. Shocked by my approach, Tam falls backward onto the wet sand. I laugh, but it sounds to him like a series of barks.

He laughs back. "What do you want?"

I want to talk to you. I want to tell you all of it. I want to dance with you at the foy like I promised, but now it is all gone and will never come again.

I inch forward until I am at his feet, my face tilted up to his. He sits up, and I can see where the sea has soaked through his trousers. His eyes are soft, liquid brown.

I lay my sea-damp head on his knee. "Rooooo," I croon, tears leaking from my eyes. They make small damp spots on his thigh when they fall. I nestle my head in his lap, and he puts his warm hand on my flank. In this moment, I no longer care if he's been true or even if he's kept his promise. I only care that he is alive and here with me. I hate myself for this weakness, but the hatred is enfolded in the tenderness I feel for him. It has been so long since I have felt anything but utterly lost.

There is only one way I can tell him, one remnant of the land that still remains, so I rest my fore flipper on the sand at his feet, fingers splayed apart, the sole reminder of my human heritage.

I wait.

"Giddy God," he whispers, staring hard at the human fingers embedded in my selkie body. "By St. Magnus and all that is holy!"

Cautiously, he lays his fingers alongside mine and looks at me, recognition playing on his face.

Yes, I am alive, I tell him with my eyes, and by the look of him, I can tell he knows.

I am not drowned. I am Elin Jean in the body of a selkie.

CHAPTER
THIRTY-TWO

I lie on the beach with Tam until daylight fades to evening glow, every part of me alive with the nearness of him. I study his face, the way his hair curls down his neck, the sinewy fingers that lay along mine, rough with scars from hard work.

"I never gave up hope," he tells me. "I could not imagine your death, and that gave me the courage to believe that you were alive. Your grandpa would not speak of it except to say that he knew the day would come when you would leave the land. He only wished it hadn't been so soon. Each day I have searched for you in the rolling waves. And now you are here. I can hardly believe my eyes."

Cautiously, Tam strokes my back, and my fur ruffles in response. As he realizes the truth of my strange circumstance, he tells me the aftermath of my flight into the sea.

The night of the foy, when Fither went to find the pelt, he discovered the aisins were empty and knew what had occurred. Eyes wild with desperation and fury, he pushed past Grandpa, knocking him down in his rush to the water's edge, searching the dark horizon for signs of Mither. Later the others spoke in hushed tones about how he called her name out to sea until his voice was gone. "Margaret! Come back! Come back to me!" But his cries were swept into the wind that howled in harmony with his pain while Midsummer's Eve revelers waltzed on the beach.

In his grief, Fither stumbled on the slick rocks, and there, floating on the water like a drowned child, was my nightdress. Tam said that Fither had the look of a madman in his eyes when he realized I was gone. "Damn you, Margaret!" he cried out to sea. "Give me back my daughter! You cannot take my daughter!"

"I saw a lone, brown-spotted selkie floating in the voe, watching," Tam tells me. "Your fither saw the selkie, too, and ran to the edge of the skerry. Some of the others tried to stop him because they thought he might drown himself in the voe. But he just stood there. It was curious, the way he called to the selkie, as if he believed she was your mither. By all that is holy, he was right, wasn't he?"

Was it Mither? Did she come back to see him one last time? Perhaps we passed one another that night in the dark sea.

"It was the oddest thing," Tam says, shaking his head. "The selkie stared at your fither as if she knew him, too. Then she bellowed once and disappeared beneath the waves. Your fither was beside himself, howling and crying, throwing whatever his hands could reach, stones, driftwood, seaweed.

"His eyes were bright with the madness. 'I curse you, Margaret!' he said. 'You cannot take my daughter!' He raised both fists to heaven, and all of us heard him. 'I swear it,' he cried. 'From this day forward, no selkie will be safe on land or in the sea!'"

I am thankful that I am hearing this terrible tale from Tam.

His warm hand rests on my head, and now and then, he wipes the tears from my cheeks as they fall. How wrong I was about him. How could I ever have thought he was like the others? There is so much I long to ask him, but I can only lie silently beside him, listening.

The cool waves lap the shore as Tam tells me that he and Grandpa have worked the croft since Mither and I were swallowed up by the sea. Without women to do the household chores, Tam and Grandpa have become reluctant experts, scrubbing and scouring, gardening and cooking. Used to the traveler life that never allows staying in one place long enough to work the land or plant so much as a stalk of grain, Tam was restless at first, but with Grandpa's help, he settled into life on the croft.

"I feel calm when my hands are coated in flour, kneading the dough for bannock. The soup ladle curving into my palm is a fine thing indeed," he says, then turns away, embarrassed that he finds such pleasure in work usually done by women.

"I have never seen such abundance, Elin Jean. It's comforting-like." I can hear the awe in his voice. "Shanks of lamb, potatoes dug right out of the ground, turnips and spinach from the garden, barley and wheat from the fields. It made me feel alive when my heart was dying from want of you."

Tam pauses, as if he needs time to gather his thoughts.

In the solemn days that followed my dive into the sea, he tells me, the three men struggled to accept their loss. They moved sluggishly about the croft, unable or unwilling to perform even the most perfunctory tasks. The goats bleated endlessly for need of milking, and the ponies all but kicked down their stalls for freedom to run the fields. Fither sat silently in the doorway of the crofthouse, as if to prevent anyone else from leaving.

Tam and Grandpa protested, but Fither insisted on building

me a coffin, gathering precious wood to fashion the narrow box. In an uncharacteristic splurge, he purchased an expensive oak lid from the mainland that he stained and polished until it reflected the light. For eight days of mourning, he guarded the coffin, bellowing at interlopers to leave him alone. Even Grandpa was not welcomed beside him. Fither's hands twined themselves into his lank hair, and clenching them into fists, he pulled away great tufts and scattered them on the doorstep, until the ground around him was littered with dark strands and his hands were bloody with the tearing. His shoulders shook with the force of his sobs, and he howled out to sea, "Margaret! How could you take her?"

Since my body was never found, there could be no cleansing the corpse for its journey to heaven. Like the unlucky fishermen who never return with their catch, I was lost to the insatiable sea. No children gathered to touch my cold form, to prevent my return to haunt those who have wronged me. And since Fither took Mither as his wife without benefit of a wedding in the local kirk, I could not be laid in consecrated ground but must lie in an unmarked grave outside the parish.

Fither insisted on burying the coffin within the borders of the croft, on a bluff not far from Odin's Throne with a grand view of the sea, windswept and clean. There the three men carried the empty coffin to its final rest, careful that no dog crossed its path to bring bad luck.

"There was naught to be done for your fither," Tam says. "He was beyond us. So your grandpa and I nursed our own wounds, and prayed." Tam fits his fingers again alongside mine. "Your fither hated my presence on the croft. 'Surely you do not think to replace our darling girl with this dirty tinker?' he said, and I hate to say it, Elin, but I wanted to kill him for it."

Tam picks up a flat stone from the beach and skips it expertly on top of the waves of the voe. It makes tiny splashes as it touches down four times before sinking out of sight.

"It was your grandpa who stood up to him," Tam continues. " 'There'll be no discussion in this matter,' he shouted at your fither. Like a sergeant at arms, he was, and the set of his mouth told an end to it. And so I stayed. I think your grandpa knew that I would not leave this place, always thinking you might come back."

As Tam speaks gently of his new life on the croft, I blink in affirmation, hoping to communicate my understanding. He tells me the details of his life, the small things that he imagines I miss beneath the sea: the smell of grandpa's pipe filling the house with its sweet smoke, the bleating of the newborn lambs in the byre, earth-colored peat crumbling in his hands.

"It is the first real home I have ever known," Tam murmurs. "My fither cared more for his friends than for me. Always under his feet, I was, getting in the way. I think he couldn't forgive me for Mither's death. It was my fault. I know that."

I ache to tell him, *No, it was nature's choice, not yours. There's nothing you could have done. You were only a wee babe.* I stroke his arm with my cheek and make the purring sound of the seals.

A muscle in his jaw jumps with tension when he speaks of Fither and his terrible revenge, of how it has given birth to the unspeakable vendetta against the selkies. He isn't sure when the slaughter began, but he tells me it has been relentless. Fither would leave early, at first light, scorning breakfast. Grabbing his coat from the hook by the door, he would heft his club over his shoulder, slamming the door behind him.

In the evening, the hard voices of men came in the open windows. As their bulky shoulders disappeared down the hill to the sea, Tam could see the blood on their clothes and knew that it had been another day of killing. Then one evening the tentative truce among the three men was shattered.

"The sky grows dark," Duncan tossed at them as he joined them at the supper table. "There'll be a storm this night, and a thrasher by the looks of it." His clothes hung tattered and filthy on his lanky frame. His hair fell in his face, where lines creased with grime mingled with the bitter look of regret. A look of perpetual hostility was molded on his face, fierce enough, Tam says, that it sent children in town running to the safety of their mithers' billowing skirts. It is a hard look, seething with fury, like soup boiling over on the stove.

"The stew is cold," Duncan complained. A stubborn smudge of blood was smeared across his cheek.

Tam tossed his plate of supper into the slop pail.

"I said my supper's cold," Duncan demanded, ignoring Tam's gesture of disrespect.

Tam ladled a portion of steaming stew into Duncan's bowl and banged it down on the table, spilling half of it over the side. Tam could smell the scent of dead seals left too long in the sun lingering on Fither's clothes.

Fither rose and blocked his passage out the door. "Sit you down, pup."

"I've no stomach for supper," Tam told him.

"Then we'll eat without you. It makes no difference to me whether you eat or not."

Fither dipped a portion of the cooling stew into his mouth while Tam stood by the door, clenching and unclenching his shaking hands. "I'm thinking of an oath I made, a promise to one whose memory is dear to me."

"No one loved her more than I," Fither growled through a mouthful of bread and butter.

"You shame her memory," Tam answered, and his quiet tone made the accusation sharper than if he had shouted it.

Fither pushed his chair back with such force that it toppled over with a crash, and seizing Tam by the front of his shirt, he lifted him up to his snarling face. "The pup has sharp teeth, but he'd best keep them muzzled or he'll find himself tethered in the byre."

Grandpa rose to defend his ward. "Leave off now, Duncan."

"He'll show me respect or find another roof to keep under."

"He's worked hard for the privilege, and a grand help he is, too," Grandpa replied. "Someone's got to work the croft while you're off hunting the selkies."

"The pelts bring good trade and put food in our bellies."

"It's wrong to let good land lie fallow, Duncan. I thank St. Magnus every night for this lad's help."

Fither released Tam and returned to his half-eaten supper. But Tam could not let it rest. "Is it true what they say, that near a hundred were slaughtered at Eaton's Bend today?"

"I did not count them."

"He stinks with the killing. He's brought the stench of blood in the house," said Tam.

"Hold your tongue, boy," Grandpa ordered, and turned to Fither. "Duncan, lay aside your grief and begin again. Stop this senseless slaughter. It will not bring her back."

"Senseless?" Duncan barked. "It is carefully thought out and purposeful. She took my daughter to an early death. She had no right!"

"You had no right!" Tam crossed to Fither in one long stride. "You had no right!"

Grandpa forced himself between them. "Hush now, both of you. Duncan, you know Margaret's not to blame."

"Wasn't it Margaret filling her head with tales of the selkies that drove her to the sea? Wasn't it Margaret who poisoned my daughter against me? And now she lies in a watery grave! Who should I blame if not Margaret? Sweet Margaret, kind Margaret. Margaret, my wife, murderer of my daughter."

"No, Duncan. It was in her blood. No one could have kept—" Tam watched Grandpa stop himself from saying my name. It is the worst kind of bad luck to speak the names of the dead. "No one could have kept her from the sea."

"How could you let her go?" Duncan's mouth yanked open in silent anguish, and he clapped a hand over it to muffle the ragged sob that rose up inside him.

"A thousand times I've asked myself that question and cannot find an answer."

"Then leave me to my own concerns," Duncan replied. "They are none of yours."

"You are my son."

"Aye. And a son counts on his fither to stand with him."

"I am bound to you by blood but cannot condone the killing. There's been enough death in this house."

"I will find her at the cull and have my revenge."

"You have gone mad."

"If you stand in my way, old man, I'll not protect you."

Tam broke the silence. "I will protect him."

"Careful, pup," warned Duncan. "Stay out of my way, lest you lose your pelt."

"You be careful, Duncan," warned Grandpa. "Lest this course you have chosen leads you on a path where a fither cannot save his son. St. Magnus deliver you from this terrible mission."

Tam's shoulders slump forward as if he is exhausted. I cannot imagine the burden of having to tell me this story and its terrible details. But Tam's eyes are clear and filled with determination when he looks into mine.

"I swear," he says, "I have kept my promise. I have taken no part in the killing. We tried to stop him, Elin, your grandpa and me. But he would have none of it."

We are silent then, and I am filled with regret. If only I could change the world. If only I could talk to Fither. Perhaps then I could stop this terrible revenge.

I drink in the sight of Tam beside me, impossibly disheartened at my inability to tell him of my life beneath the sea and all that has happened to me there. I yearn to speak of the Red and the Black. Of the Arl Teller and Arnfin. Most of all, I ache to find the means to keep the selkies safe, to find a way to prevent Fither from doing more harm. But Tam tells me of his plan to stop the cull.

"This year will be different," he says. "So many selkies have died we won't need to kill the pups. I will talk to the others. I will convince them to stop the cull."

I offer my grateful assent in the language of the seals and nuzzle his outstretched hand. *Thank you, Tam, thank you for your help,* I say silently, and he strokes my head.

"I will meet you here on the beach when the veiled midnight sun is lowest in the sky," Tam promises. "I swear to St. Magnus, I will keep you safe, Selkie Girl. I will stop the killing or die trying."

And as I listen to his heartfelt promise, I make my own silent pledge. *I will stand with you.*

The sea calls to me, and I look at its endless gray plain. Is Tam the knowin' I am meant to find? At this moment, I pray for it to be so. With Tam beside me, I might find a place to belong. I might end this loneliness that followed me from the land into the sea.

I see Arnfin watching me from the skerry. I tuck my head beneath Tam's arm and make the purring sound of selkie contentment. If I could stay here forever, I would. But Tam and I have a challenge to face, one that will take all our will.

Goodbye, I say silently, looking into his eyes, *for a short time. We will find each other again.* And summoning all my will, I rock my body to the edge of the beach.

"Selkie Girl!"

I look back at Tam. "I knew it," he says. "I knew you would come back to me. Keep yourself safe."

Tam presses his face to mine, and with a mixture of sadness and joy the likes of which I have never known, I slide into the cool sea and swim toward Arnfin.

Looking back, I see Tam waving, and I hope that no one is watching the crazy gypsy boy waving to a selkie.

I dive into the North Sea with new purpose.

CHAPTER
THIRTY-THREE

I head back to the clearing, sliding through the currents. Friendly otters swim by, poking at my sides. They want to play, but the time for playing has passed. I shoo them away, and they chatter back at me, their tiny, sharp teeth glowing white in the dark sea. Arnfin follows close behind, as if he knows that the time is coming for action to be taken.

I am weightless in the tides, buoyant with optimism. Into the crowd of dire possibilities and the ugly predictions of my dreams, a slanting ray of hope has entered and made itself at home. I smile as I plow through the sea. My selkie friends have said it over and over again: "You are not alone." But until this day, it has not been true. Now I have an ally on land, one who can fight the killers.

I hear the chanting first, the rhythmic sound of selkie voices carried by the tides. I follow the path through the crystal forest to the clearing, wondering what has brought the selkie folk together. Not wanting to miss an important announcement, I weave in and out of the trees with as much speed as I can. From the volume of the chanting, I suspect the entire selkie tribe is gathered.

The forest thrums with the ritual low humming that introduces the Arl Teller. It gathers strength, vibrating the sea, then dies slowly away until there is silence. The chanting begins. "Arl Teller! Arl Teller! Arl Teller!"

I push through the last ring of glowing trees, the saplings bending in two, inviting me into the circle, and there are the selkie folk, their noses pointed toward the fire.

In the center, her fur glowing blue-green in the firelight, is the Arl Teller. What is happening? I have never seen the Arl Teller move into the circle before. This must be a new ritual.

The Arl Teller roams among the selkie clan, weaving in and out of the circle in an odd pattern, moving forward, now doubling back, then forward again. I can find no sense in it. It seems random, yet purposeful.

Then I understand. The Arl Teller is circling the females whose bodies are so taut with life they look as though their pups might at any minute burst from their bellies. She stops at each pregnant selkie, nuzzling them, murmuring words of encouragement. With her fore flipper, she strokes the Red's belly, swollen round and full with her pup. The Arl Teller acknowledges their mates, who lie protectively near the females, touching them now and again to remind them that they are not alone in the coming event.

I take my place in the circle and wait for the Arl Teller to finish the ceremony. There's no harm in waiting. Another hour will make no difference. The selkies are safely in the sea. I see Arnfin across from me, his large head bowed. He has passed the time for a mate. I wonder if he is remembering when his mate was pregnant with his pup.

The Arl Teller settles in her usual place at the head of the assembly. She lifts her flippers in a loving benediction.

"Teach us," the selkies recite like a prayer, "the past and the future. Teach us how to live."

And the Arl Teller speaks the ancient words of the endless cycle of life—birth, death, and the inevitability of both—a truth as old as time itself on both sea and land.

"Since the world began," intones the Arl Teller, "the selkies have lived where the ocean stretches into the North Sea, the sea that gives up its herring to keep us strong, the sea that rocks us in its healing embrace."

The selkies respond with yips and barks of agreement, and when the response diminishes, the Arl Teller continues. "In the time when the Beltane Tirls whip the tides into foam, the selkies go to the land to birth the pups."

"The birthing," the selkies sing like a hymn. "The birthing. When new life is created."

"Once, long ago," the Arl Teller continues, "both the sea and the land belonged to the selkies. Then came the killers, the Norse from the east and the Picts from the south, and the land ran red with the blood of our babes."

The selkies keen a mourning song as ancient as the world.

"Our bellies grow round with life, and we return again to the land they have taken from us."

Eerie moans pierce the tides like arrows.

"Our pups need the land. In the sea, they are helpless until they are old enough to swim. Some will survive. Many will die."

A strange yowl flows from the selkies, and the fur rises on the back of my neck. With growing horror, I realize what is happening. The Arl Teller is readying the females for the migration to the beach to birth the pups.

No, it is too soon. Not yet. Not now.

"Who among you has lost a babe to the killers?" demands the Arl Teller.

One by one, the females around the fire float upright in response, their feral faces pointed reverently up to the surface in remembrance of their lost babes. The selkie males bawl their pain, and the sound rips through the currents. With no way to fight the killers, the males are helpless to prevent the slaughter. Their inability to save the pups leaves them with a gaping hunger and a terrible sense of impotence. Their part in creation has long since passed, and now they must watch helplessly as the results of their couplings are massacred. I glance at Arnfin, tallest of them all, his mouth opened wide in selkie fury. Nearly all the females float upright, except for those not of an age yet to mate or those whose wombs are quickened for the first time.

"Mourn, selkies," the Arl Teller shouts over the din. "Keen your songs into the mouth of the sea."

The females moan, and their musical tones mingle with the bellowing of the males. My fingers clench in fury at the unfairness of life, and I weep in sympathy for these creatures who cannot change their cruel destiny and so have embraced it.

I am ready for no such acceptance.

"We cannot stop the killers," says the Arl Teller. "So we speak our love to the pups and keep them close, hiding them in the shadow of our bodies. Their death is our fate."

"Our fate," the selkies intone.

"It is our way."

"Our way," the selkies repeat.

The Arl Teller nods once and drops her eyes, signaling the end of the ritual. "Selkies!" she calls. "Do you know what you must do?"

Hundreds of selkie eyes blink in the firelight. Below us, sea snake eyes flicker, and the sea shimmers with their glow. Rainbow fish, sensitive to the emotion in the clearing, disperse anxiously in all directions, their careful formations shattered by fear. The selkies wait, and I wait with them, terrified of what will come next.

"To the beach!" orders the Arl Teller, and without hesitating, she pilots the selkies into the arms of the emerald forest. Males and females alike follow her, a great mass of rotund bodies plowing through the sea.

"The birthing!" the seals chant in their golden tones as they swim. "The birthing!"

"No!" I scream. "Not yet!"

The deathly images of my dreams march through me, horrible thoughts of death and the suffering that is its companion, snowy fur streaked pink with blood, selkies skinned alive on the beach. "Arl Teller!" I scream. "Stop them! If you are their leader, tell them not to go."

Selkie bodies crowd me in their effort to follow the Arl Teller, forcing me back. I am dragged, helpless in the crush and confusion of bodies, my beloved Red and Black swimming toward certain danger. Every muscle in my body tightens, and I thrust hard to the right, until I break free from the churning throng.

Where is Arnfin? I swivel about, scanning the clearing for some sight of him, but he has disappeared.

"Stop!" I shout, but the selkies are not listening to me. Of course not. Who am I to change what has always been? Nothing more than a brown-spotted selkie girl tainted by the land. Why would they listen to me?

Torn apart by my powerlessness, I am filled with rage. "Fools!" I call to them. "Do you think a miracle will save you, that St. Magnus will appear on the beach and frighten the killers away with talk of hellfire and damnation?" But even as the anger pours out of me, I know it is not foolishness that leads them to the beach. For them, it is a simple fact. They have accepted the cull. It is as much a part of their lives as the births that precede it, and they have made their peace with it.

I do not accept it. I cannot.

The transparent forest turns darker in the wake of the churning sea, and the crystal trees lift their branches as if in solemn agreement with the clan. The rainbow fish, frenzied with excitement, dart frantically back and forth, wondering what has caused all this furor. Their faces wear apologetic looks, as if to say, *What have I done, what should I do, where are you going?* The fish scatter, hiding among the trees, their colorful gills quivering in the currents.

A heavy silence pervades the forest.

The selkies are out of sight. Even their wake has calmed to a rustle in the water, and I am alone in the thick copse of sparkling trees that tower over me, dreamlike and phantom-eyed. The trees look down at me accusingly, their arms still bending open to the path the selkies have taken. I sink down onto the shell-covered ocean floor. The tiny snake eyes beneath the scattering of ground cover wink at me.

The trees quiver gently as a figure approaches. The blue-veined branches part, and the Black drifts in with the current, Arnfin behind her. She watches me with an unreadable expression. "You burn as brightly as the fire," she says softly.

"Please, stop them—" I begin, but a sob finishes my thought.

The Black blinks her opaque eyes. "It is the way of the selkies, as it has always been and will always be."

"He will kill them all, like he slaughtered the others."

Arnfin nods his great head in agreement. "Perhaps. And you must bear the pain of it, as we all do."

"No. There must be another way. Tam is not a killer. He will help us. But I need time. Please, stop them," I plead. "You must stop them, if only for a little while."

Arnfin's whiskers wave in the tides, and his mouth lifts in a sneer. "I could sooner stop the rain or the wind," he says.

"We have all lost babes to the greed of men," adds the Black. "Did you notice the ones who trailed behind?"

I had seen them, a gathering that lingered in the clearing. Among them were the two young selkies who survived the attack on the beach.

"They are the ones who have known man," says the Black. "They bear scars from the spear, burn marks of the net, lingering damage from the wooden club that missed its mark. They are the lucky ones. They survived. No one asks them to return to the land, and so they have chosen not to." A look passes over the Black's face that travels to the center of my soul.

"Kindness is our way," she says. "The killers have much to learn about the value of life in the sea. Look." The Black lifts her front flipper. A jagged scar stretches from underneath and around her side until it disappears into the folds of her shining flesh.

"Like Arnfin, I have known man," she tells me, without a trace of self-pity. "And I have lost babes to the killers." The Black's feathery pelt ripples in the tides. "I am intimately acquainted with sorrow, like all the selkies," she tells me. "Your fither took my sister as I watched, unable to prevent her abduction. I was kept from you both for sixteen years." A half smile dances on her animal lips.

I am incredulous at her courage. "But how can you smile?"

"I smile because otherwise my tears would fill the ocean with bitterness." The Black scratches her nose daintily with her fore flipper. "Fear is part of our world. We are not the strongest animal, but not the weakest, either. And holding bitterness too close sucks the sweetness from life."

"But why are you not with the ones who stay behind?"

"My sister needs me, so I choose to be with her." The Black turns to Arnfin.

Arnfin's mouth yawns open with pride, and when he speaks, his voice is tight with conviction. "I do not fear any living creature on land or in the sea. I have met my fears and call them by name. I own them so they do not own me."

"There must be a way to stop the cull. We can fight them."

"And what shall we use to fight the killers?" the Black replies gently, and she raises her flippers in an ironic shrug.

I look down at my fingers, held together again by the webs of my flippers. Except for swimming, they are useless.

"We cannot avoid the killers, even if we try. Their determination will lead them to us. As for fighting"—the Black gazes toward the land—"that would make us like them, wouldn't it."

A deep sea moan breaks from her throat. Arnfin joins her, wailing into the sea. My throat tightens at the eerie sounds. The harmony of the two selkies echoes through the tides until the sea is still again.

Then the Black turns to me. "We are slaves to the greed of men, bound by nature and her impenetrable ways. The pups must be born on land. Better to save some than lose all to the sea. As men gain dominion over us, our numbers will diminish until eventually, we will disappear. Someday the selkie folk will be gone, but the killers will endure."

Her words ripple in the currents and are lost. The rainbow fish dart past, oblivious to the solemnity of this prophecy.

"Now," the Black says firmly, "there is no more time for talk. I must join my kind."

"Your kind," I whisper. "I have no kind."

"You have yourself." I had almost forgotten Arnfin was here. "Part selkie and part human, and both will be on the beach this night."

Arnfin dips his huge, flat head and swiftly joins the migration, the Black following, knowing that danger waits for them on the beach.

I think of the land and all I have left behind, Tam sitting near me on the beach, dark curls ruffling in the sea breeze. I think of the slaughter of the young selkies and the innocent pups that will soon die. I think of Mither, praying she is far away, and of Fither's revenge and my part in it. And I think of the Arl Teller's story about the girl who wanted to right the wrong.

Floating alone among the crystal trees, in a moment of breathless epiphany, I know what I must do.

CHAPTER
THIRTY-FOUR

$\mathcal{T}$he beauty of the birthing leaves me forever altered.

When I arrived on the beach with Arnfin and the Black, the selkie mithers were already in the throes of their labor, the air thick with their efforts. The males had made a circle of their bodies to enclose their mates, a safe harbor. Their eyes scanned the beach, keeping watch for any danger, as the females did the work of creating life. Grunts and cries filled the beach, but in between the effort to birth their pups, the mithers smiled. They knew the sacred nature of their toil, and it filled them with importance. A final push, a cry, a shudder, a small wail—all signaled a pup's emergence into the world. The mithers guided their babes to nurse, giving them sustenance after the trauma of birth.

I witnessed miracle after miracle as hundreds of pups were born, and through it all, not one moment became ordinary or repetitive. And when the last pup was safely born, a collective sigh ran through the tribe and we rested, a time of peaceful contemplation after the struggle of birth. I slept until the heat of the sun woke me, dazed with satisfaction.

Now lying on the beach among the clan, I wait for the killers. For nearly two weeks, we have waited, ever since the birthing, but there has been no sign of men. As each day passes, the time of the cull draws nearer, and although we do not speak of it, we know that our sojourn will not last much longer.

I allow myself to hope that this year there will be no cull. Perhaps so many have already died at Fither's hands the others will not kill the pups. A second hope lies in my heart. Perhaps Tam has convinced them to end the cull forever. This is the hope I hold closest. *Please, St. Magnus, help Tam convince the others.*

When I share my hopes with Arnfin, his face contorts into a mask of skepticism. "I applaud your spirit, Selkie Girl, but the killers will come, just as they always have."

So I pray silently and keep my hopes to myself.

The selkie mithers are calm, having accepted the inevitable, their round white pups lying curled contentedly beside them. The males recline nearby, ready to herd the females into the safety of the sea when the killers appear. They lumber about, bellowing now and then into the pale, darkening sky, their mouths stretched open with anticipation and dread.

The Red bends her body around her pup, a snowy bundle bright against the dun-colored sand. The pup burrows into her belly, searching for the rich milk that will nurture his growth. The Red coos softly to her infant son, marveling at the miracle of him.

The pups have nearly doubled in size in the two weeks since the birthing. Now they waddle about the beach while their mithers smile with satisfaction at the offspring they have created. The pups offer tiny barks, answered by the deeper sounds of their mithers encouraging them to stay close.

Arnfin rolls his gigantic body over the sand until he lies beside me. His fur is dappled with beach grit. He wriggles his belly, enjoying the feel of the fine sand beneath him.

"How can they be so calm?" I ask him, still dazed from the vivid memories of the birthing, awed by the innocent beauty of the pups that lie around me.

"We love while we can. What good does it do to think ahead?"

I silently offer thanks to my family for trying to protect me from the harsh reality of the cull. Now I understand the secrets, the silence in the house at the time of the cull, Mither's constant vigil of the sea. I think of Mither with a sting of regret.

"I will never see her again."

Several selkies look pointedly at me, and I realize I spoke the words aloud. I am filled with sadness at all that Mither sacrificed, the endless, painful days kept from the sea, a constant stranger among the island folk. It must have been so lonely to be adrift in a sea of others, as lonely as I have been. I turn my face to the sky and pray to St. Magnus for her safety.

Whatever comes, I will not run from it.

The Arl Teller lies among a circle of selkie mithers. She nods her majestic white head rhythmically, held in thrall by the warmth of the sun. "Roooo," she calls into the air, and the selkie mithers answer her song.

I scan the beach for Tam, my best hope, but there is no sign of him, only the birds that fly over us, claiming with squawks and cries their ownership of the beach and the sky above it. The sun momentarily shines through the clouds in spite of the dark events the day could bring, and my seal eyes squint against its brightness.

I sense, then hear, motion in the distance. The selkies turn toward the disturbance, their noses pointing in a single direction. I tense with fear, but it is only a few stray sheep that have scrambled over the hill in their endless search for fresh shoots of grass.

I am so afraid.

Grandpa would say that fear can be useful unless it keeps us from taking necessary action. I am afraid, but I will not let it stop me. Like Arnfin, I will own my fears so they do not own me.

St. Magnus, make me strong.

As quietly as the gulls skim the sky, the killers appear on the rise. They stand looking down at us, the light at their backs, and I can see the unmistakable outlines of wooden clubs hanging loosely at their sides.

How do they feel about the killing to come? Is it a chore like any other, a perfunctory task devoid of emotion, or do they ache for its grisly finish? Do they feel proud of the money the pelts and oil will bring? I doubt they have any sense at all of the meaningful lives they take. They do not realize there will be grieving this night within a society as complex and impassioned as their own. The others think of the selkies as dumb animals without feelings or souls. How wrong they are, and how misguided.

I cry out my sharpest warning, but the selkies have already seen the men, and my cry mingles with the collective realization of the clan. Pups instinctively sense the fear that flows through their mithers, and they begin to bleat short barks and cries that harmonize with the keening of their elders.

The males herd their mates toward the safety of the sea. Some females follow, but many ignore the desperate attempts of the males to save them, unwilling to abandon their babes. They comfort their pups with quiet barks and moans, covering their small bodies with their larger ones in a futile attempt to keep them hidden. The mithers rock their pups with their bodies, gentle, comforting cradles.

The killers clamber down the rise to the beach, positioning themselves for the first strike. They are not in a hurry. They know the selkies are slow on land and defenseless. There will be little struggle.

There are no women among the killers. Of course not; the women are safe at home, kept away from the killing. But they know. They know their men will slaughter babes this day. And they do nothing. I wonder if they feel sadness and regret at the injustice of it. My body shakes with anger for the land I once inhabited, a land that spawned the killers.

I search the group for Fither but do not see him. Where is he? Could it be that he will not take part in the cull?

The men discuss their gruesome plans. The killing will be organized and quick. One well-positioned strike for each pup will be enough. Then the crofters will skin the dead and ready the pelts for sale. The blubber will be rendered into oil to fuel the cruisie lamps that light the dark Orkney nights. The crofters will return home to have their suppers and cups of ale, like any other night. Tomorrow they will return to their daily work, the trade that keeps roofs over their heads and food on the table, fishing for the sweet herring that are the cause of all this destruction.

The men are in position now, waiting for the signal from their leader, a stocky man who stands at the center of the group. I recognize his face but cannot remember his name. I see Malcolm Seatter standing at the edge of the group, looking as if he'd rather be anywhere else than here. Perhaps many of the men are uncomfortable with the chore that awaits them. I hope they are ashamed.

Then I see Fither on the rise. Even at this distance, I recognize his features, sharp angles protruding from the dark hollow of his cheeks, but now his familiar face is buried in the countenance of a madman. His hair has grown to his shoulders, blowing greasy and unkempt. He does not wear a hat like the other crofters or a coat, and his ragged shirt slaps about him in the wind. I think protectively that he must be cold.

Unlike the other men, who wait for the signal to begin the cull, Fither charges with a great primal yell, waving his club over his head like a lone Viking warrior. His eyes are flat and wild, and he shakes his head from side to side as if trying to release a demon that has lodged itself there. He stumbles once, then jumps to his feet, looking around defensively, as if expecting an attack from behind. He swings his club wildly, descending the last bit of hill to the beach.

The Red and her pup are directly in his path. Fither charges toward her, head lowered like a bull, but two men have followed him down the hill. They force him down on the sand. He struggles against them, but they hold him roughly.

"Let me go!" Fither demands.

"The cull will be orderly, as it has always been," one of the men says, shaking his head in frustration at the rogue killer. "The signal has not been given."

Fither murmurs a response so low I cannot hear.

"No, Duncan," the man says to Fither. "She is not here. Your wife and daughter are lost to the sea."

"You are not the only one of us to lose a loved one to the raging tides," says a fisherman with more than a little annoyance in his voice. "Your vendetta against the selkies is shameful, and disrespectful, too. Go home. The cull will be done as always—only some of the babes, none of the mithers. We only cull what is necessary. Do you hear?"

Fither hangs his head, and the fisherman releases him, satisfied that he is tamed. Fither lies there sobbing, throwing fistfuls of sand in frustration. "Margaret!" he cries. "Give me back my daughter! Give her back to me!"

My heart swells with pity for this dangerous madman who is my fither. Memories flood through me—a baby bird passed from his cradled hands into my own, the sight of him nuzzling Mither's neck, the way he wiggled his ears until I felt sick from laughing.

Above me is the safety of Odin's Throne, and looking at it, I offer a final prayer to St. Magnus—*Give me strength*—as Fither stands and begins to close the distance between us. This time no one stops him.

Then I see Tam McCodrun running down the rocks from the rise. Hands clinging to the scrubby bushes for balance, he slips and falls in his haste. Threading his way toward us, sand flying, he shouts, "Wait!"

From his reddened wrists, frayed knots of rope hang like twin weapons at his sides. He pleads with a man who grabs him, but the man does not let go, so Tam seizes the man's arm and, wresting the club from his hand, deals him a blow that knocks him from his feet, leaving him lying motionless on the sand. Without acknowledging his victory, Tam grips another killer by his jacket and swings him aside. He sprints toward the next assaulter as if, single-handedly, he can stop the slaughter before it starts. Tam works his way to me, and I think that he must know, even at this distance, that the small, brown-spotted selkie in his path is the girl he once asked to dance with him at the foy.

I call to him, summoning all the love I can into a single sustained note. "Roooooo."

But now the others have realized Tam's purpose. "Dirty gypsy meddler!" shouts a killer wearing a sealskin jacket, and he and a companion rush at Tam, knocking him down. The men pull Tam's arms behind his back, trying to tie him with the ropes that dangle from his wrists. Tam shakes them off.

Fither shouts his fury and rushes at Tam. The men back away from the ferocity of Fither's attack, and he takes advantage of their hesitation to strike a great blow at Tam's head. Tam dodges the blow, and Fither's club lands harmlessly on the sand.

"Elin Jean!" Tam shouts at him. "Elin Jean is on the beach!"

Fither is momentarily stayed, shaking his head to clear his addled mind, and a sliver of hope darts through me.

I am here! I am here, Fither!

"Liar!" Fither spits at Tam. "Liar!" He grabs the ropes that hang from Tam's wrists and forces Tam to his knees. "My daughter is dead!"

Tam wrenches away from Fither's grasp and deftly circles out of reach. His chest rises as he takes a calming breath.

"Come, sir," he cajoles in his calmest voice, circling around Fither's ragged form. "We'll pour you a pint of ale and sit you by the fire."

Fither hesitates as though he is considering this suggestion. Then suddenly he lurches forward, renewing his attack. Tam, by far the quicker of the two, ducks Fither's roundhouse blows as they slice wildly through the foggy air.

"Stop!" Tam cries. "Stop!"

The man in the sealskin jacket moves silently behind Tam. He lifts his club to strike, but at that moment, Tam feints to the right to avoid Fither, and the blow lands on Tam's shoulder with a terrible thud. Tam McCodrun crumples on the sand and lies still.

CHAPTER
THIRTY-FIVE

I rock my body forward to Tam. Is he hurt? Is he dead? The man who hit him bends to see how badly he is hurt.

Fither turns toward the Red with mad jubilation. "Margaret!" he screams, his eyes fixed on her. "Margaret!"

"No!" I shout in the language of the seals. "She is not Mither!" But Fither cannot understand my desperate cries, and closing the gap between him and the Red, he raises his club. The Red looks up at him with stunned eyes, pleading for mercy. I cannot look and yet I cannot look away as the club falls.

There is a dull crunch, and the Red's pup lies dead, half buried by her bulk.

Fither performs an eerie dance of victory. The stocky leader gives the signal, and with a collective shout, the cull begins in earnest. All around us, the clubs fall, the crunch of bone mingling with the cries of the selkies and the shouts of men, until the beach is filled with a terrible din. Down and down again the clubs fall as pup after pup is killed.

Fither's gaze falls again on the Red.

"Save yourself!" I shout to her. "Your pup is beyond you now!"

The Red lifts her eyes to me in a silent plea, and I know she will not abandon her babe. She rolls her dead pup with her nose toward the water's edge. His skull is split open like a ripe melon, blood seeping into the sand. The Red's face is streaked scarlet with his blood, but she herds him to the safety of the sea, oblivious to his death.

Then I see Arnfin furiously pumping his body toward us. "Get out of the way!" he bellows.

But I ignore his warning. "Go!" I order the Red, and then I lie to save her. "I will save your pup!" I push the Red toward the water. She lifts her grieving eyes to me in silent refusal. We lie together at the water's edge.

"Margaret?" Fither cries, and swings his club in the air in a devastating arc. A crazed look has crawled across his face. Perhaps he's thinking of Mither standing before him as he first saw her that Midsummer's Eve in the moonlight. He doesn't notice me. I am just another brown-spotted selkie on the beach. He looks only at the Red.

Fither charges forward with terrifying purpose. The Red lies directly in the path of his raised club. I bark furiously to distract him, and he stops, surprised by the outburst of a small brown-spotted selkie aimed at him.

In that moment, I wait to die and think only that I will never find the knowin'. I will never know what I am meant to do with my life or where I belong. I wait for the crunch of wood on my forehead.

Instead, there is a huge, unearthly roar, and I see Arnfin propel his great bulk into the air, flinging himself at our attacker.

Fither falls to the beach, pinned by the weight of the giant selkie. Arnfin lifts his chest until he is nearly vertical and lets it fall. Fither lies still.

Behind my protector, the stocky leader appears.

"No!" I shout. Arnfin turns at the warning, but it is too late. The club comes crashing down with terrible force on his unprotected head, blood spurting upward from a jagged, gaping wound. Still my selkie champion wheels up toward the killer, attacking him with all the force of his body's weight. The crack of breaking bones fills the air as the killer is pinned by Arnfin's bulk. The huge selkie rolls off the dying man and lies silent on the sand. Blood pulses from his split skull.

I make my way to his side, ignoring the carnage around me.

"Arnfin," I whisper, leaning close. "You are the bravest of them all." And for a moment, the giant selkie rests his eyes on mine. The hint of a smile lights his face. Then, in a gesture of defiance, he lets loose a bellow of victory and leaps, his great bulk blocking the sun. With a final moan, he falls and lies still, his unseeing eyes pointed toward the sea. Like his ancestor Dane, he has slain his enemy.

Arnfin, my protector and friend. How can the world be such a horrible place, so unfair, so cruel? Tears of anger and frustration crowd my sight. Arnfin, with his wisdom and courage, should have grown old in a safe place, a place of honor, like Grandpa.

Like Grandpa. The connection startles me with its simplicity. Why didn't I see it before? Both Arnfin and Grandpa sacrificed so much for me. Both encouraged me to make my own choices. They believed in my reckless nature, in my instincts. They trusted me, the greatest gift a selkie can give another. Two men, one of the land, one of the sea. Land and sea.

I howl my rage into the sky. The seabirds above me scatter,

frightened by the force of my pain. Fury and tears blind me, but I don't care. I swerve to face the killers and see Fither rise, stumbling in my path. He lifts his wooden club, a trail of blood dripping on the sand.

No, not one more death.

I rise up on my hindquarters, and like Arnfin before me, I fling my body at Fither. The force of the blow knocks him off his feet, and he lies on the beach, momentarily stunned. Then, yelling with fury, he scrambles for his club. He adjusts his grip on the handle and turns to me, the club lifted high over his shoulder to strike.

The awful images of my dreams rip through me. I see my death, just as I dreamed it.

"Fither!" I scream. "I am Elin Jean!"

Fither swerves toward the sound. He stops, paralyzed with sudden recognition. From my selkie throat comes the sound of a girl's voice. "It is me, Fither. Elin Jean."

A shudder runs through me. My face shifts and peels; the layers of fur and seal blubber flay open, exposing pink human skin. Chestnut curls, stuck damply to my scalp, emerge, falling to my shoulders. The strange fingers embedded in my fore flippers separate and lift from the thick appendages that drop limply to my sides. My arms reach up, and the selkie pelt strips off me like the peel of an apple and slides down my legs until I stand before the killers as the girl I had once been. I struggle to stand on legs that barely remember the sensation of balancing upright on land. Beneath the pelt, a sea-green sheath of fabric, sheer and finely woven, clings to me like a second skin. I look down at my hands and see that my fingers are as they once were, webbed to the first knuckle.

Fither falls to his knees on the damp sand. Great rending

sobs rip from his chest, and his wooden club drops harmlessly from his opened palm. He crawls forward until he is at my feet, and his lanky arms reach out to embrace my legs.

"Elin Jean." He cries my name over and over as if hearing it for the first time. "I thought you were lost, lost to the sea forever."

"Lost?" I say. "Not lost. I am found. I have been to the bottom of the sea. I have been with the selkie folk, my other family."

I look around me, half expecting to see the selkie folk becoming human, but they lie on the beach, a clan of animals who can shed their pelts only on Midsummer's Eve. I alone have become the human I once was. I think of the legend. *A girl from the land will come among us.* I am the one foretold.

Scattered around the beach are the shocked figures of the killers, dazed at the sight of the selkie who has become a girl. The killers shake their heads in disbelief, thinking they might be imagining it, but this miracle is as true as day becomes night and the day comes again. The clubs slip from their hands, and the soft thud of the weapons falling on the sand creates the sweetest music I have ever heard.

Death surrounds us, the sand spotted with the blood of the selkies. I weep for those who have been killed. Slowly, the surviving pups begin to bleat for their mithers, and the remaining members of the selkie clan find their mates. Mithers who have lost their pups hurry to those little ones who are alone, offering them their bodies to take nourishment. I watch new families form and am reminded again of the generosity and gentle spirit of these animals.

Above us, a hawk swoops and dives, calling to her mate to come witness the strange events below. She must find us an odd lot, selkies and humans, still as stones in the aftermath of the cull. The only other sound is Fither weeping at my feet, his body racked with sobs.

The Arl Teller rises up on her hind flippers; standing upright, she is a head taller than the tallest killer. She bellows into the night in the language of the seals. "Sing, selkies. Sing of Elin Jean, the Selkie Girl. Today she has stopped the killers!" And the beach is filled with a selkie song of victory. I sing, too, in the musical language of the seals, adding a new voice, the first of a kind.

And when, at last, the killers quit the beach, their heads are bowed. Even so, their guilt is not fully realized. I think that may take them a lifetime. I have no sympathy for them. They look back at me now and again to be sure that it wasn't a dream. Let them hurry home in eagerness to tell their families of the strange sights they have seen this day. I watch them go, sitting quietly near Arnfin's body, lying where the stones of the skerry meet the beach.

Tam kneels at my feet, his hand resting on my knee. He wears a dazed look on his handsome face. I cannot tell whether it is from my transformation or the blow to his shoulder. Perhaps it is a bit of both. He smiles at me, but his eyes are grave. Today there is victory, but there is mourning, too.

The surviving pups sleep safely on the land, lulled by the nearness of the clan and the beauty of the selkie song that fills the beach with their ownership of it. And when the clan finally falls silent, the Arl Teller tells the tale of this day for the first time to a rapt audience. The selkies offer each other occasional feral smiles, their animal humor teased by the memory of the killers struck dumb by the simple sight of a selkie girl.

CHAPTER
THIRTY-SIX

The water in the voe is calm, as if it, too, is peaceful now that the violence is over. A hawk swoops into the sea searching for its breakfast, and I marvel at the trajectory of its dive. A thrill of freedom shivers through me as I watch this wild creature, and I feel a kinship. I have known the selkie folk. I have been to the depths of the ocean and have learned my heritage. Land and sea.

I sit on the sand where Arnfin fell, unwilling to leave the place where I last saw him alive. In the earliest hours of morning, I finally agree to return him to the sea that was his home. I help the selkies roll his body to the edge of the shore, and with solemn reverence, we float his body out to sea.

I follow the procession to the end of the skerry. *St. Magnus, keep him close to you,* I pray. *He is the kindest soul I have ever known.*

Throughout my vigil, Tam has been at my side, offering silent support. I am grateful for his presence and his patience. Now and then, I look at his face, the chiseled features familiar and comforting. Funny, but sometimes when I gaze at him, it is Arnfin's face I see. Not so much his features as his expression, and it occurs to me that I will see his face reflected in those I love for a long time to come.

The morning after Arnfin's body was committed to the sea, Tam and I walk down to the beach. I want to touch the sand where Arnfin died, to feel the cool salt water that was my home. I want to be among new life. Dotting the skerry, sprayed by the sea, lie the mottled bodies of selkie mithers, their white-coated pups beside them. They will learn to negotiate the land first, remaining there for six weeks until they are old enough to navigate the rough waters of the North Sea. I listen to the mithers speaking to their offspring in the musical language of the seals, and the pups reply in the short, direct words of the young.

Taking Tam's hand in mine, I lead us among them. At the sound of humans approaching, the selkie mithers are alert and watchful, ready to flee. But I speak to them in their language, and as I draw near, they recognize me, nodding their heads in the greeting of the seals.

"Do not be afraid of this human," I say, holding Tam's hand. "He is not a killer."

The selkies sniff the air and make the purring sound that speaks of their contentment.

Tam and I sit among them, watching the beauty of life sustaining life. The pups suckle and nap, then make brief forays to explore the world where the beach meets the skerry. The mithers allow them this adventure, but if they stray too far, they are called back with sharp barks. Several pups approach me and, with some encouragement, make a nest of my lap. Curled together, they are lulled to sleep by the warmth of my body. I imagine that one of the pups is mine, and I am, for a brief moment, enveloped in the rich experience of a mither's unconditional love for her child. I wonder if I will ever be a mither. I look at Tam seated near me and see a dark-eyed daughter who looks like him.

At last I rise and cross the beach to the spot where Arnfin died. Traces of his blood still mark the sand with an ocher stain. A moan escapes from deep in my throat, and the sound builds until it covers the beach with my sadness. Around me the selkie mithers echo my cries, and the beach becomes a gravesite where we mourn. It is their loss, too.

How can I express the feelings that fill me? I am torn by the battle for dominion over my heart. A legion of gratitude cheers for the love that has been in my life. Mither, Arnfin, Grandpa, the Red and the Black, and Tam—I am fortunate indeed to have known them all.

But darker thoughts clash with the delicate contentment. Arnfin is dead, and he died saving me. I will never be worthy of his loss. How can I live knowing that I will never see him again? How can I face the future without having told him how much he meant to me? Every day will be a reminder of his sacrifice and his loss.

Although I try to feel at home in the place of my childhood, I cannot. Too much has happened. I am no longer a child, and the rooms of the crofthouse do not fit around me as they once did. My box bed, an earlier haven of quiet, now feels stifling and close. I realize that I cannot live under the same roof as Fither, so I wrap my pelt around me for warmth and sleep in the byre. But even that is too confining. I ache for the vast emptiness of the sea. A strange caul has stretched over me, and I long to birth out of it.

All that I have been through and I still cannot name the knowin'. I have fulfilled my destiny as the one foretold. I feel the truth of it as surely as I breathe the air around me, feel the fine sand beneath my feet. Returning Mither's pelt, entering the sea, my solus year, Arnfin's death, and the transformation that stopped the cull—all this and I am still not satisfied.

Perhaps I am being punished. Perhaps something I am meant to do lies just beyond my reach and I am too simple to realize it. I rehearse the possibilities, but the answers elude me. *Show me*, I want to shout. *Help me!* I am shocked by the loneliness of it, this vague sense of knowledge that lies concealed. In restless moments, I am filled with fury, the unfairness of it gnawing at me, the certainty that the knowin' still eludes me.

In the crofthouse, in the garden, or wandering the fields, I am followed by a sense of longing. Will it never leave me? Is this vague sense of discontent my destiny? What will bring me the satisfaction and peace I seek? I am exhausted by the unanswered questions. My sleep is fitful, even in the byre, and as I wait for Midsummer's Eve, my mood alternates between listlessness and anger. I am poor company, even for myself.

Finally, I find the courage to tell Tam. "I used to love the land," I say to him. "The green hills, the golden fields, the smell of peat. But now it feels so small. Even the byre is like a prison to me."

Tam takes my hand. "Come with me," he says, and leads me down the path to the beach. As we walk, I can smell the sea, feel the sweet, rolling waves. Below us, the selkies roll on the beach, luxuriating in the warmth of the sun.

"This will be our home," he whispers, spreading his arms wide. His gaze takes in the beach, the fields, and the rise where Odin's Throne stands guard over it all. My eyes follow his, and I feel the sharp sting of love for this gypsy boy and the world he offers me.

"I am used to a rough life, and you have forsaken four walls and a hearth," he says to me. "I will build a boat to rock you on the sea, and we will plant a garden on the land. We will live on the riches from both. We need little besides each other."

I think of what my life with Tam might be, his fine company a safe harbor for my raging soul. I think of all that has happened, of the danger and fear that have been my life, and I long for the protection and care that life with Tam would bring.

Is this the knowin' I seek?

I lean my head against Tam's shoulder and look out to sea. The waves peak and roll, white-capped and determined. Tam's open arms cannot include the world of the selkie folk, the fiery light of the clearing, the Arl Teller's wise stories, the Red and the Black, my last tie to my family beneath the sea. How can I leave them behind? How can I leave all that reminds me of Arnfin?

The sea calls my name, although the only sounds on the beach are the lapping waves and the wind dancing in my ears mingled with the song of the selkie mithers and the sharp complaints of an angry seabird.

The sea lives inside me. It will always be a part of me.

I can smell the wildflowers that have begun to open in preparation for summer. Their scent is luxurious, and I give in to it. With Tam near me, my senses are filled with the smells of the land, the rich earth, the perfume of flowers, and the pungent animal smell of sheep. They are familiar and fine. Here on the beach, I can imagine a life with Tam, the quiet comfort of his nearness. I would never feel alone again. I would have someone to understand me, someone to share my life. I would finally belong. Could I ever have that in the sea?

In the days before Midsummer arrives, my time is filled with Tam, leisurely walking the fields, parting the stiff stalks of wheat with our determined legs. In the early mornings, we sit on the skerry, speaking of this and that, silly thoughts that only lovers share. He blows an eyelash from my cheek or throws his coat around my shoulders when the biting wind nips at our backs.

Reverently, I tell him of my year beneath the sea, the stories of the selkie folk who gather in the crystal forest. He listens carefully, now and then nodding his head in agreement. And when, lying in the sand behind the great boulders that front the sea, we touch each other, we are lost in the wonder of it. Alive with the newness of us, I begin to forget my loss, and the days take on the rhythm of routine.

Each day with Tam is a gift wrapped in colored paper, and my home in the sea begins to feel farther and farther away. But the sharp sting of worry about Mither is still with me. A part of me wants to dive into the sea and search until I find her. I remember the words of the Black. *You cannot find her until she finds you.* But what if she is in danger? What if she needs my help? Perhaps she has been looking for me and cannot find me. I cannot bear to think of her alone and lost in the vast sea.

Each day Fither weaves down the path to the beach like a drunkard to look for her. A furious anger toward him has found a foothold inside me, and instead of fighting it, I welcome its strange comfort. The rage sits quietly in my heart, but each time I see Fither, it rises to remind me that it lives there.

I cannot look at him.

One day, sitting on Odin's Throne watching Fither below me, I feel the warmth of Grandpa's hand fall on my shoulder. "You might be able to hate him forever, but I doubt you'd be the better for it."

"I have nothing to say to him," I answer.

"Aye, nor do any of us."

"Then I will leave him to himself."

"It's not him I'm thinking of." Grandpa turns me gently to face him. "It's you. If you keep the anger close, it will burn a hole through your heart. Hatred and revenge will not make you whole. Do you want to be like him?"

Grandpa's words stick to me, playing over and over in my mind until I feel sick with the weight of them. *Do you want to be like him?* But before I can find the courage to consider the forgiveness I know Grandpa hopes I'll find, Fither is taken sick with a terrible fever so pervasive and determined that, within days, his life lies suspended in the corridor of death.

And I become his nurse. I stay with him through it all, pressing cool cloths to his burning forehead, changing the linens soaked in sweat, begging him to take sips of water from a cup I hold patiently in my hands. I pray to St. Magnus to spare his life, forcing the fury inside me to become goodness so that I might be worthy to ask for this favor. Despite his actions, I love him still and cannot entertain the thought of abandoning him. Arnfin's face hovers always near me, giving me strength.

I am a boat that rocks his sickened body in a lullaby of survival. I sing to him the song of the seals, murmuring encouragement, and although I know he cannot understand a single word, I pray he will feel my intent.

He cries out from the depths of the fever—"Margaret!"—and the sound holds a plea instead of a curse. His lips form Mither's name and then go slack, weak from the effort. "Margaret," he mumbles. "Come back to me."

As each day turns into the next and Fither slips further and further away from me, neighbor women gather near the crofthouse, anticipating his death. I know they mean well, that their prayers are as fervent as mine, but their presence fills me with dread. Like carrion birds quarreling over the flesh of the dead, they wait for him to die, and I wish I could make them disappear.

One day I step outside to escape the stifling air of the crofthouse, only to overhear the women gathered nearby whispering to one another.

"He is already a ghost," a woman says, pulling her black shawl closer around her against the cold.

"Better he die quickly," adds another. "Better for the girl."

"Better for us all," a third woman agrees, and I can stand it no longer.

"He will not die!" I shout furiously at the women, and they go quiet, realizing that I have heard their dire prediction. After that, they move farther away from the crofthouse, and the next day they are gone. My determination to bring Fither back from the faraway place that smells of death has chased them away.

Then one day Fither opens his eyes. They rest momentarily on mine before they close again, and I have renewed hope for his recovery. I sleep peacefully that night for the first time since Fither's sickness and rise the next morning to find that he has left his sickbed. He sees me framed in the doorway, his haunted eyes soft with peat smoke from the fire. I see recognition in them. I wait for him to help me right the world again. Wait for the words that will begin the healing, wait for him to ask for forgiveness. But he is silent. Why doesn't he speak to me? Does he have nothing to say?

He takes a step toward me, but falters, weak as a newborn lamb from his sickness. I go to him, but he slips through my hands and crumples to the floor.

"Fither—" I begin, but he interrupts me.

"Elin Jean," he says in his fever-ravished voice. "Find your mither. Bring her back to me. I cannot live without her."

A silence settles over the house, as empty and dark as a grave. So this is what he has to say. Of all the words I imagined he might say to me, this is what I least expected. I exist only as a good daughter to do his bidding. Even the precipice of death has not altered his selfish ways.

I go blind with rage. Grandpa's question lies pulsing in my swollen throat. *Do you want to be like him?* And in that moment, I answer it. *No, Grandpa, I will not be like him, nor will I forgive.* I will not deny my anger for the wrongs that have been done, for the taking of my mither from the sea, for the death of my beloved Arnfin and the selkies whose innocent blood was shed at his pleasure. I have paid my debt to him. I am free.

Fither reaches out his hand to me, but I move away, as Mither once recoiled from his touch. "I will not be like you," I say, but Fither can't or perhaps won't hear me. I no longer care which. I walk through the door into the sweet-scented breeze from the sea, leaving him sobbing Mither's name.

"Margaret," he cries, tears crawling down his ravaged face. "Bring her back to me." But there is no one left to hear him.

From that moment, I refuse to bend to him or speak his name. I saved his life, but now, for me, he no longer exists.

CHAPTER
THIRTY-SEVEN

*E*ven when the world is turned inside out, upside down, certain constants remain. Shapinsay Island life continues much the same as it always has. But the others are irrevocably changed by the miracle that happened on the night of the cull.

When June arrives with an easy gait, leaving behind the Beltane Tirls with their high winds and lashing rain, the sun makes her entrance. The children throw off their shoes, freeing overheated toes. "Good morning!" they call to the sun. "Show your eye!"

Like the marvel it is, summer appears with its sunny afternoons and long evening light. Troops of wildflowers bravely march up the rocky hilltops, more brilliant than I can ever remember, and the puffins that nest carelessly among the rocks that frame the sea seem to know my name.

I spend time sitting on Odin's Throne, listening to the combined sounds of land and sea, hoping I'll hear some clue to the knowin' in the wind. My hearing is more acute than it has ever been, even in the sea, and here, at the top of Shapinsay Island, I can hear it all—the braying of sheep, a stallion's mating call, the voices of travelers on the road. I hear the relentless whine of the wind and the raging sea mingled with the moans and barks of the selkies. Are they calling to me? I hear them teaching their pups, speaking of the weather, of the swimming patterns of the herring, and of their longing for the clearing that they call home. Day after day, I listen for my name, but the selkies make no mention of me. Perhaps I belong to the past, the one who was foretold but now has returned to the land.

One morning I am awakened by the hooves of ponies stomping and pawing at the earth. I am surprised that Tam is not beside me since the sun is barely risen, blood-red with the threat of rain. Peeking out of the stall where I have made a bed of straw, I see Tam bridling two ponies. Their hooves paw at the ground in anticipation of an adventure.

"Up with you, lazybones," Tam calls to me. "I've a plan for this day."

I shake off the straw that clings to my hair, and Tam gives me a leg up onto my pony's back. I run my hand along his smooth, dappled gray withers. "Good boy, Paddy," I tell him.

Tam leaps on Angus, dun-colored and lean, ducks his head, and charges out of the byre, Paddy and I following close behind. And then we are off, galloping across the fields, the ponies zigzagging around the larger rocks, jumping across ditches and over the low stone walls that divide the crofts. Tam slows a bit and flashes me a smile. For a moment, we ride side by side, until Paddy decides this will be a race and lunges ahead. I drop my head low on his neck to urge him forward. The wind blows my hair off my face, and on Paddy's broad back, above his pounding hooves, I feel as swift as the prideful near-grown selkies. But Tam is urging Angus forward, closing the gap between us.

Now we race neck and neck. I look across at Tam, but his face is buried in Angus's flying golden mane. He pulls forward as I watch. I feel Paddy respond to the challenge, his muscles rolling beneath me, but I no longer care if I win the race. It is prize enough to ride the fields with Tam.

We stop at last on the southern coast of the island, and Tam dismounts. He takes my hand and leads me down the beach to the caves at Nettle Gee, leaving the ponies behind to graze on the sweet grass of the hillside. I am hesitant about being in this place. Memories of my visit here with Arnfin fill me with longing for his company.

"I know you are troubled," Tam says when our toes touch the cool sand of the beach. "I would do anything and everything to make you happy, but I do not know the cure for what afflicts you. I know Arnfin brought you here once and it was a comfort. I thought perhaps if we came to this sacred place, it might help. . . ." Tam's voice trails off, as if he is unsure of his choice to bring me here.

"Thank you," I whisper as my arms go around him. We embrace each other, and I rest in the comfort of knowing that he holds my heart in his caring hands.

Together we walk into the darkness of the cave. Now it is my turn to lead Tam, up the narrow ledge to the platform at the top of the cavern. We climb slowly; the path is steep, and loose rocks fall with each step. I am careful not to look down. As we reach the ceiling of the cave, I notice with disappointment that no light filters in to give us clues to find the opening. I grope about for a hold in the rock but feel nothing but the smoothness of stone made flat by hundreds of years of pounding ocean waves. I think of Arnfin opening the door so easily. "Trapdoor," he said, and laughed.

"Let me try," says Tam, and I slide ahead along the wall of

the cave to give him room. Tam moves his hands over the rocks. I feel a sudden thrill of fear remembering the sensation of being trapped in the cave beneath the sea with the greedy trows.

The cave is suddenly filled with light.

Tam looks as surprised as I am. "I couldn't find the door," he says, his voice filled with awe. "I didn't do this."

From above us, the light spills into the cave from a single square opening, no larger than my hand, but it burns brilliant white, illuminating the entire cave. And there are the images etched into the walls of the cave, just as I remember them. Nimble fish amid ocean waves, sailing boats and the rocks of the skerry, round sheep and tiny herring—pictures of land and sea.

I hear Tam's intake of breath as he sees the images. "By all that is holy," he murmurs.

"There," I say, pointing to the center, where the image of the three selkies, each one pointing in a different direction—east, west, and south—forms a circle. But the girl in the center of the circle is gone.

"What is it?" asks Tam, sensing my astonishment.

"There was a girl. In the picture with the selkies," I stammer. "Pointing north. She was there. She was me. I know it. She had webbed hands." The words keep tumbling out of me. "I saw her in the crofthouse the night I found the pelt and again drawn on the walls of the cave when Arnfin brought me here. But now she is gone. How can this be? What does it mean?"

"Wait!" Tam takes my arm and turns me around. He points up. "Look!" Above us, etched into the rock dome of the ceiling, is a huge mural. Multicolored and rich with detail, the mural portrays scores of people standing on the beach, all of them looking out to sea. Some of the people are holding spotted pelts loosely in their arms.

I look at Tam and realize that he knows, too. We are looking at a depiction of the selkie folk walking among the others.

"Look!" shouts Tam. "There."

Behind the selkie folk and the others rising above them, arms outstretched, is a brown-haired girl with webbed hands. Her face is unmistakably mine.

Tam and I study the pictures in the cave all afternoon, until the sky is covered with rain clouds that block the light and the cave is too dark to see the images. I am not even tempted to try rolling down the narrow ledge as Arnfin did. I am too filled with thoughts about the meaning of the pictures. So with the sun setting at our backs, the air thick with the promise of rain, Tam and I take the slower route home to the croft, walking the ponies along the beach. Now and then, we lead them into the salt water and let them splash in the waves. Angus puts his muzzle in the water and blows bubbles through his nose.

Tam and I speak of the meaning of the new images on the ceiling of the cave. Neither of us is sure about what they portend for Midsummer's Eve. Will the selkie folk walk among the others? Would they risk the danger? Can they overcome their fear? If the others see the selkie folk in human form, they cannot deny the kinship that binds them together. I pray to St. Magnus for it to happen.

That night, lying by Tam's side, I murmur my thanks to him again for this incredible day.

"Ach, it was just a notion I had," he says.

"A fine notion indeed. It has given me hope." I do not say it, but this day has brought me even closer to the gypsy boy beside me who has unexpectedly become my savior.

But as Midsummer's Eve approaches, I notice that Tam is not himself. A silence has stolen into him. He wears a look of hard resignation on his face, and he has not spoken a single word to me since yesterday except to criticize me for putting too much salt in the fish stew. Whenever I look at him, he turns quickly away.

Finally, I can stand it no longer. "Will you be kind enough to tell me what has you so bothered?" I ask.

"Nothing," he tosses back.

I know that whatever it is, it is certainly not nothing. "Have I done something to offend you?"

"No."

"Then why are you angry with me?"

"I am not angry."

"Then why are you shouting?"

"Will you not leave me to myself? Must you know every middling thought in my head?"

I reach up and, with my fingertips, smooth out the furrows that turn his forehead into hills and valleys, and he gentles under my touch like a startled mare.

He sighs. "It is only that I am content. I like this life we have together."

"As do I."

We are silent for long moments.

"Midsummer's Eve is tomorrow night," he says finally.

Then I understand. Tam knows that Midsummer's Eve will bring the selkies to the land to dance, their presence a sweet reminder of my other life. He wonders if I will leave him for the sea, if this will be our last night together. I want to reassure him, but how can I when I am torn with doubt about either choice? I am worried, too, and like Tam, I cannot bear to think of us separated. I look down at my pelt and know that the time when I must choose between the land and the sea is here. But how can I?

Either choice involves a terrible loss. And I am still not sure where I belong.

Tam strokes the webs between my fingers. I grew up hating them, but through Tam's eyes and my sojourn in the sea, I have come to take some pride in them. I wear them now like a badge of honor, earned through hard experience.

I smell Grandpa's pipe before I see him. He tunes his fiddle, one string at a time, his rocking chair creaking its familiar song. I move near the open window to hear the sound of the sea and think of Midsummer's Eve. I will see the Red and the Black, like always, but what of the other selkies? Will I see the Arl Teller? Will she help me decide what to do?

"Will you be dancing at the foy this year, Jean?" Grandpa's voice lifts me out of my reverie. I look to Tam, but he will not meet my gaze.

"I'd be wanting to see you dancing at the foy. I never did have the pleasure of showing off the finest dancer in all the Orkneys."

"I'm not sure I remember the steps," I say, thinking that I have not danced since returning to the land. I have been too preoccupied with other matters to feel like dancing.

"It would be a fine thing to have a dance with the Selkie Girl," Tam says finally.

When I do not answer, Tam takes his leave of us, closing the crofthouse door quietly behind him. Suddenly I cannot bear to be in four walls another minute and stand in such haste I knock over the stool.

"Jean."

I turn to Grandpa. The smoke from his pipe does a dance of its own toward the ceiling.

"I let you go once before, did I not?"

"Aye, Grandpa, you did."

"I am an old man, and I haven't asked for much in this life." Grandpa rises, and his arms reach around my shoulders. "God help me, it's a selfish thing to ask, but I'll ask it all the same. Do not leave us again, Jean," he pleads. "We need you here."

"I love you, Grandpa," I say, and it has never been truer.

"Will you stay with us, then?"

I want to say yes. *Yes, Grandpa, yes, Tam, I will stay with you and make a life.* The pull of their love for me knits around my heart like a woolen quilt, but I am not sure it is enough. The knowin' still lies beyond my reach. I imagine it winking in delight at its dominion over me. *Are you still searching?* it asks. *Will you give in? Will you give up?*

No matter how much I want to allay Grandpa's fears that he will lose me again, I cannot. I join Tam on Odin's Throne, and together we look out to sea and wonder what tomorrow will bring.

That night, sleeping in the half-light of summer, Tam lying warm by my side, I have a dream, the first since I have returned to the land. I was beginning to believe the dreams had left me for good, but one more has been waiting for its chance to visit my sleep.

The dream unfolds slowly, like the fattened island sheep munch their way through the fields of grass. An old man sits in a rocking chair before the hearth, a gathering of children at his feet, some with brown hair and green eyes, others with the dark curly hair and black eyes of the travelers. The set of their shoulders reveals they are listening, rapt with the story the old man lays at their feet like a gift.

At first I think the storyteller is Grandpa, but then I see that it is someone else, someone familiar. It is Tam's dear face, thickened with age, his hair shot through with gray. A wiry beard falls to his chest. His arthritic hands dance along with the tale, as animated as his voice. "And so it was that the sea married the land," he says to the children. "And in the union, the island saw a new kind of folk, the Clan McCodrun. And now, across the Orkney Islands, the stories of the sea and the land can be heard round the peat fires, and the cull is nothing more than a memory of misunderstanding and regret."

The rocking chair creaks as it bends back and forth under Tam's weight.

"Tell the story of Britta and Dane," one of the children pipes up.

"Tell my favorite, Arnfin's tale, about the bravest selkie who ever lived," declares another.

The children's hands reach out, demanding that the elderly storyteller tell their favorite story, and as Tam laughs at the antics of his grandchildren, I see the translucent webs that lie between each of their fingers.

The fire glowing in the hearth flares up, filling the crofthouse with sudden brilliance, and in Tam's face, I see Arnfin smiling at me. "Keep the selkies safe," he whispers above the crackling of the blaze. "Never let them forget."

In the morning, I remember every detail of the dream—the mellow voice of the old man Tam will one day become, Arnfin's kind face framed by the firelight, and the webbed hands of the children.

And I know. Land and sea. The first of a kind.

CHAPTER
THIRTY-EIGHT

Midsummer's Eve arrives, and with it, the Johnsmas Foy. Tam and I sit together on the rocks of the skerry and watch the island children gather long stems of heather and tie them into bundles for bonfires. Soon the torches will be lit, blazing higher and higher toward the sun, until the night turns reluctantly into day. The bravest lads will jump over the bonfires, demonstrating their courage and strength to awed island lasses, who will giggle delightedly at the attention. Like always on Midsummer's Eve, the revelers go from house to house, increasing in number until all the families are represented in their best finery, men wearing their churchgoing clothes, women with wildflowers woven into their hair as though they sprouted there.

I can hear Grandpa's fiddle in the distance playing the ancient tune that leads the procession. Over the rise to the beach, the dancers begin to arrive, bare feet picking their way down the slope, until they feel the first pleasurable give of sand. Dim sunlight glitters on the rocks, narrow rays that poke pinpoint holes in the clouds, so eager are they to join the revelers on the beach. Grandpa bows the strings, and the familiar melody hangs suspended, spreading its deft arms around the beach.

Much of the worn look has disappeared from Grandpa's face, so he appears surprisingly younger. Familiar friends acknowledge him as they troop smartly by, skirts and sand flying.

I lean into Tam's warmth and feel the sturdy ropes of muscle that crisscross his body from hard work on the croft and plenty of healthy food. He wears new trousers, and a clean, loose-fitting shirt blows about him in the wind. Tam looks handsome in the patchwork vest Grandpa sewed to replace the ragged jerkin he used to wear. His bare feet, a last concession to his former life, are dug into the cool, grainy sand. He is trying to be cheerful, but I know he is troubled by the choice that hovers over us both this night.

In the farthest reaches of the voe, the sleek bodies of the selkie folk slice deftly through the currents, covering the distance to shore. It is Midsummer's Eve for them, too, and they are drawn to the land. As their round heads break the surface to breathe, they sight their destination and dive again. The white elder who is the Arl Teller leads them, followed closely by two companions, one dark as peat and another red as the setting sun.

My heart beats hard in my chest.

"There's selkies in the voe!" someone shouts, and the islanders turn toward the sea.

The Arl Teller lifts in and out of the waves, followed by hundreds of seals swimming around her in formation, like soldiers protecting their queen. Their cries fill the air, accompanying the bright Celtic melody Grandpa plays, and the lyrics they sing declare a new regime. *Listen to the sea. There is a land far beneath.*

As I sit on the edge of the skerry, unruly curls blow in my

face. My arms are papery with the salty spray of the sea. I cry out a greeting in the language of the selkies and wave to them. They call back, and the sounds that fill my ears feel like home. As the Arl Teller swims by, I rise and walk alongside her, escorting the clan onto the land they crave.

The islanders gaze reverently at the selkies as they haul out on the beach among them, knowing that this moment is sacred. They have a kinship with these creatures, and they wait eagerly to see what miracle will happen next.

I wait with them.

The selkies shake the dripping water from their fur, spraying us with the cool sea. The Arl Teller's impossibly long whiskers lie on the sand like discarded fishing line. She touches her nose to mine, and the Red and the Black follow suit, the Red weeping as she nuzzles my cheek.

"Do not be sad," says the Black to her sister in the language of the seals. "There is much to celebrate."

"Yes," the Red agrees, drinking me in like a cup of ale. "But seeing you again, my heart is so full it will not fit where it belongs."

I stroke the Red's broad back and hold her face in my hands. "I have missed you," I say. "I have missed all of you."

"And we have missed you." The Arl Teller rises up on her tail, shudders once, and the pelt that enfolds her body peels away, like ripe fruit falls from a tree. Her head emerges first, shining in the dim northern light, the skin of her back and arms as fresh and shining as a newborn babe's. Her body is sheathed in the same shimmering, luminescent green fabric that accompanied my birth in the sea and my transformation on land. Woven with indigo and gold sea flowers, her hair falls in waves down her back. A collective gasp from the islanders accompanies this sight, followed by cries of delight and pleasure.

The Arl Teller lifts her face to mine.

"Giddy God! Mither!" My arms go around her shoulders, and we hold each other as though we will never let go. "Mither," I say, joyful at the sound of her name. "You are the Arl Teller."

A flush of happiness runs through me, enfolded in her warm embrace. I could not admit until this moment that I was certain I would never see her again. Is it possible that she is more beautiful than ever? Gone are the circles that once ringed her eyes from lack of sleep. Her back is straight and her skin shines with health, but her youthful face is haloed with hair gone completely white.

"You see me now as I am meant to be, nourished by the sea that is my home. For sixteen years, I was captive on the land. In that time, I grew old and stiff. My skin was dry and cracked for want of the sea, my bones as brittle as the driftwood lying on the shore. You gave me back to the healing sea. You gave me back my life," she explains, as if she can read my thoughts.

"But I saw you in the voe when you became a selkie. You wore a brown-spotted pelt like me."

Mither smiles and touches her hair. "Ah, this," she says. "I suppose it is a reminder of the land I left behind. I entered the sea as you saw me, but by the time I reached the crystal forest, my pelt had turned as white as alabaster."

Holding me at arm's length, she looks into my eyes. "I have always been with you," she says, and the longing for her that has been my constant companion is chased away like the clouds are blown north by the wind. I remember the Arl Teller staring, wondering why she gazed so intensely at me. How difficult it must have been for her not to acknowledge me as her daughter, to watch me struggle and let me fall.

"But why didn't you tell me?" I ask. "Why didn't any of you tell me?"

"Near-grown selkies must journey alone to find the knowin'. It is the way of the selkie folk." Mither lays her arm around my shoulder. "No selkie would cheat another of their solus time, certainly not one who loves you as much as I do."

The Red rises up on her powerful tail and leans into me until her kind face is inches from mine. "Your mither gave you Arnfin, her most fierce protector."

The Red and the Black look at each other knowingly and then turn to me. "We all search for the knowin'."

"But the journey that leads us to it is just as important."

"Would your journey have been the same if you had known your mither was beside you?"

My time beneath the sea visits me again in a rush of memories, the dangerous dive into the sea, the society of the selkie folk and their ways, Arnfin's protection and wisdom, and my choice to follow the selkies on the beach. I remember with a sense of pride my rescue of the near-grown selkies from the nets and their acceptance of me that came too late. And most of all, I think of the miracle of birthing from my pelt, the transformation that stopped the cull. I am not the same selkie girl who dived so recklessly into the sea to find my mither. I am another person entirely, one with a newfound sense of the world.

"Now it is my turn to ask you, Mither. Are you not afraid?"

Mither's gaze takes in the others scattered on the beach. "Aye, but I have been shown the meaning of courage by a near-grown selkie girl."

The Red and the Black share their knowing look. "Your mither and grandmither before her have kept the stories," the Red tells me.

"Ever since the time of Britta and Dane, a female of our family has become the Arl Teller who leads us. The legacy of the Arl

Teller is passed down through the generations, but she is also chosen."

The Red and the Black smile at Mither. "She was born in the sea but has lived on the land and knows the stories of both," the Red explains.

And the Black finishes her thought. "Like you. Who better to lead us?"

I look to Mither. In her eyes is the same intense look she often gave me beneath the sea. She sees through the cloak of protection I wear around me. As though a path has led her to it, she looks into the deepest part of my soul.

The Red and the Black dip their heads gently. "Someday it will be your turn."

I hold the gaze of the three selkies before me. I do not look away in embarrassment or shyness, or feel afraid of what they might think of me. I have earned the right to stand among them as an equal. And as I look into their eyes, I realize that there is nowhere else I'd rather be than here.

I look down at my hands. The webs that I hated, that brought me such humiliation and shame, look ordinary to me now. I realize with a smile that I no longer claw at my cuticles and bite my nails to the quick. How funny to think about that at a time like this. But this, too, is a sign of the changes in me.

I feel my feet planted in the cool sand. I hear the sea singing its mysteries, and the wind in my ears whispers, *Arl Teller*.

I hardly recognize my own voice when I speak. "I am to become the Arl Teller?"

"If that is your choice."

"It is your legacy," offers the Black.

"And your right," adds the Red. "You are our choice."

Mither touches her damp cheek to mine. "None of us decide

the circumstances of our birth. That is beyond us. But we can choose how to live. Follow the knowin' to a place of your greatest contentment. That is what I wish for you. Sea or land. Whatever you decide will be the best choice for all of us."

Above us, Fither's ragged form slides down the slope. His tortured face is streaked with tears, and his arms reach out as if trying to embrace the sea. He stumbles past the others to Mither on his hands and knees. "Margaret," he whispers. "Margaret, you've come back to me."

Mither smooths his matted hair, but as quickly as the gesture is offered, she withdraws it.

"Come back to me," Fither pleads, his hand curling like a claw for the pelt that hangs draped in her arms. But Mither gathers her skin closer, her willowy arms forming a barrier around it, and slips her hand into mine. Fither crawls closer to her. "Don't leave me, Margaret. Please stay—only another hour." Fither weeps quietly, murmuring her name, but her heart is hardened against him.

Turning back to the waiting selkies on the shore, Mither nods her regal head, and at her signal, the selkies birth from their pelts. Males and females alike lay their precious sealskins in a great bundle on the beach and walk among the humans, clad in sea-green fabric like Mither. Young and old, dark-haired and light, they mingle together.

Tam trots to the first bonfire and lights it. It flares skyward with a satisfying hiss and a golden glow. A shout of approval rises from the gathering. A crowd of rowdy boys lights the remaining bonfires until the sky is alive with flames, and the crackling sounds punctuate the whine of the wind. The selkie folk shyly join the island revelers, partnering for the dance. And the music, when it starts, is a solemn waltz, as befits such an occasion.

Tam and I look on as the islanders and the selkie folk dance on the beach, humans following the lead of the nimbler selkies, whirling faster and faster with the music, until they fall laughing together on the beach. Grandpa plays until the cock crows and the tips of his fingers are raw. Acknowledging the dawn, Mither gathers her pelt and, taking my hand in hers, leads me down to the sea just as she did a year ago today. It is time for the selkies to return to the sea. Mither kisses my cheek, and we share a smile. She shapes the pelt around her body and walks into the shallow water. There, she looks back from the gently lapping tide of the voe. "Whatever you decide will be the best choice," she reassures me.

I feel the familiar, bittersweet tug of the sea pull me toward her. I think of the society of selkies and their stories, the transparent arms of the crystal forest, and the blue liquid fire in the clearing. I think of becoming the Arl Teller, of the deep honor it would bestow. I see the selkies gathered before me offering fealty, asking for a story to help them puzzle out the dilemmas they face. I imagine the joy I would feel becoming the shepherd of their lives. I remember the sweetness of my time beneath the sea and those who have shown me the meaning of love, Arnfin, the Red and the Black, and Mither. I imagine the rich life I might lead there.

The soft water of the sea caresses my feet. I stand at the edge of land and sea, touching both, wanting both.

A hand falls gently on my shoulder, and Tam is at my side, holding my pelt in his arms. I look at Mither, then back at Tam. I think of the life we might share together. He holds out the pelt to me. "Take it," he says. "And go if you will. I will keep my promise."

Belonging's not a place. It's inside you. I wonder if the Red knew the importance of those words when she said them to me so long ago on the beach. Now I understand.

I press the softness of the pelt to my body. I can feel the eyes of the others resting on me, waiting for me to choose. The suspicion and fear that once clouded their faces are gone. No one stares at my hands.

Belonging's not a place. It's inside you.

The pelt falls onto the beach, and I hold out my empty arms for Tam to fill. "And I will keep my promise. I choose to dance. I'm fairly silted to dance with you."

Together Tam and I will ensure the safety of the selkies. Just as my dream foretold, our children and their children after them will learn the stories of land and sea. No one will question the value of the lives beneath the waves so long as a single member of the Clan McCodrun is alive. On land will be the place of my greatest contentment.

The knowin' lies in my heart like a precious jewel. Mither's eyes shine with tears but her smile reveals her pride, and it covers me like a pelt.

"Selkies!" calls my mither, who is their leader, and all eyes fall on her. "It is the seventh tide of the seventh tide. We have shared this Midsummer's Eve with humankind; now it is our time to return to the sea." One by one, the selkie folk take up their pelts and follow Mither to the edge of their watery home.

Mither turns to me. "Look to the sea," she whispers, her voice thick with emotion, "and you'll see me there. If you're hungry, fish will leap into your nets. Precious shells will wash up on the beach. Your boat will sail safely through the tides and the rocks on the shore. I will always be with you. And each Midsummer's Eve, you will see me as I am now." She turns her gaze to where the wild North Sea meets the mighty Atlantic and plunges into the sweet, salty sea. The selkies follow her. Their bodies slide through the voe, churning the water into life around them.

"Grandpa!" I call. "Have you the will to play?"

"Aye," he answers. "Haven't I been waiting a whole year to see you dance?" And lifting his fiddle, he lays bow to strings and plays a lively tune that tells a story of lovers who find each other and vow never to part. A pennywhistle matches Grandpa's fiddle note for note.

Tam takes my hand and pulls me to him until I feel the length of him all along my body.

"Dance, Elin Jean!" Grandpa shouts into the wind. "Dance the stories to life!" And feeling the warmth of Tam's hand in mine, I dance with him, dance on the beach like waves on the sea, and together we lead the others in a dance that celebrates the marriage of land and sea, a dance that foretells a sweeter future.

Acknowledgments

I wish to express my love and deep appreciation to the late Aurand Harris, who believed in "the little girl with the webbed hands"; author Susan Wiggs, for advice and encouragement; my friends in Orkney, Catherine and Mary Zawadski of Balfour Castle, Colin Firth, Fergus Brand, and the young people who taught me about the selkies; Diane, the best listener and friend ever; Jeff, Scot, Roger, Daniel, and KPK, my TYA posse; my daughters, Joanna, Elizabeth, and Stephanie, always my truest sources of inspiration; and my brother, author Terry Brooks, and his wife, Judine, whose encouragement has meant more than I can say.

About the Author

Laurie Brooks is an award-winning playwright whose Lies and Deceptions Quartet, a series of plays for young adults, includes *The Wrestling Season,* winner of "Best of" awards in Seattle, Kansas City, and Dallas. Laurie has been Assistant Professor and Playwright-in-Residence at New York University, where she earned a master's degree in educational theater. To bring the world of the selkies to life, she traveled to the Orkney Islands, north of the Scottish mainland. She lives in Phoenix, Arizona, but her heart is in Cork, Ireland, where she has written four plays for Graffiti Theatre Company. This is her first novel for young adults.

Laurie invites you to visit her Web site at www.lauriebrooks.com.